WHAT OTHERS ARE SAYING

"As a fan and author of true Christian fiction, I always love to find other authors who weave a spiritual message, lesson, into their books. Tanya Eavenson has done just that with *The Rescue*, a wonderful story of learning to trust God no matter the circumstance, to remember that He is always with you and will be your ever-present help in times of trouble. He is the ultimate Rescuer. Thank you, Tanya, for the reminder. I definitely recommend this enjoyable page-turner to all those who relish a good western inspirational romance."

—CRYSTAL L BARNES,
AUTHOR OF THE MARRIAGE & MAYHEM SERIES.

"Ms. Eavenson writes a poignant tale filled with emotions. One can't help but feel for the characters as they battle an evil man intent on getting his way. A genteel lady and a gentleman cowboy on the race for their lives. This is a historical not to be missed!"

—LAURA V. HILTON, AUTHOR OF *MARRIED TO A STRANGER*
(WHITAKER HOUSE)

"Eavenson knows how to ratchet up the action and suspense, carried all the way through to the last chapter. Rosalind and Trent are endearing characters hounded by a villain that truly gave me chills, with a supporting cast as well-drawn as the hero and heroine. *The Rescue* will draw you in, pump you up, and touch your heart."

—CAROLE TOWRISS, AUTHOR OF *BY THE WATERS OF KADESH*

The
PROPOSAL

BOOKS BY TANYA EAVENSON

UNENDING LOVE SERIES

Unconditional
Restored

GAINING LOVE SERIES

To Gain a Mommy
To Gain a Valentine
To Gain a Bodyguard
To Gain Forever

ALL ROADS LEAD TO TEXAS

The Rescue
The Proposal

GEORGIA PEACHES SERIES

The Heart of Mercy

The

PROPOSAL

BOOK 2

TANYA EAVENSON

"And he hath put a new song in my mouth, even praise unto our God; many shall see it, and fear, and shall trust in the Lord."
Psalm 40:3 (KJV)

© The Proposal
by Tanya Eavenson

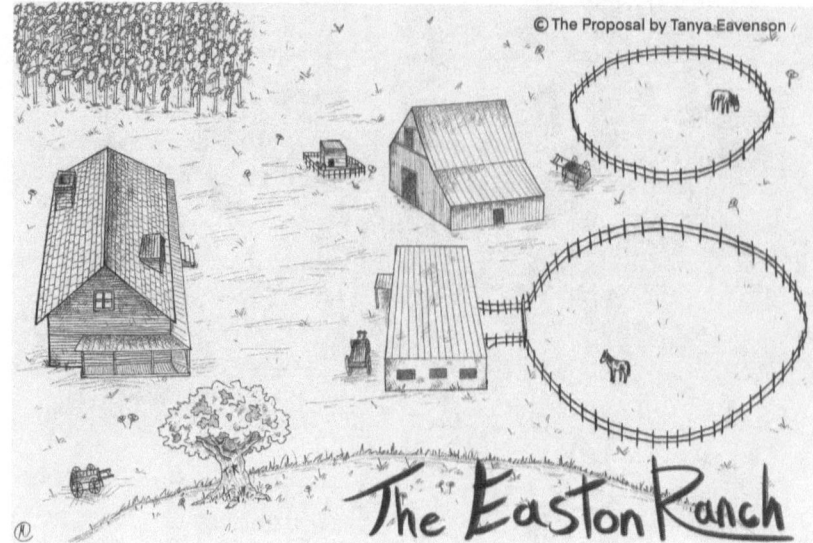

The Easton Ranch

CHAPTER ONE

Graham, Texas
1891

Blake McKenny's hand rested comfortably on the butt of his holstered gun as he leaned against an oak tree. Sweat trickled down his back—the shade did little good—but he loved it here. Several hundred feet away, the trees stopped, and wide-open prairie stretched straight to the sheriff's office in Graham, Texas, which lay a mile away, hidden by a gentle rise of land. God's country, he called it.

His office.

His land. Or soon would be.

He inhaled and silently said a prayer of thanksgiving. Seven years ago, he'd promised land to his wife—land he pictured them raising children on, land they'd work till they were old and gray. A promise he'd never been able to fulfill.

Not while she was alive.

He yanked off his Stetson and wiped his brow with his arm, thoughts shifting to the town meeting he'd left an hour ago in Fort Worth. Reports of stagecoach holdups—of men shot and killed while women and children were taken as captives to be sold to brothels—remained foremost in his mind.

He released a heavy breath. He had to find a way to keep the people in his town safe. But how could he stop outlaws, keep loved ones from dying at the hands of evil men, when he couldn't prevent his own wife's murder?

Images of long ago flashed in his mind for what seemed like the thousandth time. If only …

He shook his head against memories and pain as oppressive as the Texas summer heat and tried to refocus on his personal Garden of Eden.

In the distance, a stagecoach rounded a bend at a hazardous pace. He narrowed his eyes, tracking its movement. Two men rode up top—driver and shotgun. Dust billowed up from the ground around it, nearly obscuring the two riders galloping up from behind. The muscles in Blake's body tightened.

A light flashed in a rider's hand. The glint of sunlight off a pistol?

Four rapid booms answered his question. Was that a woman's scream?

Blake reached for his horse. He clenched the reins and leapt onto the saddle, scrambling for a plan.

The driver tumbled from the stage. The guard's body sank to the driver's bench, shotgun falling to the ground. The stage took a sharp turn.

Two bandits—one with a red bandana, one with a blue. He couldn't shoot them from this distance, having left his rifle at the office, but he could distract them. At this moment, any plan would be better than letting those in the stage be taken. Or worse, killed.

Blake rode toward the scene, pulling his bandana from his shirt pocket and quickly securing it over his face. Approaching the robbers from the opposite side of the runaway coach horses, he shouted, "Need some help, boys?"

He snatched the loose reins while Blue Bandana jumped from his horse onto the driver's box. Struggling to keep his balance, Blue Bandana yanked the reins from Blake and brought the team to a halt. The other rider, still on his horse, slowed beside his partner and pointed his gun at Blake's chest.

Lord, help me keep a cool head and save these people. Blake dismounted his horse and approached, hands raised once again, and eased toward them.

Blue Bandana on the stagecoach glared at him. The bandana had slipped to his neck, and Blake only caught a glance, one too brief to notice much.

Blake tipped his hat at the two. Their clothes were dirty and torn, but their guns—Smith & Wesson double-action—were clean. He'd seen revolvers like these only twice before. Thankfully, he was wearing one on his hip. "Heard the shots. Thought you might could use a hand."

Blue Bandana secured his disguise. "I'm afraid your rescue attempt was in vain, mister. We ain't tryin' to help nobody but ourselves."

"Stealin' is more like it." A hearty laugh came from Red. He kept his gun trained on Blake's chest.

Blake glanced at the stagecoach's door. If these men were the robbers who kidnapped women and children and sold them to brothels, he needed to do something and fast. He grunted and nodded at the stagecoach. "Take all you want. When I saw you both comin' in after the stage and heard a woman scream, I knew this was my opportunity. I'm here lookin' for a woman."

The man with the gun gawked. "Are you kiddin' me? Do you believe this, brother?"

Hard, dark eyes peered at him over the blue bandana. The robber had yet to jump down from the stage.

Blake strolled toward him as though he had all the time on this side of heaven. Hopefully, he did. "Let me take a look-see if there's a bride in here for me." He craned his neck to see inside the carriage.

One set of eyes—the color of a raging storm—glared back, brows knitted together above them. "Don't you dare touch me, or you'll regret it with your life."

Blake blinked twice. *Great.* He had a fighter on his hands. That's all he needed. "I'm in luck. I got me one *fine* filly in here." He turned back to the men.

A feminine but curt voice called out, "I'm not your woman."

"Brother, I thought you said there were no passengers?" Red, his horse antsy under him, shot a glance at Blue. "I thought one of the men sounded a little girly. There's a female in there."

The other threw the strongbox down with a thump. He jumped and landed a few feet from Blake. "Pull her out, stranger. I wanna see her."

Red chuckled, causing the gun still pointed at Blake's chest to shake. "If there's more, we could have a little fun."

Blake's jaw ticked. They knew this stage was carrying a strongbox, but not about the woman? Maybe they weren't the bandits he was looking for. Losing the strongbox with its wages would be difficult, but to a much lesser degree than losing this woman. Blake had a chance to save this from going bad. "She's the only one." Praying this woman wouldn't get him shot, Blake swung the door wide and waited, but backed against the opposite side of the carriage, she made no move to emerge.

Not having time to explain his actions, Blake reached in, grabbed her wrist, and pulled her out the door, helping her as much as possible but being rougher than he would have liked. He'd apologize later, but now he needed to play the part. Their lives depended on it.

She tumbled forward, and though he tried to catch her fall, she landed hard on the ground. He was tempted to apologize and collect the travel hat and satchel by her side, but needing to keep up the pretense, he yanked her to her feet. Her brown hair unwound from its bun and fell like silk across her smooth face. Not helpful for her cause. Neither was the becoming flush on her cheeks.

He snatched her hat off the ground and crammed it on her head in a sad attempt to hide her pretty face. "You know what's expected as a bride," he said. "Do as you're told."

Sparks of lightning seemed to shoot from her eyes straight at him. He opened his mouth to speak, and she spat in his face.

Red pointed his gun and snickered. "Well, I'll be. Look who we have here."

Blake shifted to face both men and kept the girl behind him, slipping the gun from his holster. Blue Bandana stepped toward him. "She's mine," Blake growled. "If you plan to die today, then take another step."

Something solid jammed between Blake's shoulder blades. "Are you hard of hearing?" The woman behind him spoke in a tone that shook with anger. "I am not now, nor will I ever be, yours. Toss aside your weapon."

Heat flowed through his veins. Here he was, trying to save this woman, and look where it got him. A gun in the back. "Easy with that thing, ma'am."

"I'll be easy when your gun is on the ground! Everyone's guns on the ground." The subsequent clicking sound spoke of how serious she was.

"Sure, sure." He released the cock on his own weapon and dropped it at his feet.

"Well, what a nice turn of events." Red Bandana chuckled. "C'mon, brother, we got what we came for. More money than we've ever seen in our lives. She ain't worth it."

Blue set his sights on the woman yet again. His gaze intensified, almost as if he knew her. Blake was tempted to turn around to study her for himself, but he held his stance.

But then the robber stepped back and cut the lines that hitched the horses to the stage. With two guns pointed at him—one from the woman, the other from Red—Blake stood and sweated a river while Blue Bandana heaved the strongbox onto one of the freed horses and secured it in place.

Finally, the bandit swung into the saddle of his own horse. With a wink for the woman, he shot a round into the air. The remaining stage horses jolted into a full gallop, taking Blake's horse along with them. The bandits followed.

Blake ground his teeth. If only he could use his gun on those murdering thieves, but no—he had a gun to his back. It took all the patience he could muster to wait for the men to leave, especially Blue, who turned his horse back for another look before disappearing over the horizon.

Blake had to get his horse back, but first he'd have to deal with the metal digging into his flesh. "Your turn. Put down your gun."

She hooted. "Not on your life."

Time for a new strategy. "I must warn you, if you shoot me, you'll be hung for killing a sheriff."

She laughed again, distrust tainting her voice, giving him the impression she wasn't going to lower her gun. Blake hated to manhandle her more, but he had no choice. He wasn't ready to die today. Shifting his body weight to one side, he caught a glimpse of her arm. He'd wait for the right moment.

"Where's your badge, lawman?"

Of course, when he needed his badge, he didn't have it. If his deputy could see him now, Blake would never be able to live it down. "It's in my desk drawer. At the sheriff's office."

"Your first mistake, mister. A sheriff never forgets his badge. I've seen men like y—"

Blake twisted, grabbed her wrist, pulled her forward, and yanked the gun from her as she flew past him. She spun mid-flight and fell to the ground on her backside. After opening the revolver, he dumped the bullets into his palm. "I'm sorry to do that again, but ..." He looked down.

Those dark eyes sent daggers his way for a second time, but this time, he was sure one stabbed him in the heart. Never had he seen a woman with such fire, such ... beauty.

She jumped up, balled her fists, and held them up as if she planned to fight him.

He couldn't help laughing. No. Never had he seen a woman like her. "Ma'am, you have two choices. Ride back to town with me or walk, but I have a feeling I know which choice you'll take. However, if those men return, you won't be so lucky." Blake pocketed the bullets and slid her revolver into the belt of his pants. Turning, he scanned the stage, and at seeing the lifeless guard, yanked a blanket from under the bench and covered the body.

The woman looked away, swallowing hard. "Ride?" She searched the ground. "On what horse?"

Blake realized what she was looking for and snatched her satchel from the dirt, then handed it to her. He drew his lips together, letting loose a shrill whistle to call Legend to return if he was still within earshot. "I need to look for the driver. You stay here." He holstered his discarded pistol and walked toward the area where the driver had fallen.

"What's your name?" A softer, gentler voice sounded from behind him.

He didn't turn around. "Blake."

"Is that it? Just Blake?"

He couldn't understand this woman. One minute she was trying to kill him, and the next she acted like she cared. "Why do you want to know? To write it on my headstone?"

From the south, Legend trotted to him and stood like a soldier, waiting for his command. Blake ran his hand down the horse's mane, collected the reins, and then continued his search for the driver.

"No," she said. "When I get to Graham, I'm going to find out who you really are."

"Blake McKenny." He spotted a crumpled body ahead near the trail. Dropping the reins, he ran to the man and felt for a pulse. Weak. But at least there was one. Blake wrapped his bandana around the man's bleeding head, then looked over his shoulder to find the woman holding his horse's reins. "He's alive but needs a doctor. I've got to get both of you to town." He rose and strode toward the horse.

She climbed into Legend's saddle, moving the horse farther from him. "I'll head into town and let the doctor know where to find you. It'll be quicker." She guided the horse into a canter, leaving him standing there.

Blake exhaled. Surely this woman would drive any man insane. Especially him. He had to get help, but there was no way he'd leave her alone given what had happened here or what he'd learned in Fort Worth. Her riding off unaccompanied into dangerous country wasn't an option either.

He allowed the woman her lead as he dragged the driver to partial shade under a mesquite tree. That done, he drew his lips together and whistled. His horse circled and trotted straight for him. He didn't mask his smirk as she approached. Or when one of her hands fisted as his horse stopped directly in front of him. Or when he took the reins and climbed up behind her.

It was the moment he realized how perfectly she fit against his chest that his smirk fell.

Jessica's blood boiled. Who did this man think he was, bossing her around like he did? If it weren't for the driver needing help, she'd have the mind to … what? She was trapped, pressed against this strange man's chest, and every time she tried to break their contact, the movement of the horse brought her right back.

She glanced around at nothing but flat, destitute land for as far as she could see. "How much farther?" She tossed the question over her shoulder, praying it wasn't much longer before she could be rid of him. He grated on her last nerve.

But what choice did she have? Trust the men who were robbing the stage? No. She'd rather take her chances with this man—the one who hadn't made any physical advances since claiming he was a lawman. Although wedding bells seemed to be ringing in his brain. That was a loose bolt she'd fix once she got to town and found the sheriff. She'd see who this *Blake* really was. He'd be easy to describe with that scar leaving a bare line running through his trimmed beard. A bank robber, for all she knew.

He wasn't wearing his badge. Although, to be fair, the way he'd cared for the hurt driver hadn't been the act of a villain. And here they were, riding toward town for the doctor. Could he have been playing a role?

But then again, hadn't she been deceived before?

"Look ahead."

Jessica squinted against the blinding sun. A haze outlined several buildings. At least she thought they were buildings. It wasn't even July, but the heat played mind games with her vision.

She licked her lips. If she'd been smart, she'd have grabbed her canteen from the stagecoach before trying to escape. *Impetuous,* her father had called her on more than one occasion, and now look where it had gotten her—all her belongings still in the stagecoach and her mouth bone dry.

Again she leaned forward, anxious to escape her captor's presence. "That driver looked pretty bad off. Can't we ride any faster?"

"Suit yourself." Blake spurred the horse forward, and her back slammed against his hard chest. His arm came around her waist.

Her breath caught. "Let go of me, sir." She tried to struggle out of his embrace, but he only held her tighter.

"We're almost there."

Her body tensed at his unbreakable hold, and her breath became labored as they galloped into town, collecting curious stares. Terror caught in her throat, and she fought against the memories of another man's hand on her waist as his knife dug into her flesh.

Blake halted his horse and swung off before she had time to blink, then ran into the building directly in front of her.

Her hand flew to her mouth, and she worked to swallow the vile taste on her tongue. She gasped for air and squinted against the midday sun, craning her neck to read the metal sign above the door. *Doc Adams.*

Blake and another man soon sprinted out, the latter gripping a black medical bag. Blake said something to him she couldn't hear.

The doctor, she presumed, came her way, tipping his hat as he rushed past.

She followed his movements and noted the length of his stride, still able to feel Blake's presence at her side. "He's the doctor? He looks about … my age." When she got no response, she turned to Blake, who stood beside his horse gazing at her. Questions seemed to run through his eyes. She hadn't noticed until now how blue they were, like the sky on a clear day.

He grabbed his horse's reins, breaking the trance. "He's new to town. And how old are you?"

She shook out of her thoughts and stood in the stirrups to dismount. "It's none of your concern."

Strong hands took hold of her waist and lowered her to level ground. She looked up at Blake and was taken aback by his nearness, and the pure size of him. He was a giant standing next to her, but she wasn't some helpless female. She could have gotten off the horse without him. Jessica opened her mouth to give him a piece of her mind.

"Will you be all right?"

She stopped, surprised by his words. The genuine look of concern on his face made her feel vulnerable. She hated it. Running her hands down her dress, she righted herself and straightened her hat. She clenched her hands at her side, then clasped them together. "I will be as soon as I find the sheriff's office and report this incident. Including the theft of my pistol."

The softness of Blake's eyes hardened, and his jaw clenched. He pulled her pistol from his belt and handed it to her. Before she had the metal grip securely within her grasp, he brushed past her, climbed into the saddle, and mumbled, "If I wasn't …" He turned his horse in the opposite direction and rode off.

She glanced around in search of the sheriff's office. What else could she tell the sheriff about the robbers? What had one of them said? *Come, brother, we've got what we came for. She ain't worth it.* Her throat tightened at the memory, which led to another of the life she'd left behind in Oklahoma. Her hand flew to her neck. No, it wasn't Cliff's gang. It couldn't be them. Although, she hadn't clearly seen the blue-masked robber with Blake standing like a towering wall in front of her. The other—the one with the red bandana covering his face—she hadn't recognized him. Surely it wasn't them or they would have taken her.

Hoofbeats broke into her thoughts as several men galloped out of town. With a deep breath, Jessica walked toward the livery, steeling her trembling hands at her sides. What she needed was a room at the boardinghouse for her stay in town, not haunting memories. But first, she needed to secure a way out of town.

When she rode in, she thought it was strange to find the church next to the saloon. The restaurant came up on her right, and at seeing the sheriff's office a short way farther down Main, she made a quick mental note to return after this stop. The odor of manure hit her in the nose as she entered the livery. Two young boys ran in after her, came to an abrupt halt, and clapped their knees with their palms, panting for breath.

"I won," one said.

"Nay. I did."

The tension in her body began to ease as she smiled at the two, aged about eight or nine, she'd guess. "I'd say a tie."

The boys turned their mud-smeared faces to her. The one with dark hair shook his head, flinging sand in all directions. The reddish-haired one simply stared before saying, "Ma'am, ye sure? Me da said whoever won dinna be muckin' the stalls tonight."

"Oh, I see." She peered around the livery, her eyes adjusting to the difference in light. On the left, Blake's horse waited, tied up along one of the stalls. She'd know it anywhere. Her father had taught her well.

A fire smoldered several yards away on her right, in what looked like a separate structure. "It seems your dad is the liveryman and also the blacksmith. It'd take one person a *long time* to clean the stalls by themselves, but if they had help, it'd take half the time, which means more time for fun."

The dark-haired boy drew in a breath. "Nay, I can have fun all by meself." He reached over and smacked his brother on the shoulder. "You're it!" As he took off running, his brother followed.

"Nice try, lass." A burly man the size of a mountain came out of the shadows. A severe limp to his right leg became apparent as he neared. He wiped his hands on his overalls. "Dinna pay me boys no mind. What can I do for ye?"

She straightened to her full height of five feet two inches but was still no match for the Irishman. The hard lines of his face smiled down at her. "I'm looking for a horse. It would be safer traveling."

"Right now, I dinna have none to borrow."

"I'd like to buy one. That is, if you have any for sale."

"Aye, have one that's comin' in on the train in a few weeks."

"A few weeks?" She'd be stuck here until then? She couldn't let that happen. Too much time had already been wasted this morning. She had to be out of this town one way or the other.

"Lass?"

She took a steady breath and forced a smile. "Yes. I'm terribly sorry. My mind went elsewhere."

"There's a rancher who owns quite a few horses. You could see if he'll sell ye one, though I doubt it. Maybe if ye spoke to the sheriff—"

She perked up and clapped her hands together. "Oh, yes, thank you for reminding me. I need to speak with the sheriff."

"Two buildings down. Across the street from the boardin'

house, in case ye missed it."

"Thank you, sir." She paused and pointed to Blake's horse. "Where is the man who owns that palomino?"

"Borrowed me wagon and headed out."

"I appreciate the help." She strolled out of the livery with purpose. Who was this Blake? She planned to knock him down a notch or two.

But hadn't he let her go? They weren't married, as he'd persisted in telling those robbers. And since riding into town, he hadn't acted like a robber. Her steps slowed. Blake had claimed she was his. So had Cliff. She shuddered. Blake might not be like Cliff, but no man was going to claim her. Ever.

The building held big, bold letters that read: SHERIFF'S OFFICE. Unpleasant thoughts unraveled the nice little bow she'd tied to keep her emotions intact and hidden from the world, and herself.

It was the only way to deal with murder.

CHAPTER TWO

Blake's grip tightened around the reins. Never before had a woman infuriated him like that tiny thing he'd rescued this morning. When she'd pointed her gun in his back and jabbed the barrel up into his skin, he was sure she'd drawn blood. Then later, when he'd lifted her off his saddle, pale as a ghost and weighing less than a sack of apples, the urge to care for her kicked him like a mule. But when her hands had balled into fists and her dark eyes darkened even more, he'd snapped back to his senses. How a woman so small could give him such grief, he'd never know.

She'd swallowed his robber story too easily. But she had him all wrong. Stealing went against everything he stood for … and to force a woman to marry him?

The back wheel of the wagon hit a pothole, and the trunk he'd recovered from the stagecoach shifted, slamming against the side. Hopefully, the wheel he'd fixed on the way out would make it back to town. He had to set things straight with Miss …

What was her name? He didn't think she'd mentioned it.

Blake glanced at the large trunk in the back of the wagon,

clothes and other items tumbling out. He jerked forward and swallowed. After taking the stagecoach driver to Doc's office, he'd remembered her trunk was still strapped on top of the stagecoach. Maybe it wasn't a good idea to return and collect her things, but with the ordeal she'd gone through, mercy drove him to action.

Now, as he neared the boardinghouse, where he presumed she'd stay, delicate fabrics pooled out behind him onto the wagon's wooden floorboards. What had he gotten himself into yet again with this woman? He gritted his teeth.

From the corner of his eye, he caught sight of the mystery lady entering the sheriff's office. She wasn't serious about her claims to speak to the sheriff, was she? He pulled the reins and veered the horses to the office. Once he arrived, he secured the brake and jumped down.

The office door had stood open these last few weeks due to the summer heat, so he easily heard when her voice rose in complaint, "His name is Blake, and he has plans to force me to marry him."

He rushed through the doorway.

"That's him," she said, her back ratcheting straight. "That's the man, Sheriff."

Blake scowled. This woman had his nerves on end, yet she intrigued him. The storm in her eyes, the flushed cheeks, the way she demanded to be heard.

His deputy, Jake, ignored her accusations and eyed him before a smile passed between them. "Ma'am, I'm sorry," Jake said, "but I can't arrest him. And another thing, I'm not the sheriff. I'm the deputy. Blake here has been a good buddy a long time. If he did do something, as you're accusing, I'm sure it was only to protect you from harm."

Blake clapped his deputy's shoulder. "I appreciate that." He strolled to the desk and perched against it, crossing his legs.

"When…" She bit her lip, looking less confident by the second. "When does the sheriff return?"

Blake slid open the desk drawer, pulled out his badge, then placed the star on his chest. "He has." He rose to his full height of six feet four inches and stared down at her.

Moisture filled her eyes. She seemed so vulnerable, almost childlike, that he had to stop himself from reaching out to her.

"I'm sorry I mistook you as a—" Her words cut off, and her gaze darted around the room. "Sheriff. Deputy." She gave each a brisk nod. "Please, excuse me." She turned and fled his office.

He went to the window and stared after her. Several people bustled past, but it didn't block the picture of her disappearing into the boardinghouse. Why did he have to prove she'd been wrong? To clear up the misunderstanding. But also pride, he knew. But why did what she thought of him matter?

"What else happened?" Jake asked, now standing alongside him. "Who were the robbers she mentioned?"

Blake strolled to his desk and explained what happened, from the moment the stage came into view to finding Doc. But he left out most of his encounter with the woman. "I'm not sure the men were part of the gang we're looking for, since they let us go." He withdrew from his pocket two sketches of wanted men, which he'd received in Fort Worth. "These are from the town meeting." He unfolded the pages, placed them on his desk, and ran his hand along them, then planted his finger on the forehead of one of the men. "These men, Cliff and Guy, will kill you with no questions asked and kidnap women and children." He met Jake's gaze. "Five men are dead. Women and children are being sold to brothels."

"You're kidding."

"I'm afraid not, and it seems the robberies are moving closer to us. When I was on the property, two men fired at a stagecoach. I don't know if they're part of the gang, but the only way I thought I could save the passengers would be to pretend to be one of the robbers. I feared the worst, so I didn't mind being the bait until I could control the situation."

"Do you think we should tell the townsfolk?"

"Not yet." Blake rummaged through the papers on his desk and pulled out a note. "We have a town meeting two weeks from yesterday. We can wait. But till then, I'll tell Trent and the men."

"Are you going to the Easton ranch now?"

"After I stop by the boardinghouse. Don't forget to lock up." He ambled to the door.

"See you tomorrow." Jake went toward the back room.

Blake glanced around the office one final time. He could still picture the woman standing there and the sorrow in her eyes. He'd take her trunk to Mr. and Mrs. Briggen at the boardinghouse. They'd deliver it to her. With her staying there, he'd rather pack a bag and sleep under the stars at Trent's ranch than risk passing her in the hallway going to his room.

Closing the door behind him, Blake remembered once again that she'd failed to give him her name. And why was that?

Jessica.

So that was her name. In a few days' time, Blake would ferret out Jessica's favorite color, how old she was, and if she was married—if that was something he wanted to know, and it wasn't. All via Mrs. Briggen.

Blake rode onto the Easton ranch as darkness shrouded him, but he needed little light to find his way around. A bright glow came from the house windows. He was tempted to go there now and share with Trent all he'd learned while in Fort Worth, but thought better of it.

He ran a hand down his horse's mane. "Not to worry, Legend. I'll tend to you first."

In the barn, he found Legend's stall waiting for him, clean. Blake enjoyed the smell of fresh hay and horseflesh. He'd always known his call was to tend to the Lord's animals. Perhaps one day, but for the moment, he had a job to do, and protecting his town was his priority. "It's nice to be home."

"I'd hope so." Trent Easton ambled toward him. "How was your trip?"

Blake lifted the saddle and rested it along the stall wall. "Tiresome. Would you mind if I camped out for a few nights in the barn?"

Trent pulled the pads off Blake's horse and hung them next to his saddle. "If you're planning on staying, it's not in the barn. Our house has always been yours to come and go from as you please. I must warn you though, Timothy has been keeping us up late. He doesn't want to go to bed at nights. I hope that doesn't make a difference."

How could Blake say no? Trent and Rosalind's children were the closest he'd ever come to having his own. "Thank you."

"Great." Trent patted him on the shoulder. "I'll tell Rosalind while you finish up out here." He strolled from the barn, but before leaving, he turned. "Glad you're back."

Blake gave a nod as he left. Brothers, that's what they were, regardless of bloodlines. Family.

After brushing down Legend and adding oats to his bucket, Blake entered the grand two-story home. The aroma of fresh coffee drew him in farther, although he needed no incentive. It was a godsend after his last few days in Fort Worth.

Rosalind stood at the kitchen stove, her brown hair flowing over her shoulders, nearly the same as it had when he met the new Mrs. Easton for the first time.

"You didn't have to make coffee."

She turned at his words, and her light gray eyes twinkled.

Instantly, he thought of Jessica. While their features were opposites, their eyes were somewhat of a similar gray, but where Jessica's were dark, Rosalind's were paler, as was her hair and skin. Jessica's skin was nearly as tan as his.

He quickly pushed those thoughts away.

Rosalind hugged him. "How are you? How was your trip? The kids missed their Uncle Bwake."

Blake chuckled. Trent and Rosalind's two-year-old twins could call him anything they liked as far as he was concerned. "One day they'll get the name." He opened a cabinet and pulled out a mug. "So where did Trent go?" He poured a cup of coffee, and the steam rose to his nose as he took a small sip, almost burning his tongue. Just the way he liked it.

"The children are already asleep, but Trent went to kiss them goodnight. What news do you bring from Fort Worth?"

Blake looked to the stairs. "Maybe we should wait till Trent comes down."

Rosalind remained silent.

He was aware of what that meant. He didn't mean to cause her worry, but it was better to have his friend sitting with them when he shared the news.

Moments later, Trent strolled through the living room. "What about me?" He smiled.

A frown etched lines on Rosalind's face. "Blake wanted to wait until you joined us before sharing news from Fort Worth."

Trent pulled out a chair for Rosalind, the legs scraping the wooden floor. Blake placed his coffee down, then sat alongside Trent. He went through what he learned in Fort Worth, fully aware of Rosalind's gaping mouth. "Next time you're in town,

I'd like for you both to look at the *wanted* posters I brought back."

Rosalind's hand flew to Trent's. "Oh, that's terrible. And you say they're heading this way?"

Trent covered her hand with his own. "No, that's not what he said. He mentioned that the robbers have moved closer to town, not that they're specifically coming to Graham."

"But this worries me."

"I know." Trent squeezed her hand and turned his attention back to Blake. "What are you going to do? Will you share this with the townspeople?"

"We have a meeting in two weeks at the church. I think that would be the best time since the meeting was already planned and more people will attend. I don't want to think what might happen if gossip gets started about this."

"You mean like Mrs. Briggen? If she heard of this ..."

Blake leaned on the table. "Exactly. It's my responsibility to make sure my town is safe, not in a panic."

"We understand," Trent agreed. "Who do you plan to tell besides us? Matthew?"

"Yes, and Pete. I can trust them." Blake leaned back in his chair and took a breath. If it was this difficult sharing the news with them, what would it be like telling the town?

Rosalind stood from the table. "I think I'm going to head to bed. I'll see you in the morning, Blake. I'm glad you're back." She gave him a weary smile.

Trent rose and kissed her cheek. "I'll be up after a while."

"Okay."

Trent watched his wife leave the room, then turned back to Blake. "The twins aren't sleeping well, Timothy is the hardest to get to bed. Rosalind is waking up twice a night." He went to the cabinet, grabbed a mug, and poured some coffee. "What else is going on?"

Blake lifted his head in surprise, meeting Trent's gaze. "Isn't that enough?"

He shrugged, taking a sip of coffee. "I get this feeling. Something more you're not telling me. Does it have to do with the robbers?" Trent reclaimed his chair.

He hadn't planned on this discussion, not tonight anyway. "I guess … the woman on the stage."

Trent tipped his cup in his direction. "Go on."

"I really don't know what to say about her." What could he say? Where to begin?

"A name is a good place to start."

"Jessica. Her name is Jessica. When I was trying to protect her from the robbers, I told the robbers I was going to marry her, and she believed I meant it. When she returned to town, she insisted that Jake have me arrested."

Trent tried to gulp down his laughter but failed miserably. "Oh, I have to meet this woman. She sounds perfect already." He laughed again but sobered when Steph's cry sounded from upstairs. He rose to his feet and set his cup in the sink. "You're telling me the rest tomorrow." He chuckled as he left the kitchen.

The talk of Jessica affirmed his need to sleep outside. Not that God wasn't with him wherever he went, but lying under the stars reminded him God was near, and right now, a nagging feeling within his soul drew him under the stars.

By the time he reached the barn, the heavens shone like diamonds in the clear night sky. He unbuckled his belt and hung it with his guns on a hook, along with his hat. A yawn lingered as he lifted his horse's pad and took it outside, then dropped it on the ground. Settling in for the night, he blinked, his eyes growing heavy.

Thank you, Lord. For all you did ... Protecting me ... Protecting Jess ...

CHAPTER THREE

Jessica got up early the next morning, readied herself, and left the boardinghouse before the sun rose. Traveling by foot to the ranch—the one the livery owner had told her about—was her only option without a horse. She still had a long walk ahead of her, but it was worth it if the man she'd be buying her horse from witnessed the dust on her clothes and the smudges of dirt she'd find along the way. Surely he'd have compassion and sell her a horse. Either way, it was worth the try. She couldn't wait three weeks before a horse came in. She needed to be long gone by then.

Jessica shifted her reticule from one hand to the other, thankful to have her gun back. Mr. Briggen had brought her trunk to her room last night, and when he'd mentioned the sheriff was the one who'd delivered it, her mouth had fallen open. Mrs. Briggen had even mentioned her trunk had opened because of the broken lock but the sheriff had asked her to stuff the belongings back in.

Jessica's heart twisted when she thought of what a fool she had made of herself in front of him and his deputy. What if her father had been there? He would have been upset by her actions. She hadn't realized Blake was the sheriff. It changed everything. She respected the badge, as her father had taught her with his actions, not just his words. The way he'd gone out of his way to help people stuck with her. He was a man who fought for the weak and protected the innocent. When she'd asked him why he risked his life, he'd told her as sheriff it was his job. It was God who had shown him how to love others. Protecting them came from that same love.

As she walked, an orange ball rose, meeting the horizon in the far distance. The sun's rays stretched across the land, like golden fingers spreading out from one side of the heavens to the other. Warmth raced its way up her arms. She let out a breath, and peace cloaked her shoulders like a wool blanket. She'd been on the run for close to a year and could count on one hand how many times she'd stilled enough to notice the world around her—or to thank the Creator.

She'd do better once her father's murderer came to justice. But the law had given up and now she was paying the price. She had to stay ahead of Cliff, lest he find her. And it was her fear that kept her one step ahead of him and his gang.

Her father's words had continued to come back to her over this last year as she'd traveled. *I love you, daughter. Now run. Go!*

Jessica swallowed the lump in her throat.

His last words. And she'd listened. Had been running ever since.

Tears burned her eyes. She blinked a few times to clear her vision. A tree stood in the middle of nowhere some distance away. This was where Mrs. Briggen told her the Eastons' property started.

She glanced down at her dress, its edges sweeping the

ground. Dirt. She bent and ran her fingers through the soil. Rich. She missed planting a garden, collecting eggs, and chasing her mean old rooster around the yard. She'd threatened that rooster more times than she could count, yet she loved the old thing.

At the tree, Jessica ran her hand along the bark. She fingered a heart etched into the wood. Inside were carved initials, *T* and *R*. The man she'd come to see about the horse was named Trent. Was *R* his wife's initial? This was something young children would do. Had they been childhood sweethearts? And now husband and wife?

Jessica hurried down the hill. A two-level white home came into view, unlike any house she'd seen before. A porch wrapped around the house, and two barns nestled against trees to the right. Corrals just beyond. A field of sunflowers was off to the other side.

She glanced at herself again and her dirty hands. Maybe this wasn't a good idea. It wasn't what she expected, but she'd come all this way.

Jessica slowed her steps as she reached the buildings. She cupped her mouth with her hands. "Hello in the barn."

Muffled voices sounded from somewhere inside.

"Hello," she said again, but this time with more strength behind her words.

A man sauntered out, confidence in his stride. He tipped his Stetson. "Hello to you. My name is Trent Easton. How may I help you?" He gave a friendly smile.

She swallowed, unsure of herself suddenly. "I came to purchase a horse."

He tilted his head and raised the brim of his hat above his furrowed brow. "I'm sorry, ma'am, but I don't sell horses." He glanced over her shoulder, seeming to scan the area. "How did you get here?"

"I walked."

His blue eyes widened. "From town?"

"Yes, sir. I spoke with the livery owner yesterday. He's expecting a horse in three weeks. I need to be on my way before then, and without a horse, I'm stuck."

The sound of galloping horses brought her around to find two cowboys riding into the yard. Both came to a halt, and one of them, dark hair poking from under his hat, leaned forward, his hands resting on the horn of the saddle. While he eyed her, the other got right down to business. "She's going to drop both calves at any time. The boys are out there."

Mr. Easton nodded. "God has certainly blessed us. Appreciate you both staying out."

The dark-haired fellow had yet to finish his appraisal of Jessica when he straightened in the saddle and curled a lazy smile. "And who do we have here?"

It galled her to be stared at like a prized bull for sale. She almost raised her voice to tell him a thing or two, but she was here for a horse, not to get kicked off the ranch. "Jessica Thompson. I walked from town in hopes Mr. Easton would sell me a horse."

"From town. That's about two miles." The more serious of the two glanced at Mr. Easton.

The curious one let his smile widen. "I'll take her back."

"I'm taking her to town."

At the velvet voice, Jessica turned.

None other than the sheriff came from the barn and strolled straight toward her, his steps sure. His blue eyes sparkled, and though he hadn't yet looked at her, her heart jumped.

The serious cowboy tipped his Stetson at the sheriff and gave a chuckle. "It's good to have you back. Come on, Pete. Let's get some coffee."

Her gaze followed both men to the house. The cowboy's chuckle made her curious, and she didn't want to look in the sheriff's direction anyway. He riled her in a way no other man had, and it infuriated her. Why? She wasn't sure.

She straightened, wishing she were taller, and looked Mr. Easton in the eye. "I came for a horse, and I can pay you."

"I'm sorry, Miss Thompson, but my horses aren't for sale."

"But I've come all this …" The words died on her tongue. Begging wasn't her way. "Thank you for your time, Mr. Easton." She bit her lip and headed up the steep hill.

"Aren't you going after her?" Trent stepped up to Blake as they watched Jessica climb the hill.

Blake continued to eye her as her slender arms swung and her hands fisted. "I'm debating how good it is for my health."

A smile lifted his friend's lips. "I can get Pete. He's willing."

"I know what he's willing to do. He's been lookin' for a wife for months now."

And for some reason, it bothered Blake to think Pete had taken a liking to Jessica. Yes, she was beautiful, but Pete had no idea what this woman was capable of. This headstrong, exhausting, mouthy woman. So what if she felt right nice in his arms when he held her against him. It meant nothing. She meant nothing.

"I've known you for a long time, Blake, and that daze of yours says it all. What is it about this one?"

"Maybe it's the way she stuck a gun in my back."

Trent laughed, his shoulders shaking. "I can't wait for you to finish telling me what happened yesterday."

Blake headed for the barn and saddled his horse. It didn't take him long to find Jessica. He would never let her go alone with what was happening in the area. And he might have guessed she'd have enough money to buy a horse in that little satchel. She'd be an easy pick for someone to capture and sell to a brothel. He hated the thought of anyone hurting her, touching her. And he didn't like where his thoughts had taken him.

He slowed next to her as she walked. "Want a ride?"

"No." She continued with not so much as a glance in his direction.

"Why won't you accept help?"

"Oh, I'd accept help, but it's who I'd have to accept it from that is the problem."

"Suit yourself." The words seeped through his lips before he'd realized he'd said them.

Blake had woken with praise on his lips, but now frustration doused his mood faster than water sinking a ship. He'd make sure she reached the boardinghouse safely, then avoid her at all costs. Nothing was worth the aggravation this woman caused him. The sooner she left town, the better off he'd be.

What was with this man? No matter what she said or how mean she said it, Blake wouldn't leave her be. Even now he sat in the distance on his horse and waited. Then, before she got too close, he rode up a ways and waited for her again.

She didn't like the way her heart had sped up when he walked out from the barn to her or the desire that stirred in her to be near him. It made her weak, and she had to be strong for her father's sake. He'd died saving her, and leaving town was the only way to ensure her safety, that Cliff didn't find her.

She ran her sleeve over her forehead as she looked up at the sun. Sweat ran down her back, and her mouth was dry.

Her father, he'd know what to do. How she missed him and

his guidance. Her pace slowed. She bit her lip to keep from crying. That would only dehydrate her more. Rest. That's what she needed. And water. She'd have to settle for rest. She came to a standstill and plopped on the ground.

After a few minutes, the sound of hoofbeats closed in on her. Blake halted his horse in front of her, shading her from the sun.

She closed her eyes at the relief from the heat, then opened them. "I'm not riding with you."

The most handsome smirk she'd ever seen formed on his lips, and she did everything in her power to quit staring. She failed miserably. He was aware of her predicament, and no doubt he was loving every minute of it.

He climbed down from his horse, squatted beside her, and handed her a silver canteen. "You must be thirsty."

With a sigh, she swallowed her pride and took the canteen, heat rising to her cheeks. The cool liquid soothed her scratchy throat and cotton mouth. "Thank you," she whispered. "I ... I owe you an apology. I shouldn't have said what I did." When he didn't say a word, she went on. "I also want to thank you for getting my trunk."

He glanced at the ground and ran a callused finger through the cracked dirt.

"And the water."

He looked at her then. "You're welcome. Now will you allow me to take you to the boardinghouse?"

She couldn't bear to be in his arms again, no matter how much she wanted to. "No. Thank you." She rose and held out his canteen.

Leaving her with the canteen, he jumped to his feet and stalked off to his mount. Then man and horse galloped out of sight.

Chapter Four

Jessica was determined to steal if she had to. She was going to find a horse and head to Fort Worth, and nothing would stop her.

She rolled over and yanked at the nightgown twisted around her legs before standing at the bed's edge. The sun hadn't yet peeked through the curtains, but she didn't have much time before it did.

After dressing in the dim candlelight, she crept to the stairs, where she was met by the aroma of fried ham. Her stomach rumbled, but her hunger pains morphed into something else—fear of being caught. At the bottom of the staircase, she glanced at the doorway into the kitchen. Why hadn't she thought of Mrs. Briggen cooking for her tenants?

She took the last wooden step, and it creaked beneath her. She paused. All was quiet. Maybe she'd slip out the door and no one would suspect her of being gone. Jessica tiptoed into the hall.

Mrs. Briggen met her head on, whisking eggs and sloshing them around the bowl. "You're just in time. I'm about to make these here eggs. Ham's a-cookin'. First batch of biscuits is done.

Second batch is in the oven. I need more." She spun and returned to the kitchen.

With a sigh, Jessica followed.

Mrs. Briggen poured the eggs into a pan over the fire, then wiped her fingers on her apron. "Can you hand me the jar of milk?" She pointed to the counter. "There's not much left, but we have enough for now."

Jessica hesitated before handing it to her. "Do you have another jar I can get for you?"

"I already used the fresh milk delivered this morning. The general store doesn't open for a few more hours. I'll go by later." She slowly poured the milk into the pan of egg, stirring. "So what are your plans for the day?"

"Plans?" Jessica ran her finger back and forth over the counter. What was she going to say? *I plan to be a horse thief within the hour.* Wouldn't her father be proud. "What can I do to help you?"

"There's an apron hanging on the hook near the back door. Put it on. The dough is waiting over there on the table, ready to be rolled out and cut into circles. I love the smell of fresh-baked biscuits." She spooned the mixture around the pan and sprinkled in salt and pepper. "And bring plates back with you. Everyone should be coming down soon. Perfect time to meet your neighbors."

"Oh." Jessica swallowed. The sooner she left town, the sooner people would forget she was ever here. "Mrs. Briggen, there's no need. I won't be staying long. As I mentioned before, I'm only passing through."

"Nonsense." She waved her arm in the air. "Now hurry with those plates."

Jessica turned and found the tattered, dingy-white apron on a bent nail by the back door. She slid the apron over her head and tied it behind her back. After taking the plates from the counter, she set them next to the stove and handed Mrs. Briggen a dish.

"You need to know your neighbors no matter how long you're in town. Hopefully you'll love it here and will want to make Graham your home. I've lived many places, but this is my favorite." She scooped small portions of eggs onto each dish until they were half filled.

Jessica hadn't made biscuits in so long, but thankfully, the dough had already been made. She sunk her hands into the mixture and squeezed, dough bubbling between her fingers. She pounded it out. "Do you have a roller I can use to flatten this out a bit more?"

"Oh, did I move it? Grab another from the cabinet."

Jessica glanced around, noticing a small table for two tucked on the other side of the sink. She found the mentioned cabinet, opened it, and lifted out the rolling pin, then got started on the dough. Eighteen circles were cut, and with the scraps she reformed the dough into a ball, then dug a hole with her finger. She took a slice of ham, chopped it up, dropped it into the hole, then pinched the top together.

Mrs. Briggen leaned over her shoulder. "What do we have here? It looks like a tear drop."

"I make designs and shapes out of the leftover dough, adding whatever I can. I love creating things with my hands. My father used to say …" Jessica clamped her lips together. The less people knew, the better. *No attachments. No friends. No one dies because of me.*

"You miss him."

Jessica nodded, avoiding Mrs. Briggen's gaze. Was she so obvious that a stranger could read her? She closed her eyes for a moment, and a warm hand settled on her back.

"How long has he been gone?"

She moved away from the older woman's touch. "A year." After taking a rectangular pan from the counter, Jessica placed the dough in lines down the tray. Footsteps sounded near the dining area, and she changed the subject quickly. "Sounds like a herd of cattle just rumbled through the house, down the stairs."

Mr. Briggen entered the kitchen, his glasses hanging on the tip of his nose. He squinted, then pushed the frames back up and opened the oven. "Sorry, hon." He grabbed a cloth from the drawer, pulled out a tray of perfectly golden-brown biscuits, and set it on the counter, then took the tray from Jessica's hands and slid it in.

Mrs. Briggen moved back to the counter and began filling the plates Jessica had brought her with ham. The older woman looked to her husband. "Did you put Blake's package in his room?" She handed Jessica the biscuits she'd prepared.

"I did. That's not what took so long. When I closed his door, it wouldn't lock behind me, so I fixed it. That man never complains about anything. Who knows how long the door's been unable to lock. In case he didn't have his key, I left it unlocked."

"Blake? The sheriff?" Jessica glanced at the kitchen door, then handed Mrs. Briggen plates to fill.

"That's him." Mr. Briggen lifted two filled plates from the counter. "He's been in room 219 for nearly three years, since becoming sheriff. We've never had problems with our tenants with him around."

Mrs. Briggen looked at her.

Blake lived here? Why hadn't she seen him?

"Jessica, are you all right?" The older woman pointed. "You're about to drop those plates."

She'd forgotten she was holding them. "Ah … yes. A bit distracted is all." She set the filled plates on the counter. "Is there anything else you need? I think I'm going to go up to my room."

"We have it." Her husband smiled at her, then carried the plates out. Voices rose beyond the kitchen.

Mrs. Briggen looped her arm through Jessica's. "Not until I introduce you. Come." She led her through the door into the dining room, where a handful of men and women waited for breakfast. Those with plates ate, while the others stared at her and Mrs. Briggen. "Everyone, I want you to meet Miss Jessica Thompson. She is staying with us for a while. Please make her feel welcome." The older woman smiled, released her arm, and headed back to the kitchen.

Jessica stood there dumbfounded. "Hi." Heat climbed her neck. She hated being the center of attention, especially when she didn't want anyone to remember her.

"Well, hello again," someone whispered close to her ear.

Instinct kicked in. She threw her elbow hard against a man's ribs. A plate scattered against the wooden floor, sending eggs and a biscuit to the same fate.

The cowboy from Mr. Easton's ranch—the one who'd offered her a ride—looked stunned as he held his side.

"I ... um ... I'm terribly sorry." Her cheeks flamed as she bent down and lifted both food and splinters of ceramic onto the larger pieces of plate.

He slowly knelt next to her and began picking up scattered ceramic. "It's all right, Miss Jessica." A slight smile followed. "May I call you Jessica?"

Her cheeks warmed even more, if that was possible. "I'll get you another plate." She rose, but the cowboy stood and touched her arm, stilling her movements. He wasn't much taller than she, allowing her to see straight into his chocolate eyes.

"No need. I can fend for myself." His hand went to his side, where she'd hit him. "Most of the time. That was a mighty jab."

She sensed a dozen wide eyes burning into her. "Please, let's go into the kitchen," she whispered.

"Only if you eat with me." His grin widened. "It's the least you can do."

She headed for the kitchen but halted just inside the door. "How did you know I was here? How did you know it was me? We've never been introduced."

He shrugged. "It's a small town. I had an erran' to run. Besides, where else would a newcomer go?"

Of course. Where else would she go but to the boardinghouse? She needed to breathe, try to relax. Not everyone was after her.

"I can remedy that last part." He held out his hand. "My name is Peter Stillman, but everyone calls me Pete. I'm twenty-two. I live at the Easton ranch with the other cowhands, and I want to get to know you better."

Her heart began to race. *This isn't happening.* She glanced at his offered hand and spun on the ball of her foot and moved farther into the kitchen. She had to get out of this town. She'd possibly bruised the man's ribs, and he was still following her, carrying a shattered plate.

Mrs. Briggen frowned. "Pete, what happened?"

She turned to see what the man would say, and he was smiling again.

"She threw a plate at me." He ambled over to the trash and tossed the plate and food into it.

Jessica stared, searching for a response. Who did this man think he was? "Mrs. Briggen, that's not at all what happened. I—"

The stout woman pointed a stubby finger at Pete. "You watch yourself. I won't have you scaring her off."

Jessica didn't know what Mrs. Briggen was talking about,

but it didn't matter. She walked to the sink and washed the eggs from her fingers, then grabbed a cloth from the counter and dried her hands, avoiding Mrs. Briggen and Pete's conversation. Maybe she'd be able to head back to her room without being detected.

"Miss Jessica, where you goin'?" Pete asked, hurrying after her. "I thought you said you was goin' to eat with me. You goin' back on your word?"

Great. She paused at the door. "I never gave you my word. Actually, I never said a word."

"It was understood." He palmed his side where she'd hit him.

She huffed under her breath and strolled to the small table in the corner. "I'm not returning to the dining area."

He sat across from her, and Mrs. Briggen brought them two coffees and water, then returned with plates full of food, standing over them like a mother hen.

Pete picked up his fork and glanced from one to the other. "I won't bite."

"I'll be right over here." Mrs. Briggen strolled to the stove and switched out a pan from the oven. Her husband rushed in, slid the biscuits into a bowl, and left.

"Since I told you who I was, Miss Jessica, tell me about yourself." He ripped his biscuit in two, then stuffed the first half in his mouth.

"I'm new in town, and I'm looking to buy a horse."

"I gathered as much." He lifted his mug and chugged down the contents, then wiped his mouth with his sleeve. "Where are you from?"

She took a bite of egg to stall while she decided how much she'd tell him, but moaned against the overwhelming desire to shovel her food in her mouth. "Mrs. Briggen, these eggs are wonderful."

"Thank you, dear." The older woman scrubbed a pan vigorously, water splashing on her apron.

Jessica took several bites of her biscuit. Not only did it give her time to think before she spoke, but also to savor the buttery taste left on her tongue. "I'm from Oklahoma. Born and raised."

"Do you have any brothers and sisters?"

"Nope. Only child. What about you?"

"Older brother. Owns a ranch here in town. Ma died after she brought me into the world. Pa never remarried."

She thought on this for a moment. Everyone she knew back home had remarried once a love one passed, except for her pa, but he always said loving her was enough for him. "Kinda strange, isn't it, a man not remarrying in these parts?"

"He said Ma was the love of his life."

"He's telling the truth." Mrs. Briggen reached into the sink full of soap bubbles. "My brother loved her to the depths of his very soul until the day he died."

Mrs. Briggen and Pete are related? She glanced from her to him. No real similarities. Pete's brown eyes and hair reminded her of chocolate, while the older woman had blonde hair edged with gray. Strands of it fell in front of hazel eyes.

"He told me once that they were one, in the flesh and spirit, right into eternity, and that's where he planned to see her next," Mrs. Briggen continued. "Soul mates, he called them."

Soul mates. She pictured her father reading his worn Bible under the candlelight in his favorite chair, sharing Jeremiah and how God had a plan for her life. How he had her in the palm of his hand, so she never needed to worry about her future, a husband, or the children he was sure she'd have.

None of that mattered now. Father had died. She'd never be safe until the men who killed him were captured.

"What happened to your pa?" Jessica turned the conversation back on him. "How long has it been since his passing?"

Pete dug a fingernail along a narrow crack running through the edge of the table. "Five years. There isn't a day that goes by I don't miss him. A horse thief shot him in the middle of the street while he was going after him."

Her breath caught. *Shot him. Going after him.* "Was he the …"

"Town's sheriff."

She stilled.

He inhaled a deep breath, then exhaled.

Swallowing against the lump in her throat was impossible. She grabbed her glass and drank large gulps of water, hesitating only once to breathe. As she set the glass down, the door caught her eye. "I'm sorry, Pete." She collected her plate and glass, then carried them to the sink.

All the way to her room, tears blurred her vision. She slumped on the bed, tired of feeling the pain and loneliness left by the death of her father. And the fear that followed her at every turn. Even God seemed to be silent.

Jessica flicked the moisture away from her face. She'd wait for the livery owner's horse to come in on the train. She wasn't a horse thief like the man who'd shot Pete's father. And she wouldn't forget that in the future.

CHAPTER FIVE

As soon as Jessica left her room—on the third day after arriving in Graham—the aroma of fresh bread filled her nose, and her stomach complained about missing supper the previous night. She had no choice but to skip the meal. She couldn't continue to have a roof over her head and buy a horse if she wasn't careful with her money. At least breakfast was included with her rent.

She walked into the kitchen and reached for the apron on the nail. "Good morning, Mrs. Briggen." Once the apron was on, she strolled to the dough on the counter.

"Good morning. Did you sleep well?" Mrs. Briggen finished whisking eggs in a bowl, then poured the mixture into a pan and stirred, just as she had every day since Jessica arrived.

Jessica went to the cabinet and pulled out the roller, then the flour. "Yes, ma'am." She carried them to the table. After sprinkling the flour over the table surface, she flattened the dough, then cut circles.

Mrs. Briggen sat in the chair next to her and wiped her forehead and cheek with a small cloth. "What type of design will you make today with the leftovers scraps?"

"What would you like? Something simple, like a heart or square? Or I can make a flower."

"You make flower shapes out of bread?"

She smiled, placing the circles on a tray. "I sure can. Made a few batches for the orphanage back home right before I left."

"An orphanage? Please do. I'd love to see it."

Scraping up the leftovers with her fingers, she pressed and molded the dough into the shape of a tulip. "There." She placed the flower next to the other shapes on the tray.

"Very nice, Jessica." Mrs. Briggen rose and went back to the stove. "I didn't see you at supper last night. Did you eat somewhere else in town?"

She glanced away. "No, ma'am."

"Who did you eat with?"

Avoiding her gaze, she said, "No one."

"Then I hope you weren't evading us because of my nephew Pete. I know he's taken with you, but don't let him run you off. I tell him all the time not to ask so many questions that are none of his business, but he doesn't listen. He's too nosy, if you ask me. I don't know where he gets it. So tell me. Do you like my nephew? You would be wonderful for him."

Jessica bit her lip to keep from laughing. "I think Pete is a very kind man, but I'm not interested in finding a husband."

"Oh, I understand. I just needed to ask." She took Jessica's pan and slid it into the oven. "Won't stop him from coming around is all."

Like the days before, people filed into the dining area while Mr. Briggen entered the kitchen, apologized for being late, and rushed out with several plates of food. After the food was cooked and counters cleaned, Jessica sat at the table for two and ate her breakfast. The same eggs, ham, and biscuits, but she relished each bite.

"So what are your plans for the day?" Mrs. Briggen stood on her toes and slid a plate into the cabinet.

"I thought I'd head over and speak to the livery owner. He told me he was expecting a horse in a few weeks."

Pete entered with his empty plate in hand. "Aunt Martha, have you seen …" He caught sight of Jessica in the back of the kitchen, and a boyish smile raised his lips. "Never mind."

"Since Pete's here, ask him to show you the town. He can introduce you to Tom, the livery owner." Mrs. Briggen faced her nephew. "You won't mind showing Miss Jessica around, will you?"

Jessica knew what Pete's answer would be, just as she knew wedding bells were ringing in Mrs. Briggen's ears. She rose and set her plate in the sink. "That sounds fine. I planned on walking around town but haven't had a chance. Give me a few minutes, Pete, and I'll be right out."

She hurried upstairs, her thoughts turning to Blake as she passed his door. Her pulse raced. She entered her room and grabbed her reticle, which held her gun and money, then left.

"There you are." Pete grinned and held out his elbow as she neared.

She hesitated. "We're friends, Pete. That's all."

"I know." He dropped his arm and opened the door for her. "Doesn't mean I can't hope for more."

There wouldn't be more, as far as she was concerned. Friendship was all she had to offer, and that was more than she was willing to give most men. But she liked Pete.

The dry air stole her breath as they exited the boardinghouse, and it took a moment to recapture another. How had the weather gotten so blisteringly hot in only one day?

They strolled in silence, side by side, down the boardwalk,

and she didn't mind it one bit. It was nice being with someone and not having to fill the time with useless babble. It also felt nice trusting someone again, and somehow, she trusted Pete.

"Where would you like to go first?" he asked. "The livery to see about the horse?"

"I would. The man mentioned only one, so I want to make sure he'll sell it to me."

They strolled past the seamstress shop, and she immediately fingered the brown fabric of her shabby dress. Longing to own one of the dresses in the shop window almost made her pause, but she continued to the livery with Pete.

"Hello? Tom?" Pete called as her eyes adjusted to the darkness.

No answer.

"Wait here, and I'll see if he's in the house."

Jessica glanced around as Pete walked away. There was no sign of the two young boys she'd seen before. Next time, she'd ask Mrs. Briggen if she could make the bread scraps into something the boys might like. Jessica missed being around children and working at the orphanage. She'd prided herself on making the children smile, even for a short time, as her small gifts had. Yes, she could make a bow and arrow just fine out of the dough that was usually left.

Two carriages awaited use on one side of the livery, while horses were being fed on the other. Blake's horse was nowhere in sight. A strange twinge fluttered within her stomach. She pressed her hand against it. Surely she couldn't be hungry so soon.

Pete came out of the house with the other man limping close behind. "This is our blacksmith and livery owner, Mr. O'Connor. And Tom, this is Miss Thompson. I believe you met earlier."

"Nice to see ye again. Did ye have any luck findin' a horse?"

"No, sir. It's the reason I'm here. I want to purchase the horse you have coming on the train."

Tom glanced at Pete, then back at her, shoving his hands into his pockets. "Ye have that kind of money?"

"It depends on what you're asking. I can pay you half now to hold the horse and the rest when it comes. I think that would only be fair."

The silence lingered until Pete said, "I agree. I think that's a perfectly sound arrangement for both sides. Don't you agree, Tom?"

The livery owner looked at Pete, then at her. "The cost of me horse is three hundred."

She gasped. "You aren't serious?"

"Aye, ma'am. The horse is a mustang, and with the cost to ship him—"

Pete took a step forward. "Mustangs around these parts are free for the catchin'. You can't possibly—"

"Right sorry Mr. Easton wouldn't sell the little lady a horse. I know he's a fair man, but that's me price. I've got mouths to feed, so take it or leave it."

Pete took another step forward, but she placed herself between the men. This wasn't anyone's concern but hers. "Fine. I need a horse."

Pete stared at her, brow furrowed. "You have that kind of money?"

She opened her reticule and pulled out a wad of bills, her family's savings, and began counting. She took out enough for the down payment, then stuffed the rest back into her bag and snapped it closed. "One hundred and fifty dollars. You'll have the rest when my horse is delivered. Pete here is my witness."

Tom clenched the bills between his long fingers, and a wide smile spread across his cheeks. "I might raise me prices, but I'm an honest man, Miss Thompson."

Somehow "raised prices" and "honest man" didn't seem to fit together. It really didn't matter though. Finally, she'd have a horse. Even if it cost her everything she had, she'd be on her way out of town in a few weeks.

Jessica turned to head outside, leaving Pete speaking with Tom. Whatever they were discussing didn't matter, but Pete's raised voice gave her an idea as to the topic. With a little over two weeks to go, she'd need to acquire a job and make certain Cliff, or his gang, couldn't find her.

Pete ran to catch up and fell in step beside her. "We can find someone else who will sell you a horse. That's a lot of money."

"It is, and I know he took advantage of the situation, but what other choice do I have?"

"I can speak with Mr. Easton. He's a generous man. When you went to the ranch, did you explain the situation? I'm sure—"

"He turned me down, Pete. There's no one else."

"That's not true. Blake has several horses. They're fine horses, like Mr. Easton's. They've been raised together. We can go ask him now." He veered toward the sheriff's office at a full jog.

"Pete! Wait!" She lifted the hem of her dress and hurried after him, but he didn't stop. "Pete! Please. Don't!" People stared at her now as she stepped onto the boardwalk and grabbed his arm.

He entered the building, pulling her inside with him. "Blake," Pete said loudly, covering her hand with his own, "we need to talk to you about something."

Blake looked up from a stack of papers on his desk. His crystal blue eyes peered from under his Stetson, piercing her. "What can I do for you both?"

Jessica pulled her hand free of Pete's.

"She needs a horse from someone who'll give her an honest price. Tom's being unreasonable."

Blake leaned back in his chair. "You're still looking for a horse, are you? Well, Tom is the man to buy a horse from, owner of the only livery stable in town. Besides, none of my horses are for sale." He sat forward and returned his focus to his papers.

Of course they weren't. She looked to Pete. "It doesn't matter. He doesn't care. Let's go."

Pete didn't budge. "Three hundred dollars is quite a bit for a mustang. Even you would admit it's an unfair price. And I thought with you having seven of your own ..."

Blake scowled as he gazed at her. "You didn't give Tom that kind of money for a horse, did you?"

She swallowed. "No. But—"

"Good. Only a fool would pay three hundred dollars for a mustang."

Jessica clenched her reticule to her waist. His words and the way he looked at her infuriated her to no end. "Then I'm a fool, Sheriff, since I just gave Tom half the money. When the horse arrives, I'll pay him the rest."

Blake shook his head. "I'm afraid you've been taken, ma'am. No mustang is worth that price."

She gritted her teeth and moved forward. "If men in this town would be straightforward and honoring of a woman, as God intended, instead of manipulative and deceitful and downright rude, then I wouldn't be in this predicament."

The corners of his mouth lifted ever so slightly. "By predicament, do you mean unwed and stubbornly fending for yourself? If you've changed your mind about marriage, the *men in this town* are always looking for a helpmate."

"You insufferable man! What I meant to say was ... I was

speaking of loving thy neighbor as thyself." She turned and hurried out the door, almost tripping on the boardwalk.

She couldn't wait to leave this town, to never see this place again—and especially Blake McKenny.

Blake chuckled to himself as he shook his head. "She's a handful, that one." Again resting against the back of the chair, he met Pete's narrowed gaze.

"Why did you have to tease her that way? It was my idea to come to you because I knew you would help. What Tom did was wrong, and we both know it." He turned to leave.

"Pete, wait."

The younger man stopped with his hand on the door.

"I'll ask Tom about it, and I'll see what I can do."

"Thank you. That's all I ask." Pete closed the door behind him.

Blake rose and strolled to the window. Pete stood on the edge of the street, head turning as if looking for something. Or maybe someone.

He inhaled. A light fragrance lingered in the air, the same as before when Jessica had stood in his office.

Pete waved and dashed out of view.

With a deep breath, Blake rounded his desk, grabbed the two *wanted* posters, stuffed them inside his shirt, and scribbled a note to Jake letting him know he'd be at Tom's and then the boardinghouse.

Outside, a group of quilters from the church walked in his direction. Two women held bundles of fabric in their arms.

"Good afternoon, ladies." He tilted the brim of his hat. "May I carry something for you?"

"Oh, how lovely. Yes, please." The youngest of the group,

Mrs. Patterson, gave him a weary smile. Dark circles hung under her eyes. She was the newest mother in the community, so he could only imagine how tired she must feel. He still remembered how both Rosalind and Trent looked after their children were born.

Blake held out his hands. Yards of fabric with a blue-flowered pattern crossed his arms first, then a yellow gingham the color of the sun on a bright day. "Where're you heading?"

"To the church. We have a quilt to make. You know us ladies like to have a few on hand. You menfolk never give us advance notice before you pop the question, and we find ourselves rushing to get a wedding ring quilt finished in time. Prime example, Mrs. Briggen tells me her nephew Pete has his eye on the newcomer in town. What did she say her name was again?"

"Jessica Thompson." One of the other women spoke up.

"Yes, that's right. I think there'll be a wedding soon."

"Is that so?" Blake inhaled deeply, then glanced around. He didn't want to think about weddings, Pete, or Jessica. Or how Pete seemed to have won her confidence in such a short time. How many days had she been in town? Four? The image of Jessica's hand on Pete's arm when they entered his office came to mind. His steps slowed.

"Are you all right, Sheriff?" another woman asked.

"Um … yes … fine."

As he left the church a few minutes later, Blake made a mental note to stay as far away from Jessica as possible. She did something to him every time she neared. It wasn't the name calling or the irritation that seem to swell within him from nowhere, but an emotion he'd buried so deep it frightened him that she could unearth it.

CHAPTER SIX

Tom's kids came running from the livery and sped past Blake.

"Hey, boys. Your dad at home?"

They kept running, but one hollered over his shoulder, "Aye, sir."

Blake kept walking, then waved as he caught sight of the livery owner. Tom had a hold of Doc's horse's reins and was guiding the black carriage from the livery.

"Someone sick?" Blake asked.

"Doc's regular house calls. What can I do ye for, Sheriff? Need me to board ye horse?"

"Not this time." Blake lifted his Stetson above his brow. "I came to find out about the horse you sold to a Miss Thompson."

"Aye, sold her me horse. Hasn't arrived. Will be here in three weeks." Tom paused and met his gaze. "Why ye askin'?"

"Well, I heard you sold the horse for a higher price than expected. Three hundred dollars to be exact."

"She agreed, Sheriff. I didn't twist the lass's arm. When she first came to me, I sent her to the Eastons' place, but he turned the little lass down. That's none of me concern. All I know is she needed a horse and I happened to have one for sale." Tom strolled to the feed bags, grabbed a couple of handfuls, and added them to a horse's bucket.

"It's your horse, Tom, but I hope when it arrives, your conscience will get the better of you. You and I both know no mustang is worth the amount you're asking." Blake's gaze followed Tom's boys running around the building. "How's everything going? Are you planning to allow your sons to attend school this year?"

"Aye. It'll give them something to do other than be under me foot." Tom cleared his throat. "I put an ad in one of them fancy newspapers back East for a mail-order bride."

Blake took his hat off and hit it against his leg, giving him time to respond. He had known Tom as fair and trustworthy, so when Pete had accused the man of cheating Jessica, to say Blake was surprised was an understatement. But he was starting to see the big picture. "So you actually did it. Is that why you sold the horse so high?"

"I need the money for the horse just as bad as me boys need a female to tend to 'em. I've got to provide for me new wife when she comes. If she comes."

Blake nodded his understanding. If his mail-order bride did come, it would cost him more than the man had. Tom wasn't much older than Blake, but he had many responsibilities Blake didn't, and two of them ran past the livery chasing each other.

Securing his hat on his head, Blake nodded. "I hope things work out. I'll be praying God brings the woman He handpicked for you."

"Appreciate it." Tom climbed onto the carriage and met his gaze. "Blake, ye should order yerself a bride. It'd be nice to have a woman to cook for ye and keep ye warm at night."

"If I ever find myself in need of a woman, you'll be the first person I ask for advice to write one of those letters."

Tom smiled, tugged the reins, and drove the horse down the street, past the general store, then out of sight.

Blake shook his head as he headed toward the boardinghouse. He wondered what type of woman Tom's mail-order bride would be. Nothing like Miss Jessica Thompson. That he was sure.

He nodded to a passing carriage and hoped he wouldn't run into Jessica while at the boardinghouse. He needed a few things, and trouble wasn't included. There was too much to do today to rein in a wild filly. A pile of papers waited for him at his desk when he returned. Then there were the *wanted* posters—there was something about them he couldn't put his finger on. *But what?* Then there was the wire about another robbery right outside of Fort Worth. No word if the man who'd been shot survived. Blake prayed, not only for the man but for his town. Was that connected to the robbery he didn't stop? Thankfully, the driver of the stage was on the mend. But he reminded himself the two outlaws had left Jessica behind, and he was alive. Yet, he might have to call a meeting sooner than he expected.

The boardinghouse still smelled like sunshine and breakfast when he entered, though it was close to lunch. He shut the door and climbed the narrow stairs, then entered his musty room. After drawing back the curtains, he opened the window to allow the fresh air in. Thunder rolled in the far distance. It wouldn't be long before the storm made its way to town, but he'd have enough time to make it to the ranch before it hit.

In the street below, he caught sight of Pete and Jessica walking side by side. There was no hand holding, or much talking on Jessica's part. It seemed Pete's mouth was the only one moving. Pete pointed to the sheriff's office, and Jessica's head never even turned in the direction indicated. She looked to the opposite side of the street instead.

The corners of Blake's mouth rose. He was becoming accustomed to seeing her frustrated. She had looked beautiful standing in his office, face flushed, pleading her case.

Blake shook his head, closed the window, and moved the curtain back. He rummaged through his dresser, pulling out three days' worth of clothes. He dropped them on the brown quilt on his bed, grabbed a sack from the corner of the room, then stuffed his clothes inside. All the while, Jessica and the *wanted* posters pushed through his thoughts like a raging river—uncontrollable. Thinking of wanted men was better than the other option though. That one would just get him into trouble.

Blake yanked the rolled-up posters from inside his shirt and set them next to the sack. The only ones who knew about these men where Jake, Trent, and Rosalind. He needed a few more days to think and make a plan of action. For what? He wasn't sure, but he didn't want to be taken by surprise—or worse, find a town member dead.

He unraveled the sketches and stared, then stared some more. One man could have been anyone as far as he was concerned, but the other, there was something familiar about him. The eyes, perhaps? What could it be? Had this man come to town before?

A knock sounded at the door. "Blake, you here?"

Blake rose from the bed and quickly set the *wanted* posters on his dresser. "Come in, Mr. Briggen."

The man entered and pointed to the door frame. "I fixed your lock. Please tell me the next time something needs to be done. I know you don't like to complain, but we enjoy having you here, even if you haven't been around much lately. So next time …"

Blake snickered. "I appreciate you fixing my door. I planned on doing it myself, but I've been a bit preoccupied."

Mr. Briggen gave him a hard nod. "Don't you worry. You tell me what needs to be fixed, and I'll do it."

"Yes, sir." Blake grabbed his sack. "I'll be staying at the Eastons' ranch for a few days."

"Oh? You're not leaving us?"

"Just visiting." He smiled, not wanting to worry him. Being the sheriff, Blake wanted to live close to town in case something happened, and the Eastons lived a bit farther away than he liked. Besides, he couldn't avoid Jessica for the rest of his life. It was obvious it wasn't working seeing her everywhere he went.

"Good." Mr. Briggen patted his back. "I'll lock up for you."

Blake slid his room key from the shelf, threw the sack over his shoulder, and headed out the door, wishing he had a moment to go back for the posters. He needed to keep the posters hidden until he had a plan. Just a few more days.

A horse and rider trotted past Jessica and Pete as they strolled along the boardwalk. She'd know Blake's dark Stetson anywhere. Well, maybe it wasn't the Stetson itself, but the man wearing the Stetson. He sat tall in the saddle, and the muscles in his shoulders rippled beneath his shirt.

She forced herself to turn away. "I dislike him so."

"Who?" Pete glanced around.

"The sheriff, that's who. He irritates me."

"I know what happened earlier upset you, and I feel like it's my fault. Blake shouldn't have teased you as he did, but he's as honest as they come. He said he'd talk with Tom, and he will."

Jessica slowed to a stop. "This might come as a shock to you, but I knew what I was doing back there in the livery. I also knew I was going to pay too much for the horse. I just didn't realize it was going to be so much, but I had no choice. I need a horse of my own. There's something I've learned traveling, and that's most men take advantage of women and what they believe to be our helpless state. They either take what they can or try to marry up for the rest. The only thing they think about is themselves. Money and a pistol are the only things that will help a woman stay alive."

Pete frowned. "Do you truly believe that about all men—taking advantage, only caring for themselves?"

"I've met only one man in all my twenty-one years who thought about others before himself, and that was my father."

Pete hung his head. "I guess you see me as no different than the others."

Her heart fell. She hadn't meant that. "Pete, I …"

"It's all right. It's true. Since you've come to town, all I've wanted is to make you my wife because I wanted you." He met her gaze. "I'm sorry."

"Please, Pete …" She touched his hand. "I didn't mean …"

He took a step back. "I should be going." He turned away and walked to the boardinghouse. After untying his horse from the post, he climbed up into the saddle and rode out of town.

Jessica kicked the heel of her boot into the dirt. Why couldn't she keep her big mouth shut? She'd talk with Mrs. Briggen about what had happened. Pete was her nephew. Surely she'd have some advice on how to fix this.

After putting her reticule in her room, she found Mrs. Briggen in the kitchen stirring something. "What do you have there?" Jessica peeked into the bowl. "Potatoes?"

"Makin' shepherd's pie. Want to help?"

"If I can work and talk to you about Pete at the same time?"

"My two favorite subjects: cooking and my nephew." She chuckled. "Grab your apron."

Jessica nabbed the apron from the peg and tied it on. "What do you need me to do?"

Mrs. Briggen poured the contents of her bowl into a larger bowl. "There's tomatoes by the table over there. You can peel and cut while I finish mashing and smoothing the potatoes."

Jessica found a knife and two bowls waiting on the table and a barrel beside it. She reached into the wooden barrel, grabbed an apple-sized tomato, and began peeling.

"So what do you want to talk about? I know my Pete can be a little pushy, but he's a kind boy."

"He is kind." She paused, searching for the right words. "I said something I believe hurt his feelings. I didn't mean to, but it's truly how I felt. I was being honest."

Mrs. Briggen paused her stirring and glanced her way. "What did you say?"

"Told him men treat women unfairly, and they only want to marry for selfish reasons."

"I see." Mrs. Briggen set her bowl down and sat in a chair across from her. "What happened today? Did Pete do something?"

"Oh, no. That's why I wanted to speak with you. When I said it, I wasn't thinking about Pete but of other men I've met along the way. I've been treated like property and once almost found myself wed before I could reach for my pistol."

Her eyes widened. "Heavens, Jessica. I can't imagine. Pete would never treat you in such a way, but I can understand how he took it. He's been trying to court you since you came to town." The older woman let out a deep sigh. "I haven't helped matters any. I've encouraged him."

"I'm sorry, Mrs. Briggen, but I'm only interested in Pete as a friend. One I hope I haven't lost."

"Not to worry." She patted Jessica's hand and rose from her

chair. "Pete will come around. If not, I'll speak to him about it."

Jessica lifted another tomato. "Thank you. You know, Mrs. Briggen, it will be strange not seeing Pete tomorrow morning for breakfast."

She smiled and pointed a plump finger in her direction. "That's my Pete. Grows on a person. Maybe one day—"

Jessica raised a brow and shook her head at the woman.

"I wasn't going to say it. I only thought it. I can't help it if this old woman thinks you two would make a nice couple."

"Not to change the topic fast enough, but today I put money down on a horse the livery owns. Should be arriving on the train in nearly three weeks."

"Good for you. What will you do first when your horse comes?"

Jessica couldn't very well tell Mrs. Briggen she'd be leaving to never return. Not yet anyway. "Head to Fort Worth."

"Make sure you visit Millie's Shop. She has some of the finest chocolates I ever did taste."

"Oh, it's been a long time since I've eaten chocolate. Hopefully, after I pay for my horse, I'll have enough money left to try some."

Mrs. Briggen stayed quiet so long that Jessica met her stare.

"Is everything all right? Something about Pete?" Jessica asked.

"How would you feel about working for me? As you can tell, I can use your help. My dear husband wakes up when breakfast is finished, leaving me to do all the work. It's been wonderful having you here. Look, half the barrel of tomatoes has already been peeled."

"If you're sure, Mrs. Briggen. I can use the money."

"Of course. You can start now."

Jessica laughed. "Sounds wonderful."

Once dinner was finished and the kitchen cleaned, Jessica hung her apron on the peg and hugged the older woman's neck. "Thank you." Tears formed in her eyes, and she hurried from the room. For the first time, Jessica felt like she belonged. She'd forgotten what it felt like.

CHAPTER SEVEN

Horse hooves pounded toward the Eastons' barn and then stopped abruptly.

As Blake stepped to the side to drop the brush he'd been using on Legend into the bucket and see what the commotion was about, Pete stormed in. He could only guess what—or make that *who*—had Pete all riled up, but he was fairly certain the name started with a J.

"Blake." The younger man yanked off his hat and shoved a handful of mail in Blake's direction. "Give this to Trent."

Blake eyed him. "Don't you wanna go in and give it to him?"

"No." Pete shoved the bundle closer to Blake's chest.

Blake took the letters and placed them in his saddlebag, which was hanging off a stall, then strode back to Legend and picked up his brush. He tried to return his attention to the task at hand, but with each brush stroke on his horse's back, he reconsidered. "I spoke with Tom."

At the open barn door, Pete turned around. "What did he say? Did you tell him he was being unfair and needed to return some of the money?"

"Basically. But he said he needed the money to support his wife."

"What wife? Tom ain't married."

"Well, it seems he might be soon enough. He placed an ad in one of those newspapers back East for a mail-order bride."

"You don't say." Pete got a faraway look in his eye. "That old coot."

For some time now, the poor boy had wanted to get married and start a family, but he scared away any prospects with his persistence. Women liked to be courted, fall in love, then marry. Not the approach Pete was taking. So Blake thought. Although Jessica seemed to like his company—and him.

"Do you think he'll give back the money?" Pete asked.

"I'm not sure. They did make the deal, and she agreed. You were their witness."

Pete shook his head. "Still doesn't mean it's right." He glanced outside. "I guess I should head to the bunkhouse. The boys are a nosy bunch. They're all in my business." He met Blake's gaze. "What do you think about Miss Jessica?"

Blake almost choked, then chuckled to hide his cough. "She's stubborn ... bossy ..."

"Oh, but what about her smile? You ever seen a smile like hers?" Pete leaned against one of the barn doors. "The way the corner of her mouth lifts a little when she does, and she gets that dimple in her cheek."

Smile? She never did anything but frown at Blake, stomp off in another direction when he was near, or jab a weapon in his back. "Can't say I have."

"Well now." Pete continued to stand there and babble on about that dimple and other fine features about Jessica that Blake *had* noticed. By the time Pete headed for the bunkhouse, Blake was even more determined to stay as far from Jessica as possible. He didn't know how, but he would.

With the horse brushed and in his stall, Blake walked out to the barn and propped a foot on the bottom rail of the corral fence. One of his horses, Bucky, eased his way to him. "Hey, boy. How are you?" He stroked his head and back.

The front screen door slammed shut, and Blake glanced over his shoulder. Trent held one of the twins in his arms.

Blake stroked the horse's mane once more before turning. "Pete left for the bunkhouse. He gave me the mail, and I stuck it in my saddlebag. It's hanging on the stall in the barn."

"Why didn't he come in?"

"It has to do with a woman."

"You mean Miss Thompson. When he asked for the mornings off, he mentioned her name."

"Let's not discuss Miss Thompson. Pete did enough of that for the both of us." Blake watched the sleeping child in his friend's arms for a moment. He had to focus on the job at hand. Keep his town safe, including Trent's family—his family—but he wasn't sure how. "I think I need to tell the town about the robberies. A stage is due next week. I'd feel responsible if somethin' happened because they weren't prepared to defend themselves."

"When?"

"Sunday after preachin'. Most of the town will be there."

Trent nodded. "Rosalind and I will help get the word out."

Blake held out both hands for Trent to relinquish the drooling child to him, but then wiped the little girl's chin with his sleeve. He took her and tucked her to his chest. Her bare feet dangled at his waist.

Trent strode off to the barn as Blake crooned to the little girl. When Trent returned with Blake's saddlebag, his friend indicated the house. "Let's eat before we share the news about the town meeting with Rosalind. I don't want anything to steal her appetite."

"Is she still not feeling good?" he asked. The little girl nuzzled her cheek against his.

"Her strength is gone before the day even starts. I know it will get easier when the twins get a little older and sleep through the night. She's been invited for tea with several ladies from church, so she can help spread the word as well."

Blake inhaled the soft fragrance of soap and child as he entered the house. A yearning he tried to keep at bay filled him, a sentiment indicating part of his life was missing. He had hoped that loving Trent and Rosalind's children would make that emptiness subside, but it had only grown. What would it be like to have a child of his own?

Trent paused at the stairwell. "Did you say a stage is coming in?"

Blake eyed him for a moment before Jessica flashed in his thoughts. He gave a slight nod.

"You should tell her."

Jessica swiped at the sweat along her forehead with her sleeve. The sun bore down on her as she stooped over the tub and washboard in the boardinghouse's small backyard. Eyes safe from salty drops for now, she continued scrubbing the old apron. When she finished, it might not be useable, but after wearing it for days on end, it needed to be cleaned, along with the rest of her clothes. If she had some fabric, she'd make a new dress and apron, but as it was, she had not a penny to spare. All she had would be going to the livery owner once her horse came on the train.

With a huff, she snapped the apron in the air, then hung it to dry on the line next to her other clothes. She lifted the tub, and water sloshed over her shoes, soaking her feet. She turned the tub upside down, showering the brittle grass. It crunched beneath her wet shoes as she walked back to the house with the empty tub.

Mrs. Briggen stood gaping at her from the stove when she entered the kitchen. "Jessica, how long you been out there? You're as bright as a red apple."

Her father had told her on more than one occasion her skin was like her mother's. Any exertion in the least bit of heat caused her cheeks to flush, even when her skin was already tan from the sun. "Not long." She sat at the table in the kitchen and unlaced her soggy boots, then placed them outside to dry. "If it's all right with you, I'd like to keep the leftover dough?" She went to the sink and washed up.

"That's fine."

"Thank you. I have plans to take them to the livery."

"To the livery?" Wrinkles spread over Mrs. Briggen's forehead. "Tom's place? But I thought he overcharged you for the horse. Why would you go over there again?"

"His boys. I met them when I first came to town. They reminded me of the children back home. I think they might like the shapes I've come up with."

"You're not interested in Tom, are you?"

"Mrs. Briggen." Jessica shook her head, stifling a chuckle, then walked to the icebox.

"Sorry, dear. I know it's not my place, but I'd rather you marry Pete. You can't be upset at this old woman's romantic heart."

Jessica brought her the milk jar and set it on the counter, grinning. "No, I cannot."

"Maybe you could take your little breads to the general store. Mr. Vines is always looking for something different, especially if it doesn't cost him anything. Besides, if it works out, it will be an extra way for you to provide for yourself."

Jessica turned to look at her. "Do you think he'll like them?"

The older woman turned to her and smiled. "Of course. Now, let's get busy with breakfast. We have mouths to feed."

Two hours later, Jessica set out with a basket packed with her "little breads," as Mrs. Briggen called them. She'd take them to the livery, but first she had a stop to make at the general store. She passed the sheriff's office, trying to avoid a glance in that direction, but failed miserably. She still couldn't understand why she hadn't seen Blake since moving to the boardinghouse. Or had he been there but she'd missed him completely?

The bell rang as she entered the general store, breaking her thoughts.

"Hello. May I help you?" asked the balding man behind the counter. He slid a pencil behind his ear and pushed a stack of papers away.

She set her basket down on the counter and opened the lid. Nervousness grabbed at her stomach. What happened if he said no and sent her on her way? She cleared her throat. "Yes, Mr. Vines. My name is Jessica Thompson. I'm staying with the Briggens at the boardinghouse. Mrs. Briggen suggested I stop by and show you my little breads to see if you'd be willing to sell them in your store." She placed a towel on the counter.

"I've never heard of little breads."

Neither had I. Swallowing hard against the lump in her throat, she took a few samples from the basket and placed them on the towel. She gestured to the heart, the star, and then the bow and arrow she'd made for Tom's children. "These are little breads. I make them from biscuit dough and form them into all

73

different shapes."

"These are interesting, Miss Thompson, but I'm afraid—"

"I'll make a dozen of different shapes, and if they don't sell within two days, you're free to eat them," she said.

His eyes narrowed. "I can't promise you anything, Miss Thompson."

"I understand." She held her breath.

"Fine. Bring a dozen in the morning." He removed his pencil from his ear, yanked back his papers, and scribbled something.

"Yes, sir." Jessica placed the breads back in her basket and headed for the door. Tears of gratitude welled in her eyes as she stepped through the doorway onto the street. With lightened steps, she strode to the livery.

"Miss Jessica."

She glanced around, shielding her eyes as she looked in the direction of the sun.

Pete came toward her. "Hi."

"Hello to you."

He fell into step with her. "I'm sorry about yesterday, leaving as I did."

"And I'm sorry as well. I didn't mean …"

Pete stopped her when they reached the boardwalk. "It's all right. If friends can't be honest with each other, then there really isn't a friendship, is there?"

She nodded. "Does that mean we're still friends?"

"I need to say my piece before I agree to being only friends."

Her hands tightened around the basket handle. "All right."

"You were right about what you said yesterday. When I first met you, all I thought about was you becoming my wife. Don't get me wrong, I still do, but I like you as a person too. I want to be your friend, with no expectations, but you'll have to give me time. I can't help it if I find you attractive."

Her cheeks warmed. "What are your plans for the day?"

"Running an errand for Blake. He wants me to tell folks about a town meeting this Sunday after church."

Blake's name caught her attention, and she glanced toward the livery. "A town meeting?"

"You need to be there. It's important. But I also came to let you know that I won't be in town until Sunday."

"Does it have to do with the meeting?"

"No. It's just time to stay at the ranch."

She understood it wasn't because of her—their friendship—but she did enjoy his company. Was it wrong? "If you have time now, do you want to come with me to the livery?"

"What's at Tom's?" His brow furrowed. "Did your horse come in already?"

How she wished it had. "No. But I have something for the boys I hope they like."

Pete chuckled, taking the basket from her. "I'm sure whatever it is will be just fine. More than fine. You amaze me, Miss Jessica. To the livery it is."

She smiled as they approached the livery. The boys ran to her, much as they'd done when they'd first met. They halted at her side, out of breath and hands planted firmly on their knees.

"I won."

"No, I won."

"I beat ye to her." The nine-year-old met her gaze. "Tell him I won."

Pete set the basket on the ground. "Hey, boys. Miss Thompson here brought you a surprise."

They looked at each other with wide eyes and gaping mouths, then stood upright and inched forward. "Did you really bring something for us?"

Jessica gave Pete a sideways glance as she leaned down a

bit to the children's level. "I wasn't going to tell you yet." She held the basket lid ajar. "I did, but it's for the loser of your race. Tell me who lost the race, and I'll give him what's inside."

Both jumped up and down. "I lost. I lost."

"Of course you both did. How did I guess you'd say that?" She pointed to the smaller boy. Dirt that reminded her of coffee grounds covered his head. "And what is your name?"

"Chase. I chase me brother everywhere. Does that mean I won?"

"I believe you lost the race, so yes, you won a prize for being last."

The other boy planted his hands on his hips and kicked the dirt. "That's not fair."

Pete started to say something, but Jessica held out her hand. "What's your name?"

"Tommy."

"Well, Tommy, life's not fair. People look at others who are last or weak, and sometimes they are treated poorly, like they aren't important. But you know what? God cares about those who are last. They are special in God sight."

"'Tis still not fair."

"I know it seems that way." She reached into the basket and carefully pulled out the arrow-shaped little bread, then held it out to Chase.

His eyes widened in amazement as he took the bread.

Tommy turned away.

"Wait, Tommy," she said. "I have something for you too."

"But I won. I don't get anything."

"And you see, that's where you're wrong. With God, everyone gets a chance to accept His free gift, if they will only accept it whether they win or lose, whether they're good or bad or smart or poor. His gift is for all. Come in first or last."

He dropped to his knees beside her basket. "I get one too?"

"If you want it." She pulled out the bow and handed it to him.

"Look, Tommy, ye got a bow. Mine's an arrow." Chase held his down for his brother to see it. "It smells good enough to eat."

"You can eat it," Pete said as he leaned over her shoulder.

Tommy wasted no time in taking a bite. "Mmm." He chewed and swallowed. "Chase, if ye don't want yours, I'll eat it."

Chase put it behind his back. "'Tis mine, and I'll eat it when I want to."

"Suit yourself." Tommy took another bite, jumped to his feet, and strolled away into the livery.

Jessica closed the basket lid and stood, then smoothed the hair from Chase's eyes. "Aren't you going to take a bite?"

"'Tis true? What you said?"

"What was that?"

"About God? Thinkin' me special?"

She knelt again and said a quick prayer within her heart that he could understand what she was telling him. "God thinks you're very special. Do you know you have an angel watching over you right now?"

"Ye joshin', ma'am?"

"Nope. In the book of Matthew—that's in the Bible—it says you have a guardian angel, and it's because God loves you something awful."

"An awful good thing? Like me candy on Christmas morn? Or awful like me brother's smelly socks?"

Pete chuckled behind her, but she stifled her own laugh. "An awful good thing. Like candy on Christmas morning."

He tilted his head as if taking in all she said, then ran toward the livery, calling for Tommy.

Pete reached down to help her stand, and she accepted his hand. She collected the basket, but Pete took it from her. "You believe in God," he said.

"I do."

"The more time I spend with you, the more … Let's just say you're making it difficult to be just friends." He smiled and handed her the basket, surprising her. "I need to talk with Tom real quick. Can you wait for me?"

"Sure."

He tilted his hat and hurried inside. A few seconds later, the air stirred with the sound of running children. Tommy ran past, but Chase stopped beside her.

"Did you enjoy the little bread?" she asked.

"I didn't eat it."

She frowned. "You didn't? What happened to it?"

"Me pa has been sad lately, so I gave it to him. I told him what ye said: it was God's free gift, and that if me pa wanted it, he could have it. I guess he did, 'cause he ate me bread right then."

She smiled as Chase ran off.

Pete came out of the livery, bringing Tom with him. The big man's limp was very noticeable. Why didn't he use a cane? Perhaps pride. Was his limp the reason he was sad? Or was it something more? He wasn't a clean-looking man, much like his boys. Maybe she could help him somehow. Be a neighbor. She could always do that no matter how long she stayed.

Yes, that's what she'd do. All she needed now was a few tree limbs.

CHAPTER EIGHT

B lake rode out early from the Eastons' ranch in hopes the townspeople, including Miss Thompson, would still be asleep when he entered the boardinghouse. But when he arrived, Jessica's voice carried from the kitchen. He glanced at the stairs, then back at the kitchen. He'd come to grab the *wanted* posters and a shirt for the Sunday meeting, which would be the day after next, and had intended to be quick, but he couldn't help himself. He stood there and listened.

"Thank you again for allowing me to use the scraps," she said. "I can't tell you how grateful I am. Let's hope someone buys my little breads."

"I'm sure they will." Mrs. Briggen's voice softened, and he couldn't hear anything more.

Blake frowned and inched forward. Jessica's voice whispered back. Two more steps forward, and the whispers stopped, and everything became still.

You'd better leave. As he took a step to do so, Jessica collided into his chest. Instinctively, he caught her by the waist and held her there. Time seemed to stand still as he breathed her in. She smelled of fresh-baked bread, and the closeness of her body against his stunned him. He lowered his hands from her waist. "Are you all right?"

Avoiding his gaze, she backed away a foot, then paused to raise the basket's lid.

Curiosity getting the better of him, he leaned over and tried to look inside while she checked the contents, but he came up short as the lid fell.

She let out a sigh. "Thank goodness." She patted the basket. "I am now."

"What's in there?"

"Bread."

"I thought I heard voices." Mrs. Briggen came out of the kitchen. "Hurry, Jessica, or you'll be late. Mr. Vines won't accept them if he thinks you're not reliable."

Jessica scurried past him and out the door.

Blake stared after her. Almost two weeks in town and he'd never seen her obey anyone.

"Sheriff, I need a favor."

He turned to Mrs. Briggen.

Her eyes settled on him with a hard stare, and within a split second, Blake knew he was doomed.

"I hope you didn't make that child late." She pointed toward the door. "Go down to the general store, and after Jessica leaves, buy a little bread. She needs them to sell so Mr. Vines will allow her to make more for the store."

"What's a little bread?"

"Does it matter?" Her eyes softened, and she smiled at him. "Did you come to stay this time?"

"No, ma'am. I needed a fresh shirt for Sunday's service. We'll be having a town meeting right after. Please make sure you attend. Oh, and will you do me a favor in return? Share about the meeting. It's important."

"Fine, I will. But, Sheriff, my favor will cost you." She went back into the kitchen.

Something within him agreed, but was he willing to pay the price?

Blake grimaced, realizing he was leaving yet again without the *wanted* posters, and now without his shirt for Sunday.

As he exited the boardinghouse, Doc Adams walked across the street with a smile on his face. "How are you, Sheriff?" He stepped onto the boardwalk as if he'd intended to talk with him.

"Fine. Heading to the general store to buy a little bread. I think it's edible. Want one?"

Doc chuckled. "I'm a single man. I can't afford to turn food away."

"Then we better hurry." They walked together, soon passing the land office and saloon. "So, Doc, is there something you need?"

"About the town meeting Sunday. How important is it? I'm heading out to the Fosters' right after lunch." They crossed the street to the general store.

"You need to be there. Some are speculating it's about the new school teacher. I haven't said otherwise. Curiosity will drive many to come."

Doc met his gaze. "It's serious?"

"I'm afraid so." Blake opened the door to the general store, and the bell chimed.

Henry was scribbling something on a notepad as they headed toward the counter. He looked up, pushed his glasses to his nose, and slid his pencil behind his ear. "What are you men looking for today?"

Blake scanned the glass counter, suddenly feeling foolish. How did women get him into these things? "Henry, I hear there's little breads in the store?"

He gave a slow nod. "And how did you hear? She only dropped them off minutes ago. Let me guess. Briggen?"

"Yep. Told me to buy one, so I invited Doc here."

Henry leaned over and opened the glass case, then placed two stars on a napkin. Blake lifted the bread to his nose. It reminded him of Jessica and the scent of her hair. His stomach rumbled. "Smells good." He took a bite, and his mouth watered at the taste of the flaky crust. "Not bad. Go on, Doc." He shoved the rest in his mouth.

Doc stuffed the entire star in.

Blake and Henry chuckled.

"What?" he said with a mouthful of bread. "Single man here who hasn't had his breakfast."

"How much do I owe you?" Blake reached in his pocket for change, then looked at Doc. "Want another?"

"I'll buy this round." Doc tapped the counter. "Two more."

By the time Blake and the doc left the general store, they had eaten every one of the little breads Jessica had baked, except for the two Blake planned to take to Trent and Rosalind. Now he was as stuffed as a turkey before Thanksgiving.

As they reached Blake's horse, Doc moaned. "Boy, that was delicious. I'll have to stop by there before I head to the Fosters'. Thanks for breakfast."

"Anytime." Blake glanced at the brown paper sack in his hand. He stuffed it in his saddlebag, his thoughts finding their way to Jessica.

Jessica needed a few branches and a way to cut them down, but first, she'd head to the only spot where several trees grew and hope for an oak. She could always cut a root from a tree for the handle. She almost skipped as she headed down the boardwalk to the cemetery at the end of town.

Jessica's gaze sought the general store as she passed. Had any of her little breads sold? She wanted to stop and ask but paused when a man strolled into the graveyard next to the store. *Blake?*

With the general store forgotten, Jessica hid within the shadow of the building and watched Blake slip off his hat, say a few words to a weathered black-and-gray stone, kneel, and bow his head. She couldn't hear what he said, but his lips moved.

Her heart mourned for him, and for the loss she still hadn't dealt with herself. That was the reason she pushed herself so hard. She didn't want to think, didn't want to feel, for if she did, she might never survive the hurt from losing her father, and from losing him the way she did. She closed her eyes, fighting back tears as she remembered the day her father was laid to rest.

She shook her head. No. This wasn't the time to think about it. She opened her eyes to find Blake staring back at her from the fence separating them. His teary blue eyes held hers, and a yearning called out to her heart. When a tear slid down her cheek, she broke eye contact, bowing her head to wipe her face.

Oh, what must he think of her, hiding in the shadows watching him? Heat rose to the back of her neck as dark-brown boots stopped in front of her.

"May I walk with you, Miss Thompson?" He didn't ask about or mention her behavior.

She met his gaze. His eyes were dry now, searching hers for answers. "Thank you, Sheriff, but I've come to look at the trees." She pointed behind him to the cemetery, hoping to take his gaze from her, but failed.

"Please ... call me Blake." He reached out his hand and wiped a gentle finger across her chin.

Her breath caught as her skin tingled. She tried to breathe, tried to find the words, but once again failed. Never had a man touched her so tenderly.

Blake stepped to her side and looked out to the trees. "They are beautiful, aren't they? God's creation."

She nodded, finally finding her voice. "I need to cut down three limbs, about four feet each, from one of the oak trees."

He chuckled. "I can only imagine what you need them for. How do you plan to cut them?"

Seeing there were no lower limbs the size she needed, Jessica swallowed hard and forced a request through her lips. "Sheriff … I mean Blake, would you help me cut them down? I'd like to make Tom's sons an atlatl."

He glanced at her and quirked a brow. "An atlatl?"

"Yes." She straightened her shoulders. "A stick used to propel a spear. I'll have you know—"

He held up his hand. "There's no disrespect in the question. I haven't seen an atlatl since I was a boy myself, and you took me by surprise is all. Never mind you asking me for help." His mouth lifted into a smile.

His handsome grin did her in, and she smiled in return. "Does that mean you'll help me?"

"I will, Miss Thompson. I'll get them down for you after Sunday's service."

She took a few slow steps toward the general store, and Blake followed. "I can't pay you for your help," she said, "but there's something in the general store I can give you as a thank you."

"There's really no need." The bell rang over the door as he pulled it open and waited for her to enter. "I'll wait for you out here."

She nodded and hid her face as she passed him, not wanting

her emotions to show. Why did it hurt her that he'd rejected her offer? She didn't have much, but she'd thought a little bread would do.

Mr. Vines stood at the counter filling a jar of candy sticks. "Back so soon, Blake?"

She turned in surprise to see Blake walking in behind her after all. The look on his face stopped her. Was it fear?

Blake gave Henry Vines a look that he hoped conveyed his thoughts. Under no circumstances did Blake want Jessica to know he and Doc ate all but two of her breads—and then flipped a coin to see who bought the rest.

Henry smiled at him in understanding, but when the corners of the older man's mouth lifted even more, Blake knew he was in trouble. Why did he care that she'd seemed dejected when he'd mentioned staying outside? Of course, he'd probably misunderstood. The good it did him now when he was about to be humiliated in front of the woman.

"What can I do you for, Miss Thompson?" Henry capped the jar of candy sticks and placed it on the shelf behind him.

Jessica scooted past two barrels of rice and potatoes. "Hi, Mr. Vines. I wanted to see if the sheriff here could have one of my little breads?"

"Oh, do you now." Henry leaned over to the fresh baked goods counter and stared at the spot they should have been. "I don't think that's possible."

She bent low and fingered the glass. "What happened to them?" Her brow creased.

"I admit I was tempted to devour them, but another man beat me to it."

"Someone ate a dozen so fast? Well, who?"

Great. "I ate them." Blake lowered his hat to cover his eyes, but he didn't tip it down far enough, because when she spun, he didn't miss the surprise on her lovely face. The smile Pete spoke of flashed at him full force, almost knocking him to his knees. Trying to recover, he tipped his hat to her and took a step back, gazing at the dimple she rewarded him with. "Me and Doc. We were hungry."

"Miss Thompson, I'd say it was a little more than both men being hungry. They flipped a coin to see who won the last two. Can you stop by before church with two dozen? We open on Sundays for two hours after service to allow those who travel such distances to get their supplies."

Her smile never faded as she agreed to two dozen, or when they left the store in silence.

As he walked her to the boardinghouse door, he planned to mention the stage coming in, but she spoke first. "Thank you."

"Yes, ma'am." She started to go inside, but something pushed him to speak. To say anything. He wasn't ready to let her go. "Will you stay after the church service for the town meeting?"

She turned around, dimple-smiling back. "I thought I would."

"Good. I'm asking everyone who can attend to come."

"I'll be there. Bye, Sheriff." She went inside.

Disappointment settled somewhere in his chest as he headed through town.

He preferred Blake.

CHAPTER NINE

B lake ran his fingers through his hair, then shuffled his papers on his desk, glancing out the window all the while. If he could will a person into the room, it'd be Jessica. She'd invaded his dreams last night, and today it still shook him. He hadn't woken from a dream with sweat rolling off his person for a long time, not since his wife died.

A nightmare was a better word for what he'd had.

Jessica had been running. Fear shone in her eyes. And though he ran after her, he could never catch up. A stagecoach was waiting in the distance. She entered and vanished inside.

Sunlight crept into the stillness of the office, its rays running a narrow finger along his desk, landing on the speech he'd prepared last night. Two items had pressed on his mind as he'd written the speech: Jessica and the robbers. He was sure his subconscious had joined the two, but the fear he'd woken with was unfounded. But if so, why did his heart race even now?

He reached for his speech, and his eye caught on the part that terrified him. *Women being sold. Men dying ...*

A lump grew in his throat. He'd do whatever it took to keep

his town safe. He wouldn't let the townspeople down.

His deputy came in and hung his hat on the peg by the door. "How's it going?"

"Not sure I should answer." Blake mumbled through his speech, sounding uncertain to his own ears. Uncertain wasn't what he wanted his town to feel as he spoke to them. "It's all here." He pointed to his head. "Somewhere. I wish I could remember it."

"Why are you nervous? You've spoken to them before, and everyone knows you in these parts."

Blake lifted his pencil to write another sentence but then threw it back down.

"Oh, I get it." Jake grinned, strolling to the chair in front of his desk. "I admit, it's odd to see you this flustered, but it's about time you found a likin' to the womenfolk. A shame it's going to break many a woman's heart."

Blake rose. The chair he'd been sitting in fell backward, but he caught it in mid-air.

"I rest my case, Sheriff." His deputy chuckled under his breath.

"I'm going out." Blake swiped his hat from the peg and jammed it onto his head.

Jake shouted as he exited, "Tell Jessica I said hello."

Blake stomped his way across town with nowhere to go. But he didn't care about where he went so long as Jake wasn't around teasing him about feelings he didn't have. Yes, yesterday with Jessica—he hadn't planned or expected that. In one day's time, she'd made him laugh, truly laugh. Her kindness for others poured through her words and actions. Her vulnerability shocked him. She wasn't what she'd appeared when they'd first met. Jessica was a complex woman, one that baffled him—and turned his nerves on end when she was near.

His eyes caught on the general store sign. Yes, he'd go there. Surely he'd find something to buy. Oil. He needed to wipe down his saddle.

He threw open the door harder than he intended, and the bell clanged loudly as it fell to his feet. He sighed and swiped it from the ground.

Henry met his gaze. "I'm sure you're in a rush for more little breads, but Miss Thompson won't bring more until tomorrow." He taunted him with a knowing smile.

Where's Doc when you need him? Blake needed a cure. Besides, he and Doc understood each other. Blake marched to the glass cabinet by the register and plunked the bell down in front of Henry. "I need some oil for my saddle."

Henry unlocked the cabinet, took out a bottle, and set it down. Clinking the register buttons with his finger, he totaled the purchase. Blake paid, and Henry slid the coins into the drawer. "Anything else I can help you with?"

Blake muttered his no and strode out of the store. Where to next? He certainly didn't want to head back to the office, no matter how much he needed to do. He took a deep breath and glanced around, and his eyes fixed on the trees in the graveyard.

Why was it when he was in town, he'd forget about God's creation, the sights and smells of the earth, but when he was on his soon-to-be land or at the Eastons', he lived and breathed it? Everything came alive. He took another deep breath. The dry air tightened his chest, much like being in Jessica's company had yesterday. He still couldn't get the picture of her with fresh tears in her eyes from his mind. He'd wanted to wipe away every one of them, and when he'd reached out and run a finger against her chin, she'd shaken against his touch.

That's when he'd known no man had ever touched her the way he had. Protectiveness rose up within him, even now as he remembered how soft she felt.

But he wasn't the right man for her.

He glanced over to the spot in the graveyard where he'd buried his late wife's silver hairbrush. It had been all he'd had left of her, except for the memories. He used to comb her hair at night. She'd claimed it felt right nice, and he'd wanted to please her, love her anyway he could. He had loved her from the very depth of his soul, always had since they were children. Had known from the start they would marry. They did. And it was his fault she'd died so soon after their wedding.

How many times had he tried to wash those memories away with whiskey? He didn't know. He'd lost count long ago, when he'd left everything behind and moved to Graham. Even now, at the thought, his mouth grew thirsty.

Blake entered the cemetery and knelt once again where he'd buried the memory and prayed to be free from the past. Yet here he was, chains of sorrow and regret binding his heart, thoughts of that terrible night haunting him.

He could still hear the gunshots. See the blood oozing from her body. Shouting, he'd rushed to her, reached for her, but his world had gone black before he made it. He hadn't seen her alive again.

He touched the scar on his cheek. Why did he have to survive?

Blake rose to his feet, and in the distance, a tree dropped a branch. He gritted his teeth. *Jessica.* He needed to keep his distance from her for both their sakes.

He'd promised her three tree limbs, and that would be it.

Jessica left the boardinghouse and headed toward the general store. Thankfully, Mrs. Briggen paid her wage in advance, allowing her to buy a ready-made blouse for church tomorrow. She couldn't remember the last time she'd purchased anything new, but she wanted to look nice. She continued to tell herself it wasn't for Blake. Although it did cross her mind. Once. Or maybe twice since this morning. She'd enjoyed his pleasant voice as it had filtered through her dreams, and the way he'd slid a finger along her skin. His warmth had seared her straight to her toes.

She reminded herself she couldn't stand the man, but it was fruitless. She'd wished him near her the moment her eyes had opened, and every minute since the sun had crept through her window.

As if in answer to her desire, there Blake stood, in the graveyard behind the general store, on a ladder, beneath an oak tree.

She hurried to the end of the boardwalk and stepped to the ground near the front of the graveyard, shielding her eyes from the sun rising behind the trees. "Well, hello!"

Blake flailed. The ladder wobbled.

Jessica gasped in horror as Blake tumbled sideways from the top rung. He landed on the ground, and before he'd settled, she'd lifted her skirt and was running to him.

He lay sprawled on his back, his eyes closed.

She knelt beside him. "Oh, Blake." Leaning over, she gave him a little shake, searching for blood and finding none. "Are you all right? Please, say something." A firm press to his chest confirmed his heart beat strongly.

Relieved, she gently wiped dirt from his forehead. "Blake?"

Nothing.

His utter stillness afforded opportunity to study him. She took in handsome features marred by a red welt on his forehead and a scar almost hidden by facial hair. Brown hair cut short at his neck, over tan skin, and around the curve of a strong jaw.

That scar ... She couldn't help herself as she ran a finger along the remnants of the jagged cut that stretched from his ear to the bottom of his cheek.

Blake's blue eyes flickered open and instantly found hers and held them. Her heart jumped within her chest. His callused hand caught hers gently against his skin. She stilled as a tingling sensation spread through her fingers. He closed his eyes, breaking their spell, and didn't open them when he spoke. "Miss Thompson, I'm fine. Thank you for your concern." He released her hand.

Miss Thompson? What happened to Jessica? He kept his eyes closed. He didn't want to look at her? Whatever was she thinking to caress his face so intimately?

She stood quickly, wringing her hands as she backed away. "I'm terribly sorry. I thought you were hurt. I shouldn't have ..."

His eyes flashed open. "No, you shouldn't have," he said, his voice husky. His eyes had darkened several shades, mesmerizing her.

For the life of her, she couldn't move. She wanted to move. Flee was more like it. His words pierced her, but something akin to a fire burned between them and drew her. He rose, and as he came close, soap, sweat, and other manly scents swarmed her senses. Her breath caught at his nearness.

He studied her, his gaze on her lips. "You need to find yourself a husband, Miss Thompson. It's not safe for you in this town."

I need to find a husband. "Are you offering? *Again?*" Her voice quivered as she tried to disguise her shock at his words.

A shadow passed over his eyes. He glanced away and took a step back. "I'm not the marrying type."

She bit her lip, wanting to feel the pain there instead of in her heart. Biting a little harder, she planted her hands on her hips. "Neither am I, Sheriff. No matter how many times you try to marry me off. But don't worry. I'll be out of your town soon enough." She turned, but Blake snagged her arm.

"It's dangerous for a woman like you to be alone."

She spun and balled her fists. "And what type of woman am I? Weak? Fragile? That I'd need a man—"

"Beautiful."

The word wrapped around her thoughts, suffocating her. Jessica's fingers eased to her sides, her voice softening. "I can take care of myself."

"For how long? I've called a town meeting because there have been robberies, men killed, and women and children taken to be sold to the highest bidder. I cannot protect you."

"It's not your job to protect me."

"You're wrong. I'm the sheriff. It's my job to protect my town and its people, and that includes you. Marry Pete. He'll have you. He loves you."

She closed her eyes for a moment, swallowing around the knot in her throat. He wanted her to marry Pete? She hated her traitorous heart when it came to Blake. Hating the man but wanting him to want her at the same time. She was breaking her own promise to never allow herself to love another lawman. She didn't want Pete, or anyone else, for that matter. Her father's death was her fault. He'd saved her from the clutches of a wanted man. She would protect herself to honor his sacrifice. Any other way and the pain would be too great.

"As I said, I'm leaving your town soon enough." She stalked away, then threw over her shoulder, "Besides, I'm as good a shot as any man."

Jessica turned the corner out of Blake's sight and leaned against the general store. She took a deep breath and gathered her emotions, then entered.

Mr. and Mrs. Vines, talking with customers at the counter, hadn't noticed she'd come in.

"Hello." She smiled at them, walking toward the ready-made wears. "What happened to the bell?"

"Our dear sheriff." Mrs. Vines smiled. "Where did you say he went, Henry?"

"I think he mentioned something about cutting a few limbs down from one of the oak trees in the cemetery."

Jessica had forgotten about the tree limbs. That's why Blake was out there and fell off the ladder.

A swish of the door and the scraping of wood against the floor sounded behind her.

Mrs. Vines looked past her. "Did you get them down?"

Jessica didn't hear the answer but expected it was Blake. She forced herself to not turn around.

Blake set three branches by her feet. "I'll replace the bell." He went to the counter, swiped the bell, and stalked off.

She tried not to care what he was doing but couldn't stop her wandering thoughts. She eyed him as she made her way to another clothes-filled table and reprimanded herself for not looking away. Only moments ago, his breath had tickled her face. Now they were states apart.

She lifted a cream-colored blouse and carried it to the register, fingering the puffed sleeves. Firm steps brought Blake close to where she stood. His gaze darted to her as his brow furrowed. He didn't say a word but replaced the ladder, then turned and left.

After paying, she lingered in the store until he strolled out of view. "Bye, Mr. and Mrs. Vines. See you tomorrow morning." She grabbed the branches from the floor and walked out.

In a little over a weeks' time, she'd be done with the boys' atlatls, her horse would have arrived, and she'd be on her way. Where? She wasn't sure anymore, but it would be far away from Sheriff Blake McKenny.

CHAPTER TEN

Jessica buttoned her cream blouse, then each cuff, tucked the hem into her skirt, and ran her hands down her hips. With a heavy heart, she exited the boardinghouse and headed for the general store. Preparing for church had been harder than she'd thought it would be, as memories of her father had continually washed over her. She hadn't stepped foot in a church since her father's death, and now she wanted nothing more than to leave town and never look back. Her feet slowed, and her gaze caught on the row of horses in front of the church.

No. She wasn't a thief no matter how bad she wanted to leave. No matter how bad it hurt to stay. She was becoming attached to the people of this town whether she wanted to or not, and it was affecting her, clouding her judgment. Especially with regard to spending time with the sheriff.

"Miss Jessica, you're standing in the middle of the street. You all right?" Pete peered down at her from his horse.

It had been a couple of days since she'd seen him, and he was a sight for weary eyes. She needed a friend right now, no matter how much Pete wanted more. "Lost in my thoughts."

"Would you mind if I sat with you during the service? As friends, of course."

"I'd be honored." She gave him a mock curtsy.

Pete dismounted and bowed to her.

She chuckled. "I need to go to the general store to deliver my baked goods. Will you save me a seat?"

"I'd be glad to. I thought you'd make something for after the town meeting."

After the town meeting? She inhaled. "I wish I'd known, but these are for Mr. Vines."

"No need to worry. There are always plenty of leftovers when the town gets together for a picnic." Pete bowed to her again, then tugged his horse into a slow walk toward the church. "Look for me when you come in."

Jessica gave a small wave. She reached the general store and knocked. Mrs. Vines came to the door, wearing a grin. "Good morning, Jessica. How are you?"

Jessica slipped inside, and Mrs. Vines locked the door behind them.

"Doing well, Mrs. Vines. Here are the little breads your husband asked for." She set the basket on the counter and began taking out the little breads one by one.

"The way my husband talks about your breads, I'm buying one now before I miss out."

Jessica smiled, warmth from the compliment flooding her. It did her heart good to hear her breads were wanted, even if she herself was not. Blake's words still pressed on her: *Marry Pete.* "Thank you, Mrs. Vines. Very sweet of you to say so. There seems to be a lot of people out today. I don't remember ever seeing so many before."

"With a town meeting, the sheriff can draw a crowd. Without a town meeting, he draws the women, if he only noticed." She chuckled.

Jessica nodded and forced her smile to remain as Mrs. Vines walked her back to the front.

"See you shortly," she said as Jessica stepped onto the boardwalk.

Jessica's thoughts and steps carried her toward the crowded boardwalk in front of the church. Judging by Mrs. Vines' words, it seemed Blake had his pick of women to marry, and here he was trying to marry her off to Pete. Blake claimed she was beautiful, but the reality was he didn't want her, and with a heavy heart, she admitted it hurt.

She glanced at the entrance and noticed Pete had waited. When he caught her eye, his gaze never wavered. Pete did care for her, as Blake had said, and she believed if they were to marry, they could be happy. She did want a family. But what of love?

Pete strolled to her and held out his arm. "Are you all right, Miss Jessica?"

No. She wasn't. Why was she thinking about marriage anyway? She was leaving town as soon as she acquired her horse.

She glanced up at the white, steepled church. "I think so." With a deep breath, they entered. She'd never seen so many people in one building. The wooden pews were filled with women and children, and the men stood along the four plain-white walls. She caught a glimpse of Blake, Mr. Easton, and another man she recognized as a cowboy from the Easton's ranch—whom Pete said he was called Matthew—speaking to each other near the pulpit. In the middle of the small platform forming the pulpit was a simple wooden stand. An older man— the preacher, she assumed—walked to the pulpit, laid his Bible on the stand, and opened it. The people who were scattered around the room talking began to find their seats.

"Sit here." Pete led her to the edge of a pew. She sat on the simple wooden bench, taking everything in. The man she assumed was the pastor welcomed everyone and began to pray.

Throughout the service, thoughts of her dad, Blake's gentle touch, and his declaration she must marry Pete, made her mind a boggled mess. Her father wouldn't be happy she hadn't paid attention during the service, especially since it had been so long since she'd attended church.

Another thing to add to the growing list of disappointments her father would have faced if he were alive. She folded her hands in her lap. It was odd that within a crowd of people, she could feel utterly alone.

The seemingly sudden switch from preaching to singing caught her attention, and she glanced up to find Blake watching her with an emotionless expression. Of course it would be devoid of warmth. Why did her heart wish for more? She forced her gaze to her lap.

Throughout the service, Jessica seemed to wrestle with herself. Blake watched her from afar as she gnawed on her bottom lip. Her eyes flashed back and forth across the room. Her shoulders eventually slumped inward and stayed.

Then she looked up, seeing him for the first time. He wanted to hold her, plead with her to share what burdened her heart, but her gaze fell and her shoulders caved in even more. Whatever her sorrow was, he wanted to take it away, make things right for her, but he was aware he couldn't. Distance was what he needed.

As the church service ended, the preacher asked the congregation to stay and then turned the pulpit over to Mr. Vines, who swiftly called the town meeting to order. "Sheriff, the floor is yours."

Blake took the stand. "I've called this special town meeting because I want you and your families to be aware of a situation that has been brought to my attention and which is now getting closer to town.

"Almost two weeks ago, I met with officials in Fort Worth, and while there, I learned that several stagecoaches near Dallas had been robbed. The problem isn't only the robberies, but the vermin responsible are killing any male passengers and drivers with the stagecoaches. And if there are women and children, they take them as captives and sell them to brothels."

Gasps filled the air. Mothers held their children close, and the men around the room stood taller. Someone yelled out, "How can we stop it?"

"Right now, we are doing all we can to apprehend these men, but working together with other counties, and keeping our towns aware of the situation, is the best way to protect ourselves. I know a stage is coming in on Tuesday. If you are taking the stage, be vigilant. Take your weapons. I know some of you aren't for violence. I commend you, but you need to protect yourselves, and I'll do all I can to protect you as well."

Jake and Matthew came and stood on the stage alongside him. He motioned to them. "Everyone knows Deputy Jake, and our fill-in deputy, Matthew, from Mr. Easton's ranch. Both men will be in town if you should need them. I, on the other hand, will be riding out to your homes to make sure all is well.

"I want to thank Mrs. Easton for another idea. I know this idea might be a bit unusual, but I believe it holds great merit. Mrs. Easton, please come and share your thoughts with the town." Blake moved from the pulpit to stand beside his deputies, arms crossed against his chest.

Rosalind stepped up to the stand and began, "When the sheriff first mentioned to Trent and me what was going on, fear filled me, and my first thought was how I would protect my family, my children. I began to pray and ask God to take away my fear and fill me with peace. He did, but He also gave me an idea. How many women here have your husband's guns in the house?"

Blake glanced at the crowd. Every woman raised her hand.

"How many know how to use a gun or can actually shoot something?" she asked.

Blake glanced around again. Not many raised their hands this time.

"I'm opening my home next month for the First Annual Women's Shooting Day. It will be the first Saturday, at nine in the morning—a time for us women to learn how to handle a gun, how to shoot, and other safety measures. We will have lunch afterward."

"Can the men come?" someone hollered.

A few "Yeahs" came in response.

Trent stepped from the line of men along the wall. "Everyone is welcome to come. However, the women are the only ones allowed to shoot on the property. We will have our cowhands to help the women, if their menfolk are unable to come. Bring only one gun, the one you want your wife to learn with. We will have plenty of food, so no need to worry about going hungry."

Blake touched Rosalind's shoulder and spoke to the crowd. "Any other questions?"

With silence the only response, Rosalind stepped down.

A soft voice lifted to Blake from the crowd. "Do you know what they look like?" Mrs. Bligh, the pastor's wife, asked. "The men doing these terrible things?"

He reclaimed the stand. "I do. We have *wanted* posters we'll nail up in front of the sheriff's office as soon as I get them from the boardinghouse."

"Where was the last robbery?"

"I'm not certain the robberies were related."

"Just tell us, Sheriff."

"Outside of Fort Worth." Blake found Jessica's gaze intent on him. "And Graham. The day I brought Miss Thompson to town. The difference, the robbers let her go."

Gasps rang throughout the church.

Jessica's eyes widened, and she covered her mouth with her hand. Her gaze flicked to the left, then to the right. She rose from her seat and quickly left the church.

Blake wanted to stop her. She wasn't safe with the entire town at the church, but he couldn't. Pete glanced up at him, then quickly followed Jessica.

"Any more questions?"

There were.

Many.

Chapter Eleven

Pete caught up to her outside the church and walked her to the boardinghouse, thankfully not asking questions. Jessica waited for him to leave, then gathered as much strength as she could and strolled up the stairs to Blake's room. *Could it have been Cliff?* She had to see for herself who had robbed the stagecoach. To think if it had been him ...

She ran a shaky hand along the wall, glanced back and forth down the hallway, and, without blinking, turned the knob. The door opened. Relieved, she slipped in and quickly closed it behind her.

The smell of spice and leather mingled in the air like it had on the day she and Blake had met, with her gun pointed in his back. She inhaled deeply, wanting the feel of Blake by her side—his strength. Somehow, his presence had gone from agitating her to calming her.

But if he caught her here, it would be agitating again. She glanced around, hunting the posters. The bed flanked the right wall, and a tall dresser stood to her left. Red-and-brown quilted curtains, in the same pattern as on the perfectly made bed, hung from the open window. A package next to his pillow drew her notice. She fingered the edge of the square bundle. The brown paper wasn't thick but thin, like wrapping paper. Who would he have bought a present for? She almost lifted the gift, but a glance at the dresser stopped her. The word *WANTED* drew her to it.

Lifting the yellowed papers, Jessica eyed the first sketch. *Henry "Guy" Smith.*

No. He wasn't the man she was looking for, yet he could have been one of the four men who'd come to town that day in Oklahoma. She'd only seen Cliff. She shook her head. It couldn't be Cliff, the robber on the stage.

She moved the poster aside to see the one below it. The face was familiar. The papers slipped from her grasp, and bile climbed her throat as she gripped the dresser to keep herself upright.

He'd found her. Her father's killer had stood so close, and she hadn't even known it. How could she not have recognized him? But hadn't she trembled in fear after hearing what sounded like his voice? Yet, she focused on Blake as her immediate threat.

Her breaths grew rapid as panic from Cliff's attack came back to her. She was no longer safe in Graham.

She staggered to the window, threw the curtains back, and hung her head out, desperate for even the tiniest of breezes, but her stomach still clinched. She grabbed the wastebin by the dresser and became sick. A noise sounded behind her, but she couldn't move.

"Jessica!" Blake's panicked voice rang in her ears, adding to the pressure already in her head. Then he was beside her, lifting her hair out of the way and gently rubbing her back in slow movements.

"I've been looking for you," he said worriedly as her

retching stopped. She sank to her knees and set the wastebin on the floor. He opened a drawer, then handed her a handkerchief.

"Thank you," she whispered, unable to think with Cliff possibly on her trail even now. Unable to talk with Blake even nearer. She took the white cloth and wiped her mouth. "I'm sorry."

"It's …" Blake released her hair and bent down, reaching for the posters she'd dropped. "What are you doing in my room?" He rose with the posters in hand, questions dancing in his eyes, distrust lacing his words.

She squirmed, sensing his gaze even as she stared at the floor. "I …" She tightened her grip on the bin. "Excuse me. I need to empty this." She stood, swallowing the return of bile to her throat, and headed for the door.

He stepped in front of her, took the bin, and set it aside. "Jessica, I asked you a question." He threw the *wanted* posters on the bed, and one landed at the edge and curled back into its scrolled position before falling back onto the floor. "What are you doing in my room?"

Jessica pointed to the window as a distraction. She needed to think. "Look out there. What do you see?" While his gaze bounced to where she'd indicated, she steeled her nerves and decided to slip from town and never look back. She had no choice but to leave tonight, before it was too late. "If what you said at the town meeting was true—"

"Every word." He stepped closer, frowning. "Do you think I'd make this sort of story up for my own pleasure?"

"I don't know. Would you? You neglected to tell me about the stage coming. You knew I was trying to leave town."

Blake flinched like he'd been struck. "You never answered my question. You better start talkin' or you might find yourself in jail."

She gasped. "You wouldn't dare."

"I can and I will," he hissed. "Don't try me."

Accepting his bluff, she walked around him and turned toward the door. "Don't worry, Sheriff," she threw over her shoulder, "I'm leaving town. You won't have to deal with me again."

He grabbed her elbow and steered her through the door into the hall.

Heat rose to her face as he guided her down the stairs. Who did he think he was, manhandling her? She yanked her elbow away and tripped in the process. Blake's fingers gripped her arm, steadying her. He didn't say a word, nor did he let go. Instead, he tightened his hold. Maybe he thought she'd run, and he'd be right.

She would, if given the chance.

Blake marched Jessica right over to the sheriff's office and swung open the door, slamming it against the wall. At his desk, Jake jumped to his feet.

Blake released her when they entered, then followed close behind. He wanted to shake her, hold her, and he didn't care which. "Put her in the cell. I found her in my room. She won't tell me why."

She'd be safer there until he could control his anger. *Lord, please show me what to do with this woman. She twisted my heart when I couldn't find her after the town meeting, and now she's ridin' on my last nerve because she won't talk to me.*

"I … I'm sorry, ma'am." His deputy opened the cell and gently took her arm, then led her through.

Blake forced himself to settle at his desk. He rubbed his hand over his forehead, fighting the jabbing pain in his head. He didn't want to keep her in there—he just wanted her to talk—but what else could he do? She was worse than a coffee stain. He threw open the bottom drawer and reached for a sheet of paper. After pulling one out, he reached in again, fingers fumbling for something to write with, until they landed on the necessary instrument. Out of the corner of his eye, he saw Jake grab a rag and start wiping down everything in view, even the cell bars.

"What is your full name?" Blake asked.

When Jessica didn't answer, he glanced her way. That storm in her eyes struck him and hit its mark. He swallowed.

"Jessica Lyn Thompson," she barked back.

He scribbled on the paper, avoiding her stare. "Where do you live?"

"At the boardinghouse."

"That's not what I meant, and you know it. Before you came to town, where did you live?"

"Here and there."

He dropped the pencil, sucked in a long breath, exhaled, then repeated the question through clenched teeth.

She actually answered, but her voice softened to the point he barely heard the words. He cocked his head to look at her again. She had turned from him, arms encircling her waist.

"Can you repeat that?"

She cleared her throat. "Oklahoma. But I haven't lived there in a year. Been traveling since."

"Alone?"

"Yes." Her head hung.

What had happened to her family? How she'd made it this far alone amazed him. These parts were rough, hard on a man and that much more on a woman. She would be considered property to most, with no one to protect her from the harsh realities of life in the West. Yet here she was in Graham.

"How old are you?"

"Twenty-one last week."

The light from the window outlined her slender frame and curves that could drive any man crazy. He'd known beautiful women before, but none with fire that churned his blood or vulnerability that tugged his heart and pulled at him.

He glanced away and swallowed hard. *Lord, how has she made it all this time? Please protect her.*

He stood and strolled over to the cell. "Non-violent breaking and entering is punishable by time served. You'll be serving time. You have two choices, Jessica. You can ride out with me to the Easton ranch to serve your time there, or you can be locked up in this cell with no privacy of any kind."

"I didn't mean any harm. Just let me go," she pleaded. "I could leave tonight. You can keep my horse. It should be arriving soon on the train."

"How could you leave tonight without a horse?"

"I can walk. That's why God gave us feet. I won't be a burden to you any longer."

Is that what she thought she was? A burden? Yes, he might have tried to push her into Pete's arms, but it had nothing to do with her being a burden. It had everything to do with his growing attraction and how his heart seemed enamored by her presence. And today, as he'd studied her at church …

No, she couldn't leave. It was for her protection. "You'll be here a month."

She grabbed the cell bars. "A month? I have to be on my way. They'll be …" Her hands slid from the cell bars to her side.

It was his turn to clench the bars. Better them than her shoulders. "They? Who's they?"

She began to pace. "What about my horse?"

"Who's *they*?"

"I can't afford to keep it at the livery."

He glanced at Jake, who watched them. She wasn't going to answer his question. Could Jake get her to talk? And what was she hiding? He inhaled a deep breath and forced himself to return to his desk. "I will collect your horse and keep it at the ranch. But you need to choose now. Serve your time here or on the ranch? I don't want to embarrass you any more than I have to. I'll keep things quiet at the ranch. If you stay here, then I can't help you. The town will find out, and the gossip … let's just say it won't be kind."

"I'll go to the Easton ranch."

He strolled to the jail with keys in hand. "Jake, will you take my horse around back? We'll leave from there not to draw attention."

Jake nodded, threw his rag on the desk, and left through the front door.

Blake grabbed his rifle and some extra bullets, then unlocked the cell. "Follow me." He led the way down a long hall to the back door and opened it.

"No need for the extra gun. I won't try to escape."

"It's not for you. Besides, I hope you'll keep your word about not escaping."

Jake rode around the building to them, dismounted, and handed Blake the horse's reins. "When will you be back?"

"Later today, or tomorrow at the latest."

Jake entered the building and tipped his hat at Jessica before closing the door.

Blake held out a hand to her. "Do you need help up?"

She avoided his gaze. "I can manage."

"Suit yourself." He took a step back and waited as she placed her foot in the stirrup and swung her leg over, grabbing the reins.

She looked at him. "Where's the horse you're riding?"

"You're sitting on him."

She pulled the reins away from him. "You're not serious."

"Yes, ma'am, I am. Haven't you learned my words aren't to be taken lightly?" He tightened the strap securing his rifle and the canteen to the saddle horn, then climbed into the saddle behind her. He snaked his arm around her waist and held out his hand. "Reins."

She handed them to him, and he began to regret his decision. It was bad enough she smelled like soap and sunshine, but when the leather straps slipped into his palms, her fingers grazed him. His skin burned.

He really should have thought this through.

Chapter Twelve

Jessica rested heavily against Blake's chest. Not that he minded. The contempt she'd held for him had fizzled the farther they'd traveled, but he needed to stop before he made a mistake and wrapped his arm around her waist once again and kept her there.

Blake slowed his horse. "We're a little over a mile from the Eastons' ranch. Do you need to rest a moment?"

She nodded. Strands of her hair caught in his whiskers, tantalizing him to remove them from his face. To rub the soft silk of her hair between his fingers.

He'd deal with it.

Slowing the horse to a stop, he handed the reins to her before slipping off and planting his feet on the ground. "Ready?" He held out his hands.

"I can get down."

Of course she could. He backed away as she climbed down, then he unhooked the canteen from the saddle horn and handed it to her. She nodded her thank-you, unscrewed the top, and drank.

What was wrong with him, just staring at her? He shook his head, clearing his thoughts. She was now essentially his prisoner. The prettiest prisoner he'd ever had. "Do you want to walk around a bit?"

"I think I'm good now. Needed to stretch my legs mostly." She walked to the horse's side, climbed up, and settled herself.

He followed close behind, expecting her to lean against him once again. Instead, she sat with her back straight. But it wasn't long until she'd inched her way back to the exact spot she'd previously occupied. He had to admit, he liked the feel of her and wanted to keep her right where she was. Realizing where his thoughts were taking him yet again, he prayed the rest of the mile would go quickly.

As they rode past the tree marked with Trent and Rosalind's initials, Blake inhaled Jessica's scent one final time before releasing it in a sigh. He had to let whatever his feelings were go. She was his prisoner, and she was hiding something. He halted the horse in front of the barn.

"Hello there." Rosalind shielded her eyes as she came from the back of the house with a sunflower-filled basket hanging from her arm.

"Hi, Rosalind." Blake climbed down from the saddle and turned to help Jessica, but her feet were already planted on the hard ground. "Rosalind, this is Jessica Thompson. Jessica, this is Rosalind Easton, Trent's wife, the man you met the other day."

Jessica's eyes lit with recognition. "Yes, you spoke at the town meeting this morning. Nice to meet you."

"It's wonderful to make your acquaintance, Jessica. Would you both like to come in for some tea or coffee? I have an apple pie warming."

The horse nosed Jessica's hand, and she giggled, patting his neck. Pleasure at seeing the way Legend and Jessica had bonded settled sweetly in his stomach, and he felt it to the tips of his boots. No, this woman wasn't any prisoner. Not by a long shot. He turned quickly to Rosalind. "We'll be right in."

Rosalind grinned and left him standing there with Jessica, unsure of himself. Unsure of everything at the moment. Had he done the right thing in bringing her here? He looked to the house. "I think I should tell Rosalind right away of our agreement."

"I know you don't want to give your friend the wrong impression."

He turned to her. "And what impression is that?"

The corners of her mouth lifted slightly. That dimple of hers was showing off again. "She seems quite pleased to see me with you."

He cleared his throat. "Don't read into it. It's that no one has ever ridden my horse but Trent. We trained our horses together so they would know us and the routes we take to get home, in case anything were to happen."

She met his gaze. "Has anything ever happened before?"

He ran a palm down Legend's back. "My work is fulfilling but dangerous. I can never be too careful."

Jessica nodded. "I can understand." His horse continued to nuzzle her fingers, and her smile returned.

"I take it you like horses. You must have been around them growing up?"

She tilted her head, continuing to pet his horse. "My father was a wonderful horseman. He had a special way about him when it came to horses. He was so gentle and kind, with people too. They'd do anything for him."

"Are we still talking about horses?"

"Both. Growing up, I'd spend hours sitting on the fence trying to take in all he said and did." Her pretty face crumbled. "One day I'd like to raise horses of my own, but it won't ever happen."

"And why do you say that?"

"It's only a dream, Sheriff." Her hands fell to her sides. "Don't you know dreams don't come true, no matter how much you wish them to? I'm sure being a lawman, you understand my meaning. The only thing true in life is right and wrong, and justice is the only thing that keeps hope alive." Jessica walked to the porch steps.

She wanted to raise horses? It was a dream only a few knew Blake claimed, along with having a wife and family. Was she right? All he had was a hope for those dreams?

Once she reached the house, Jessica turned back for a moment. "Are you coming?"

"Go ahead. Tell Rosalind I'll be inside in a moment." He continued to study her until she disappeared beyond the door. Oh, he wished she'd return. He wanted to hear that soft voice she used when she spoke of her father. It reminded him of a brook, water trickling against the rocks, the gentle flow, guiding leaves to their destination. Jessica had many sides to her, he was learning, and a part of him wanted to explore those sides, but hurt ran too deep, no matter what he told her.

He'd tried to heal himself at one time, marry someone to take away the pain. Thankfully, she'd left him when he became sheriff, not wanting his way of life. It was for the best. Was Jessica right? Did dreams not come true?

He touched the side of his face. Work-roughened fingers made it difficult to feel the jagged scar that was a constant reminder of what he'd lost. Yet it was death that had left him with a hole that ran straight through his soul, never to be filled.

"God, why is she here?" His words came out gruff. He turned and started for the house. He'd collect Jessica's things from the boardinghouse and tell Mrs. Briggen where she'd be if she needed her for some reason. Heck, the whole town would know she was at the Eastons' by suppertime. At least they wouldn't know why. He'd make sure of it.

He wanted nothing more than to travel a different path—the one to his land. He was close to owning it. And he would. Jessica's dreams might be dead, but Blake had one left that he and his wife had shared. A dream and a promise, the only one he could ever fulfill.

As Blake pushed through the door, he caught Jessica saying, "I'm his prisoner."

Rosalind's smile faded as he entered the kitchen. "Oh." She glanced up at him, then back at the guest she'd invited into her home. "What happened?"

The ticktock of the clock in the other room echoed in his ears as he considered how much to say. "I found her in my bedroom at the boardinghouse, and she wouldn't tell me why she was there. I gave her two options: stay in the jail or come here and work."

"I see." Rosalind hesitated a moment before looking at Jessica. "Do you like to cook?"

"I do."

"Then we can start with supper. How does that sound, Jessica?"

Blake held his breath for her answer. He should have discussed this with Trent and Rosalind before bringing her here.

"Just fine." She turned to Blake. "Mrs. Briggen will be concerned if I'm not there to help her cook. We need to tell her."

Mrs. Briggen was the last person on his mind. "She can wait until I get there."

Rosalind cleared her throat. "Blake, I think Jessica is right. Would you want the entire town concerned for her safety— which they would be due to the meeting today—because you hadn't told Mrs. Briggen Jessica was staying with us?"

"You have a point." And though she did, it quickly became an opportunity to put space between him and Jessica. "I'll find Trent and let him know what's going on before I leave. I'll stay in town tonight. See you both in the morning."

Trent wasn't in the barn or in the stables, so Blake rode out to the bunkhouse, where every cowhand, along with Trent, was cutting and chopping wood. "What do we have here?" Blake lifted his Stetson and crossed his arms over the saddle horn.

Trent stuck his ax into the block of wood and wiped his brow with his arm. "I thought we needed some targets for the ladies to shoot. What has you out this way?"

"I brought Jessica Thompson here to stay on at the ranch for a while. I should have thought it through first and asked if it would be all right. I made a mistake."

Trent turned to his cowhands. "Be back, boys." He grabbed his shirt from the ground and yanked it on. "Let's go for a walk."

Blake exhaled and climbed down from his horse. They took several strides before Trent spoke.

"Jessica Thompson—the same girl who came here looking to purchase a horse? The same woman who made the bread you brought us the other day? The same woman your eyes bore into during the church service?"

Heat climbed the back of his neck. There was no use hiding it since Trent knew him better than anyone. "The same."

Trent stopped. "First of all, you don't need my permission for anything. Second, you know I will help you any way I can, but you have to tell me what's going on."

"I arrested her. I found her in my room at the boardinghouse, and she wouldn't tell me why."

"Did she take anything?"

"Nothing that I could see."

"Why did you bring her here? Be honest with yourself, Blake. Why is she here at the ranch?"

"To help Rosalind around the house. You said it yourself. Rosalind hasn't been feeling well, and I thought she could help. You already know she can cook. Besides, she committed a crime, breaking into my room. I couldn't let that go."

Trent met his gaze. "You mean you couldn't let *her* go. If she travels from town to town, when was she planning on leaving?"

Blake opened his mouth, then closed it.

Trent clapped his shoulder. "I take it sooner than you were willing to let her go. Be careful, Blake. If you haven't already, you're closer than you think to falling for this girl."

"Would a man in love with a woman try to push her into another man's arms?"

"Yes, if he was afraid of what he felt. Who's the other man?"

"Pete."

Trent smiled. "I take it she turned him down?"

"It remains to be seen. Speaking of Pete, I'm staying in town tonight. Have him sleep in the barn while she's here. Matthew's the best shot, but he's in town. Pete is next of the men."

"Do you expect trouble?"

"She's hiding something, and I have this nagging feeling it has to do with one of the men or both from the *wanted* posters."

"What is it?"

"I'm not sure, but I've had it ever since the robbery. One of the men ... it was the way he looked at her. I can't put my finger on it."

"Your instincts are the best I've ever seen, but Pete? Are you sure?"

"I'm sure. I wasn't able to protect my wife. What makes me think I could protect Jessica?"

"Blake, it wasn't your fault."

He wanted to believe it, but he knew the truth. "Good night, Trent."

Twilight was beginning to fall, trapping him in memories of a past he couldn't escape, when he finally arrived back in town. He'd ridden slowly so as to not overtax Legend, and consequently when he entered the boardinghouse, Mrs. Briggen was close to hysteria.

"They've taken Jessica!" She grabbed his shirt, fisting the fabric. "You have to find her!"

He pried her fingers away and held them in his hands. "Jessica was with me all afternoon. I've taken her to the Eastons' ranch for a while. She asked me to tell you so you wouldn't be worried."

Her wide eyes narrowed. "I know that girl. She wouldn't have gone without saying goodbye."

"Please come with me, Mrs. Briggen. I'd like to explain in private." He led her to his room and shut the door behind them.

Refusing a seat, the stout woman planted her hands on her hips. "Now what is this about?"

"I arrested her for trespassing today."

"Trespassing? Where was she?"

"Here. In my room."

"Oh, heavens, Blake. Have you lost your mind?" She waved her hand in the air as if dismissing the idea. "That girl wouldn't steal anything. You'll just have to release her and bring her back home."

He thought it interesting Mrs. Briggen had already grown attached to Jessica. Hadn't he done the same? "I know you don't understand, but the law is the law."

"Blake McKenny, I'll have you know—"

"Mrs. Briggen, she's keeping something from me, something important and it's connected with my job as sheriff. I can't shake the feeling she's in danger. Something about the robbers ... I wish I knew, but I want to keep her safe, and she will be safe at the ranch. Even now, Pete's watching over her and the Eastons."

The annoyance in Mrs. Briggen's gaze faded, and a smile lifted her lips. "Pete, you say? Fine. Fine." She waved her hand again as she moved to the doorway. "I won't stand in your way, Sheriff. But make sure you tell Jessica that Mr. Vines expects those little breads every Sunday morning before service. She needs the money, Sheriff, to support herself, because after she pays for that horse of hers, she'll have nothing left. Tell her not to worry about her room. I'll hold it until she returns."

Blake closed his door behind her and stared at his things. Something had to be missing, but what did he have that Jessica would want? He grabbed the posters from the bed, then stuffed them in his dresser drawer.

After cleaning out the trash can Jessica had vomited in, he moved the curtains about. When he found nothing, he stared out the window, thinking about where Jessica had been standing when he'd entered the room.

Graham was busy tonight, with most of the people who'd come for the meeting staying in town. Matthew walked along the boardwalk as sure of himself as if he were born to be sheriff of a town like Graham. Blake smiled at his friend, although Matthew couldn't see him.

A shadow caught his eye. Something or someone moved away from Matthew as he approached. Blake grabbed his extra rifle from the closet and headed downstairs to join his friend for night watch. There'd be no sleep for him tonight.

CHAPTER THIRTEEN

After one night on the ranch, Jessica felt refreshed and energized, despite being under arrest. With breakfast still two hours away and the house still dark, she dressed and headed outside to the barn to milk the cows she'd seen yesterday when she and Rosalind had walked the property. How she missed her daily routine and the feeling of home and belonging.

Once in the barn, she found a lamp and lit it, then hauled a three-legged stool and several buckets over to the first of the six milking cows. After putting a bucket into position, she sat, pressed her cheek against the cow's flesh, and began gently milking the cow, studying her surroundings as she did.

Manure smelled just as bad as she remembered, but there was peace about the place, and a promise of God's provision, that He would raise her out of the muck of her life. She began humming an old hymn her father used to sing as they milked together every morning. After finishing the fourth cow, Jessica took the bucket and poured the milk into a container by the door. She returned to the stool just as Trent walked in and stopped short at the sight of her.

"Good morning, Miss Thompson. I didn't expect to see you this early. How did you sleep?"

"Wonderful. It's been a long time since I felt so rested."

He grabbed a stool and sat next to a cow she'd already milked.

"Mr. Easton?"

He glanced down at the depleted udder and smiled. "You've already milked her. You've been up for quite some time, it seems. I appreciate your willingness to help. Actually, I dreaded milking this morning without Matthew or Blake. When Blake's here, we get done in record time."

"Glad I can help. So how long have you known Blake?" She pointed to the end of the row. "The last two need milking."

He stood, picking up the stool as he did, and moved to the cows she indicated. "Since I was a teenager. He was a cowhand before he turned sheriff."

"Had he always wanted to be sheriff?"

"Never. We planned to train horses together."

"What changed?"

Trent tilted his head away from the cow's flesh and grinned at her. "Maybe you should ask him yourself." His smile faded, and he glanced around. "Have you seen Pete?"

She scowled, following his gaze around the barn. "Pete? Why would I have seen him?"

Trent turned to her with concerned eyes. He stood from the stool and walked to an empty stall, then came back with a gun belt wrapped around his waist. "He was staying in the barn last night. Wait here until I come back for you." He started for the door just as Pete ran in, his face flushed and his hair and clothes in disarray.

"Mr. Easton." His breath came out ragged. "I can't get them back. Blake's horses. They're gone. I must have left the gate open after I fed them. I chased one on foot, but it got away."

Trent rushed for his horse, bridled it, and hopped on without a saddle. "If we lose any one of those horses … Saddle up, Pete. Jessica, we can finish milking later. Please go to the house."

Jessica remained seated and looked up at the man. "Mr. Easton, I can help."

"I don't think that's a good idea." He kicked his heels into his horse's side and took off through the barn.

She moved from the cows' side, frustration filling her gut. She wasn't useless. Her dad had taught her well. "I could have helped."

Pete came to stand next to her, shaking his head. "Blake's horses. I couldn't repay him in a lifetime." He eyed her for a moment. "So you think you can help?"

She stood up straight. "Could if I had a horse."

"I have to head out, but if you're sure, I can help you get a horse ready."

"Of course I'm sure." As Jessica walked through the barn, a neigh sounded at her side. She turned to see Blake's horse there. "Is Blake back from town?"

"He has two horses he rides. This one is his favorite. Legend. Blake said he rode him hard yesterday and needed to let him rest. I fed him warm oats this morning before I learned about the others."

She reached toward Legend. "Hi there, boy. Do you remember me?" He nuzzled her hand, and she smiled. "You do. Want to go for a ride?"

The horse raised his head up and down, as if he understood. "Then let's get you bridled." She unlocked the gate, and Pete hurried off while she led the horse out of the barn.

Pete came running after them with bridle in hand. "Aren't you going to saddle him?"

She placed her cheek next to the horse's nose. "I think we'll be fine. The bridle will be enough."

Pete nodded, then knelt and cupped his hand. "Let me give you a foot up."

Although she really didn't need the help, she accepted since Pete seemed anxious about it.

Once she was settled onto the horse, he touched her hand. "Please be careful. I'm not sure this is such a good idea."

"Thank you for believing in me. I won't let you down." She rode out slow, allowing the horse to feel the pressure of her weight against his back. She stroked his mane. "Good boy. Now let's find us those horses."

Blake had once said his horses would know the way home if there was ever trouble. Surely this horse was trained on other parts of the land too, so she allowed Legend to guide her.

A neigh carried on a light wind, and she turned Legend toward it. One of the missing horses, a palomino, stood tall along the flat land. Land much like she'd known in Oklahoma. She slowed to a stop several yards away from the other horse, slipped to the ground, and slid the bridle from Legend.

With steady steps, she turned to the runaway horse and held out her hand. She spoke in a soothing tone, as her father had taught her as a child. Relief rushed over her as her last steps brought her to the palomino. She stroked the horse's nose and spoke soft whispers close to his ear as she set the bridle securely in place.

The palomino sidestepped to the right, then to the left, much like Pete before she left, undecided and unsure of what to do. She, on the other hand, made the easy choice to walk the horse back to the barn. When she reached Legend, she smiled. "You're such a good boy. If you knew how to kneel—"

The horse did just that, and she stared in disbelief. "Blake has taught you well."

Legend rose to his hooves, then swung his head toward her.

The next moment, one hand held the reins to the palomino, the other a furry nose that tickled her fingers. She chuckled. "Legend, you're a flirt."

He nudged her toward the ranch house.

The horse's strides back to the Easton ranch soothed Blake's tight muscles. He'd spent all night searching for the shadow he'd seen through his window, but found nothing. Matthew told him he'd keep his eyes open and would tack the *wanted* posters in front of the office.

He recalled how Matthew had given him a knowing smile when he'd handed his friend the keys to his room at the boardinghouse. Matthew was aware Blake had no place to stay now that he'd given up the keys, and it would bring him home to the ranch every night to see Jessica. At the thought, Blake grinned and pushed his horse into a gallop.

The sight of the ranch caused his heart to race. Not much longer until he'd set eyes on her again.

Trent's voice rose as he reached the barn and dismounted. "It wasn't yours to give."

Blake strolled inside but then stopped, taking in Trent's hard stare and Pete's downcast eyes.

"What happens if she gets hurt?" Trent continued. "You shouldn't have allowed her to take the horse."

The hair on Blake's arms stood on end. "Are you referring to Jessica?"

Trent glanced over, seeing him for the first time, and sighed. "I'm sorry, Blake. Pete left the gate open. Your horses are gone. I was able to bring one back, but I haven't had a chance to search for the others. When I returned, Jessica had left with Legend."

"She wanted to help," Pete said stubbornly.

Trent gave him another hard stare. "And you helped her leave."

Pete lifted his chin. "She said she could find them. I believe her."

Blake gritted his teeth, breathing in and out, grabbing the little control he had of the situation. He spotted his saddle on the stall door where he'd left it. "She rode out of here without a saddle?"

Pete gave him a nod.

Blake clinched his fingers. "If anything happens to her, Pete, I'm holding you personally responsible."

Trent strode to Blake and placed a strong hand on his shoulder, helping him to focus. "Let's find her."

Blake nodded. He'd deal with Pete later. Trent was already mounted by the time Blake had grabbed the reins of his own horse and swung into the saddle. He whistled a long, steady call for Legend, hoping if his horse was in earshot, he'd come. Once they passed the barns, Blake whistled again, scanning the fields. Nothing. "God, please, take care of her."

"He's coming." Trent pointed and whistled again.

Blake's gaze followed where Trent pointed. There was no rider.

"Ha!" he shouted, plunging his horse into a gallop. He caught up with Legend and dismounted, running a hand along the horse's back and legs, looking for a possible injury and finding none. *Where is she?*

When he looked up, Trent had disappeared down the path from which Legend had come. Blake smacked Legend's backside. "Go home! Ha!" He mounted his horse and headed in the direction Trent had gone.

On the other side of a patch of trees, he found Trent, stopped, sitting tall in the saddle as if looking for something.

Blake slowed. "What is it?"

"See for yourself." He pointed to the field beyond them. Where a woman was walking a horse.

Never had Blake seen a lovelier picture than Jessica walking through a dry, withered field, leading one of his horses by the bridle. Her soft brown hair cascaded over her shoulders and down her back. His heart squeezed, and he could barely breathe.

He bowed his head, swallowing down his tears. Trent was right. More than right. He'd fallen in love with her. "Thank you, Lord, for keeping her safe."

Trent cleared his throat. "I'll leave you both. I have horses to find."

Blake nodded, directing his horse toward Jessica. Seeing his approach, she smiled, and his heart squeezed that much more. "I see you found one of my horses," he said, closing the distance between them.

With the back of her hand, she pushed her hair from her lovely face. "He's a tricky one."

Blake leaned over his saddle horn. "My most difficult tamed horse. How does a woman of your small size manage such a feat?"

"It's not the size of the woman that matters, but the size of her heart." Her smile brightened as she looked up at him.

What he'd learned about her from others finally came into focus. Her heart overflowed with compassion, leading her to show kindness to Tom's children and risk her safety to find what was dear to him. Did she love with the same sense of abandonment with which she helped others? Oh, how he wanted to know.

"The size of the heart. That is what matters most, for the

heart is where loyalty, truthfulness, faith, and love grow." Blake regarded her profile when she looked away. "May I walk with you?"

"If I might ask you a question." She tightened her grip on Bucky's reins, bringing the horse closer, then scratched behind his ear.

Blake jumped down from the saddle and fell into step beside her. "Ask away."

"How many horses do you own?"

"Seven." He sneaked a quick look at her, unable to help himself. "Two are kept in the stables. Five graze the land. It seems my five wandering horses escaped."

"Four." She looked at Bucky. "I hope we find the others. This one needed a bit more coaxing than most, so it's taken me longer than I had planned to return him to the barn."

"Your father must have been a patient man, teaching you how to calm a horse."

"Not only calm them, but care for their needs and read their personalities. They're like people, different in every way, and you learn which ones to trust."

"With horses or people?"

She grinned as she glanced at him. "Both."

"You know you can trust me, Jessica." Blake collected the reins from her, his hand grazing hers in the process. His fingers burned from her touch. It was a controlled burn, slow and consuming. He needed to be careful because he had no intentions of giving in to his desire. He'd already lost one woman he loved and wasn't about to lose another. If he allowed himself time to adjust to what he felt, he could control his passion and fight it altogether before it blazed and all was lost.

"Trust is earned, Sheriff. But sometimes truth is withheld out of love, no matter how much the heart desires to give it."

"And does your heart desire to trust me?"

Jessica's lips parted as if to answer, but she looked away.

Blake's heart jerked at the sag of her shoulders. He handed her the rein to his saddled horse. "Go on. I'll walk him back."

"Thank you," she accepted the reins and mounted. "To your question, I don't know. I want to, but … it doesn't matter." She turned the horse's head in the opposite direction and clicked her tongue, sending both her and horse away.

Blake pressed out a slow breath as he watched her ride off. He didn't know what she'd been about to say, but to him, it did matter.

He ran his hand down the horse's nose. "I think you need a brushing down tonight."

The horse whinnied as if in agreement.

"Let's get you home, and after I find your friends, you'll be the first for a good brushing. Besides, it'd give me time to think." He mounted Bucky and headed home.

As he rode into the yard, Blake passed Matthew's horse, feeding on a hay bale. He led his horse through the gate and dismounted, then slipped off the bridle and hung it in the barn before steering the horse through the fence.

There was no sign of Jessica or Pete. He was tempted to look behind the barn to see if they were there, but then he shook his head at himself. He wasn't used to these feelings, and jealousy didn't fit him. Besides, Matthew was here. Three hours ago, they'd walked the streets of Graham. What had happened since?

Blake walked to the house, took off his hat, and hung it on a peg by the door. Matthew sat with Trent at the table in the kitchen, clasping a mug in his hand.

"Everything all right?" Blake asked.

Matthew nodded. "Everything's fine. Thought I'd ride out. I told Jake about the man you saw. He'll keep his eyes open."

Blake sank into a chair. "Then why are you here?"

Matthew took a sip of his coffee. "I wanted to get the other *wanted* poster from you."

"Didn't you find them on the bed? They couldn't have been hard to miss."

"Checked. Found one. Thought you might have the other here."

Blake ran his fingers through his hair. "I saw them. They were both there when ..." Blake glanced back at the door. He'd put them on his dresser but had found them out when he'd ...

Jessica.

Sometimes truth is withheld out of love, no matter how much the heart desires to give it.

Blake stood. "Trent, where's Jessica?"

"Rosalind told me she and Pete went looking for the last horse. They were gone when I brought Sable in."

Matthew eyed him and chuckled. "You don't honestly think she was in your room for the *wanted* posters? Why would she be interested in wanted men?"

Blake's gut twisted. "Good question."

CHAPTER FOURTEEN

The blistering dry air blew against Jessica's cheeks. She didn't want to slow Legend's pace, but Pete galloped toward her in the open field. Moisture rolled down her back and along her face. She wiped her forehead with her hand. No sign of the last missing horse.

He halted in front of her. "See anything?"

She looked out over the land, scanning the area again. "No. Haven't seen him. But he couldn't have gone too far." At least, she hoped not.

"All right, I'll keep looking. Why don't you head back? There are a few more places I'd like to check."

She wasn't going anywhere. There was still a horse on the loose. "I'm helping until the last horse is found."

He eyed her. "I'm taking a great risk allowing you to do this. If anything were to happen to you …"

"Nothing is going to happen, except maybe you getting beat by a woman. I've put two horses in the gate compared to your one." She smirked.

Pete yanked his hat over his brow. "Are you challenging me,

Miss Thompson?"

"I believe I am." She bit back a grin and raised her chin for effect. "How about it?"

"Are we wagin' a bet?"

"I don't bet."

"Then how will I ever take you out for lunch?" he teased, pouting.

She chuckled. "I'm sure you'll find another way." Flicking the reins, she sent Legend into a trot and then a run. Another set of hooves pounded the ground. She looked back over her shoulder. Pete chased her. The wind hummed in her ears and whipped through her hair, sending strands every which way as she cut through the field. It was as if her heart was one with the horse and time stood still. She indulged in the freedom. Pure, heart-pounding freedom.

Pete waved as he passed, then veered to the right.

To her left, something brown caught her attention against the greenery of the tree line. A chestnut horse was grazing. She slowed and withdrew the rope she'd attached to her belt, then made a lasso. If she could get close enough, she'd use it. It had been years since she'd tried, but her father had taught her well.

The horse spotted her and bolted. The chase was on.

As Legend caught up to the runaway, she readied the lasso, but the horse darted to the right. It was obvious this horse wasn't fully broken.

She couldn't let it get away though. She swung the lasso three times overhead and sent it through the air and around the horse's neck. She had no saddle to wrap the rope around the horn, and fear jumped in her stomach when the horse refused to stop. Jessica tightened her hold on the rope and wrapped it around her hand for a better grip. She didn't want to release him, but if he darted in another direction again, he'd pull her to the ground.

The chestnut horse must have sensed something, because it opened a greater space between them, cutting the rope into her palm. It was turning. The rope dug deeper into her flesh, and she cried out. She leaned forward in hopes of loosening the pull, but the rope tightened that much more. She'd be dragged to her death in moments.

Another set of hoofbeats signaled someone joining the chase. She couldn't see where. She prayed for Pete to hurry before it was too late. She was slipping off Legend.

But when the rider flanked the runaway, it wasn't Pete but Blake. She swallowed back tears at the pain in her hand, trying to hold on a few minutes longer as rider and horse worked in perfect sequence to finally halt the runaway.

After tethering the chestnut to his own horse, Blake jumped from the saddle and came to her. He never met her eye, but he gently took her hand and untangled the rope from it. She was about to speak but his jaw twitched, and anger flashed in his eyes, sending the tears down her cheeks, unchecked. A moan escaped at the last tug to her skin as the rope came off.

"Don't move." His hard voice made her flinch. He returned from his horse with a knife, took hold of the edge of her skirt, then cut off a long strip. After throwing the knife to the ground, he wrapped the cloth around her hand, which was trembling and bleeding.

What would have happened if Blake hadn't come to her rescue? A thank-you was in order, but she ground her teeth so they wouldn't chatter as her entire body began to shudder uncontrollably.

He shook his head, mumbling under his breath, "Are you in your right mind?"

"My father would say that I need to think before acting, but that I'm too headstrong to listen to my own advice." She flexed her injured hand to test it, but regretted it a moment later when she had to bite her lip to control the pain. "I did this for you … at first, anyway. I enjoyed my freedom and got carried away. I'm sorry."

Without warning, Blake grabbed her waist and dragged her off the horse. Once he'd set her on her feet, he went to the horse he'd been riding, took the saddle off, then brought it back to her. "Since Legend has taken a liking to you"—he threw the saddle on the horse's back and strapped it down—"he's the only horse you may ride while you're here. No more riding without a saddle either." He spun and met her gaze for the first time, his blue eyes piercing.

She wasn't sure what she saw there, but she didn't like the feeling that she'd disappointed or even angered him. She looked away.

"I'm going to lift you up."

"No." She took a step back, but not far enough. His hand still grazed her waist. "I can do it." She hoped. Being short, it always took all her strength to pull herself up, and now with an injured hand, it wouldn't look pretty. She tried twice and still fell back to the ground.

"You're wasting time. Let me help you. You need to have the doc look at your hand."

Aggravation played on her nerves. "I can do it."

He walked over to the chestnut and stood, waiting.

It took a little longer than she'd hoped, but she was finally up. "Okay, Sheriff."

"Legend will take you back. I'll be close behind." His voice came out gruff.

She held on with her good hand and rested her injured one palm up in her lap. Blake had asked if she was in her right mind.

She would have said yes, but she wasn't sure anymore—not since she'd met him. She'd have time to think on that as they rode back to the Eastons'.

"God, are you testing me?"

Blake watched Jessica, then looked into the blue sky as he held the reins to his runaway horse and the rope to the one he rode. "If you are, I'll fail. I can't keep doing this, saving her. It's too much. I failed the wife you gave me to love and protect."

He had gone looking for Jessica to ask her about the *wanted* poster when he came up on Pete chasing her through the field. Jealousy almost made him leave, but Pete had turned in a different direction, leaving her alone. He'd watched her from afar, admiring the way she rode his prized horse, trusting Legend as he wished she would trust him. She soared through the air like an eagle spreading her wings.

But when his runaway came into the picture, he could hardly believe what he'd witnessed. She'd lassoed him. Pride had filled his chest. Never had he seen such a bewildering sight. She amazed him and, just as quickly, frightened him into action when his runaway didn't stop.

Blake closed his eyes, still able to feel Jessica's tremors when he'd peeled the rope from her hand, her skin adhering to it. If he hadn't been admiring her and the way she handled herself on a horse, none of this would have happened. Common sense told him he should have stopped her and sent her home. Why hadn't he listened to the common sense God had given him?

Blake pulled the rope and started his way back. Finding his rhythm with the two horses, he met up with Jessica and slowed to the same pace. "Are you doing all right?"

Jessica opened her mouth but only a sharp breath escaped.

His heart ached at her pain. "We'll ride into town to see Doc."

Pete rode hard across the field toward them. "You found him! Thank goodness. Blake, you have to know I'm sorry for leaving the gate open. I don't know what I was thinking. It won't happen again."

Jessica remained silent. She bit her lip and turned her focus ahead as the horse picked up his pace nearing the barn. The three of them rode in together.

Blake hopped down from his horse, shoved the runaway's reins in Pete's hand, and hurried to Jessica's side. "Let me help you down."

She nodded her thank-you with a half-hearted smile.

He took her by the waist, and the mere contact jolted him straight to his toes, much like at the cemetery when he'd wiped her tears. With a deep breath, he carefully set her on her feet and reluctantly released her middle. A long strand of hair fell over her eye, tempting him to tuck it behind her ear, but Pete watched them.

"What happened to your hand?" Pete asked, climbing down from his horse.

Blake carefully collected her injured palm, covered with the strip of blood-red cloth. He gritted his teeth at the now-hoovering Pete. "I cut the edge of her skirt to wrap her hand." He huffed. Taking a breath and turning to Jessica, he spoke with more control. "I'll hitch the wagon and take you to see the doc. Go into the house and have Rosalind help you into another skirt."

"But my trunk is still at the boardinghouse."

"I'm sure she'll have something for you to wear. While we're in town, we'll grab your things."

"Jessica, is it bad?" Pete asked.

Blake wasn't sure why he did it—he'd think on that later—

but he didn't release her. "I'm taking her to town. In the meantime, feed the horses and brush them down."

"It's nothing, really. Just rope burn." Jessica met Blake's gaze, questions passing over her eyes. "I'll go inside now."

She slipped her hand from his, and instantly, the warmth from her touch left him. He stared after her, wondering what she thought of him and his unwillingness to release her. When she entered the house, Blake turned to Pete.

The cowhand took a step forward. "Your words earlier in the barn ... and now ... you care for her."

"Well, of course I do. I'm responsible for her care. She's my prisoner." He stalked off to hitch the wagon.

Pete followed. "Prisoner? If you cared for your prisoners the way you *care* for Jessica, you'd be the laughingstock of Graham."

Blake opened one of the stall doors, pulled out a horse, and walked it to the wagon by the corral. "In case you're unaware, what I do is my business. This has nothing to do with you."

"I disagree. This has everything to do with me. I plan to marry that woman in there."

Blake continued to work, ignoring the man following his every step.

"I saw the way you were holding her hand. It wasn't necessary. What else wasn't necessary while you were tending to her? Did you touch her while you were at it?"

"I have no idea what you're talking about." Blake went to the other stall and led out another horse.

Pete stepped in his path. "Did your hand *accidentally* graze her legs while cutting her dress? What other liberties did you take while *helping* your prisoner?"

Blake threw his fist, making contact with Pete's lip and sending him against the barn wall with a thump. "I'd never do such a thing. So help me, if you tarnish Jessica's reputation, I'll finish what I started here, sheriff or not."

Pete staggered up, holding his mouth. Blood stained his fingers. "I never thought you'd hit me."

Blood boiling, Blake ignored him and marched the horse to a stop at the front porch steps. Pete took the runaway horse from the post where he was tied and walked him to the barn.

The front door opened, and Trent came out saying something about Rosalind helping Jessica.

Matthew followed close behind and whistled. "It looks bad. Good thing you're taking her to Doc."

"Yep." Blake caught Pete's glance as he returned to put the other horses in the stalls.

"Pete," Trent called as he came down the steps. "What happened to you?"

"Ask Blake. He'll tell you." Pete and the horse disappeared into the barn.

Trent's face contorted. "What happened?"
"He said something about my cutting Jessica's skirt, and then I hit him." Blake took the steps to the house two at a time.

Matthew's hearty laugh could be heard from there to Kentucky.

CHAPTER FIFTEEN

Jessica gritted her teeth against the pain in her injured hand, while fingering her hair with the other. Her tresses draped over her left shoulder and were tied with a yellow ribbon that matched the dress Rosalind had shared. She couldn't remember the last time she'd worn something so lovely. What would Blake think when he saw her? Would he think her beautiful? Or would he be blinded by his anger at her carelessness? She wasn't sure which twisted her nerves more: seeing Blake or the doctor.

She heard whispers as she descended the stairs to the living room. Rosalind and Blake stood waiting for her. Blake's stern expression gained in displeasure as he watched her. He didn't care for how she looked?

Rosalind hugged her neck. "I'll see you tonight. Blake will take good care of you." She pulled away with a smile.

"Thank you for the dress."

"You're so welcome."

Blake stepped to her and touched the small of her back, sending chills up her spine. "We need to head out. I hope to get back before dark." He escorted her to the waiting wagon, and before she could object, he took her by the waist and set her on the wooden bench. He rounded the horses and climbed up next to her, then took the leather reins.

Matthew and Trent came out from the barn, carrying on a conversation.

From the corner of her eye, Jessica watched Blake as he set the wagon into motion toward town. She'd anticipated riding to town together on horseback, remembering those moments on the way out when she'd relinquished control and rested against his chest. How different it was now in the wagon, being close to him but not close enough.

Remembering the first time they'd ridden together—after the stagecoach robbery—and how she'd fought him, brought a smile to her face.

"Your hand feels better?" he asked when she caught him staring at her.

"Not really. Trying to keep my mind off the pain. I was thinking about the first time we met."

"And that helps with the pain? If I remember correctly, you pointed a loaded gun at my back."

She chuckled. "True, but I thought you were someone else. Being forced to marry … I'm glad I was wrong about you."

They hit a pothole, and she swayed, unable to grasp the seat with her injured hand. Blake caught her by the waist and pulled her alongside him. His blue eyes pierced her. "Stay close."

The whispered words sent her heart racing, and she yearned for more of his voice, more of him.

Hooves sounded behind them, and she tensed.

Blake turned. "It's Matthew."

She nodded at Matthew as he caught up and rode beside Blake.

Matthew tipped his hat. "Ma'am, since it seems I know little about you, and we have the time, what brings you to Graham?"

She focused on her injured hand. "Just passing through. I'm waiting for my horse to come on the train, and then I plan to head on." She looked at Blake, his sentence of a month as his prisoner still fresh on her mind.

"Where to?"

"Not quite sure." She couldn't allow him to continue asking questions. Over the last year, she'd found most men enjoyed talking about themselves, adventures they'd been on, or their wealth, and she expected Matthew to be no different. "How about you, Deputy? What brought you to Graham?"

"My father. He was a marshal. Traveled through here often, and when he'd come home, he'd talked about how much he loved this land. He became ill about five years ago, and when he passed, it was an easy choice. He was right about the land."

"A marshal? Pete said his dad was a sheriff at one time." She turned to Blake. "And you're a sheriff. How did you all come to the Easton ranch?"

Matthew chuckled heartily. "One thing you need to know is the Eastons are a God- fearing family. I'm not sure how Blake feels about this, but I believe God brought us here."

Blake smiled. "I've been told on several occasions that the Eastons have some of the best gunmen around working as cowhands. Truth be known, they do."

Jessica fell silent, thinking on their words. Her father was a sheriff. She knew how to shoot and ride better than most men she'd known. If God had brought Blake and the others to the Eastons', had God brought her to them as well? If so, why?

"Jessica, we don't understand. Why?"

Blake's voice drew Jessica from her thoughts. Only then did she realize the wagon had stopped.

Matthew leaned into his saddle, eyeing her, while Blake's

gaze begged for truth.

"You don't understand what?" she asked. "What are you talking about?"

"Where is the other poster?" Matthew pulled a yellowed paper from his saddlebag and handed it to Blake. In turn, Blake handed it to her. "This is the only one we have."

"Why were you in my room at the boardinghouse?" Blake asked. "Are you traveling through looking for these men?"

A queasy feeling made her stomach clench as she took the paper from his hand. She didn't need to look at it to know it was one of the posters from Blake's room, but she did anyway. Cliff's dark eyes stared back, hard and as cold as ice. The eyes of her father's killer.

Her injured hand flew to her neck. She still could feel Cliff's fingers on her skin. Her blood ran cold. Nausea leapt, and she quickly leaned over the side of the wagon and became sick. When there was nothing left within her, she sat up, avoiding eye contact with the men.

"Are you all right?" Blake asked, handing her a handkerchief.

No. I'm so scared. "I'll be fine." Jessica wiped her mouth. She had to be fine. She couldn't tell them how Cliff had tried to force her to marry him. How when she'd said no, he'd tried to abduct her. How it was her fault her father died. "And no, why would I take *wanted* posters? Did you check under the bed?"

Blake rolled up the poster and handed it back to Matthew, then angled her way on the bench. "Ready to explain?"

She folded Blake's handkerchief and wiped her mouth a final time. "I've met Cliff Berkley before. I realize now he was one of the robbers on the stage."

Her words swirled in the dry air, and Blake couldn't grasp them if he tried. What did she mean they'd met before? When? How? Were they friends? Lovers? And Cliff was one of the stage robbers. Why hadn't he taken her with him when he'd rode off with the loot?

Blake scooted to the far side of the wagon bench. If he didn't, he'd grab her and do something he'd regret. Instead, he grabbed the reins. "Can you tell us anything about him? Anything that will help us catch him?"

Matthew cleared his throat. "Is he looking for you?"

She bit her lip and wrapped an arm around her waist.

"So, he is." Matthew eyed her.

Blake didn't want to believe a man like Cliff meant anything to Jessica. But her silence wasn't helping her. He shifted in his seat. "Is he so important you'd go to jail for him? What are you hiding?"

The color drained from her face, and she gripped the side of the wagon as if about to get sick again.

"We need to get her to Doc," Matthew reminded him.

Blake snapped the reins, and the three of them headed to town in silence. Matthew followed them to Doc's office and dismounted. "I'll wait for you outside."

Blake came around to help Jessica dismount, but she'd already jumped down. Although her color had returned, she swayed. He reached to steady her, but she swiped her arm away and turned her back to him. Avoiding both him and Matthew, she entered Doc's office.

A bell rang, and Jessica quickly sank into the first available chair, which was near a glass cabinet of medicine bottles.

The doc came from the back of the office and smiled. "Well, now. How are you both today?"

Jessica rose, her lips pinched together. "I hurt my hand

lassoing a horse. He wouldn't stop. The rope cut into my skin."

Doc glanced at her bandaged hand. "You both come on back, and we'll take a better look."

"No." She paused then, looking him square in the eyes. "Blake can wait out here. He has no claim on me."

"I'm going," Blake said. "I'm responsible for you for the next month, whether you like it or not."

"Send me to jail." She stalked through the office and disappeared behind a curtain.

Blake took a step after her. He was going with her whether she liked it or not.

Doc placed a hand on his shoulder, stopping him. "Let her go. She's wound up tight."

"You don't understand. It's my fault she's hurt. It was my horse."

"Let me tend to her, Blake. Go outside. Take a walk. Cool down. Then come back."

He wanted to be there, to know she was all right. But Doc was right though. Pushing his way in would only rile her more. "I'll be outside if you need me." He looked over Doc's shoulder. She was still hidden from sight. "I don't know if it's related, but she became sick twice on the way."

Doc nodded, then disappeared behind the same curtain Jessica had.

Or sick at the thought of Cliff? Blake found Matthew outside, leaning against the wall. "She told me to put her in jail."

"The idea did cross my mind, but something doesn't feel right about this. Did you see how the color drained from her face when you mentioned going to jail for Cliff?"

Blake recalled how she became sick in his room at the boardinghouse too. "The day I arrested Jessica, she was in my room, sick. I found the *wanted* posters moved and on the floor."

"I wonder how their paths crossed."

"Tell me, if she really *knew* him, wouldn't she have recognized him during the robbery, even with a bandana covering most of his face? She wouldn't have gone looking for the posters to discover it. And when the stage was robbed, Cliff recognized her."

Matthew stood from the wall and glared. "How do you know he recognized her?"

"It's been haunting me since, but now I know. When the stage was robbed and Cliff heard her voice, he wanted to see her. Then when he did, he took a step toward her and something passed over his eyes. His brother was the one who broke the trance and called for him to get the strong box."

"There's a lot more to this. If only she'd tell us, then we could figure this out."

Blake ran his hand along his scar. "Maybe I scare her?"

"If that was true, the little lady in there wouldn't be attracted to you."

Blake shook his head. "You're thinking too hard, because you're losing your mind." He pushed his friend's words aside and handed him the poster. "Post this for everyone to see. And check under the bed, as Jessica had said. Maybe we'll find the other, but at least we'll have Cliff's picture. If he's looking for her, he might come to town."

Matthew took the poster, folded it, and shoved it in his shirt pocket. "Want me or Jake to head back with you?"

"We'll be fine. Keep your eyes open. If you see anything, send word."

"I will. Oh, Rosalind found a gun in Jessica's dress. Thought she might want it." Matthew went to his horse and came back with a Colt handgun.

Blake took the offered weapon. "This is the second time I've seen this gun."

"If she rides like you say, I'd watch out if I were you." Matthew chuckled as he headed back to his horse. He slipped his rifle from the saddle and walked toward the general store.

Blake entered the doctor's office, and with no sign of Doc, he paced back and forth.

Doc joined him sometime later. Holding out his hand, he gestured to the strip of his palm corresponding to Jessica's injury. "The width of her palm is severely burned. Her hand is swollen and weeping. I added an ointment to try to stop any infection. If fever doesn't get her, numbness will. The rope cut through a nerve, and the feeling in her hand might not return."

He grimaced. "What can I do?"

"Tell her family that the dressing needs to be changed several times a day."

Blake met his gaze, mouth going flat. "She has no one, Doc."

"Then you need to listen. I can be blunt with you. Infection can set in quickly, without warning. I've given her something to help with the pain. Right now, she's fine. Soon she'll become tired and the pain will increase. She might not mention it because she seems to have a high tolerance for pain. I would suggest soaking the hand in warm salt water. Pus might start oozing from the area. If it does, send for me." He strolled to a cabinet with medicine bottles, unlocked it, and withdrew a small, narrow bottle. "Give her half of what's recommended, since she's a petite woman. A full dose would make her ill and might kill her. She needs this once a day. I suggest giving it to her at night so she can sleep, but give it to her whenever the pain is unbearable. Although, I'm sure you will have to ask her to find out when that is."

Blake gripped the bottle, and fear settled within his chest.

She has to be all right. "Can I see her now?"

Doc took him to where Jessica sat on a bed behind the curtain. She looked up at him and gave a small smile. His fear lifted at the sight of her.

"I'll come by tomorrow," Doc said. "Where's she staying?"

"At the Eastons'." Blake took her arm, and she rose to her feet, leaning into his chest. His heart galloped. "How are you feelin'?"

"My hand hurts."

Doc took her bandaged hand, checked his work, then looked her in the eye. "If the pain becomes too much, tell Blake. I gave him some medicine. I'll stop by the ranch to see how you're doing."

"Thank you," she said, stifling a yawn.

"Well, we should go. We need to make a stop at the boardinghouse to collect her things. See you tomorrow." Blake took Jessica's arm and laced it through his. He was glad to see that not just the color in her cheeks had returned, but also her smile.

Once they reached the wagon, he lifted her onto the bench and scooted in next to her, trying to forget how small her waist was and how light she felt in his arms.

"Where are we going?" she asked.

"The boardinghouse. I know Mrs. Briggen would love to see you."

"I can't cook today."

"No. No. Just to say hello while I grab your things."

She nodded, swaying to the motion of the wagon until they stopped at the boardinghouse.

Blake hopped down. "Stay here. I'll send Mrs. Briggen to you."

Jessica covered her mouth, trying to hide a yawn as he left

146

her sitting on the bench.

"Mrs. Briggen," he called, entering the boardinghouse. "Where are you?"

She came hurrying from the kitchen. "Where's the fire, Sheriff?"

"No fire. Jessica's in the wagon outside. Will you sit with her while I grab her things?"

"Well, she could have come in." She stormed through the door.

He'd explain later. Right now, he had to collect Jessica's trunk. When he walked into her room, it struck him that the room would have appeared unrented if not for the trunk in the corner, for no personal items or even clothes were visible.

Had she even unpacked? He opened the dresser drawers. Empty. Closet. Empty. He glanced at her trunk. Rifling through it seemed wrong in so many ways, but she was under investigation. He unlatched the lock and opened the trunk.

Blake stared at the dark-colored clothes, representing mourning and hard work, filling it. Had her life been one of sorrow? Who was this Jessica who'd stolen his heart and captivated his mind? If only she'd open up and allow him in.

But was that what he truly wanted? What if Cliff was involved in her life? How would Blake react to her deepest secrets? They would surely affect him.

With a heavy breath, Blake closed her trunk and carried it to the wagon.

Mrs. Briggen, sitting with Jessica as he neared, released her uninjured hand when she saw him come through the door. She waved a finger in his face. "You tell that nephew of mine he'd better take care of her, or I'll have a word with him when I come for the Women's Day of Shootin'."

Blake set the trunk in the bed of the wagon. "Yes, ma'am. I

will. Do you have a blanket I can lay in the back for Jessica? I think she would be more comfortable there."

"Of course." She scurried inside.

Jessica sat in the seat, leaning to one side.

"We'll be leaving shortly," he told her. "Anytime you want me to stop, tell me and I will."

She licked her lips. "Thank you."

He scooped up the canteen from the back and unscrewed it for her. "I think you need this." She grazed his hand as she took it, and a yearning he'd tried to suppress hit him full force, almost knocking him to his knees. As a flower breaks through the ground after being planted, Jessica had found a way to break through the hurt of his past and bring new beginnings to his life. A protectiveness stronger than he'd ever felt surged through his veins straight to his heart. The thought felt like a punch to the gut.

No.

But standing there, he knew. He'd fallen in love with Jessica, and there was no turning back.

"Here you go, Sheriff." Mrs. Briggen held out a quilt.

He spread the quilt out in the bed of the wagon, then climbed up next to Jessica on the bench.

"Take good care of her." As Mrs. Briggen stood on the boardwalk and fanned herself with her hand, he tilted the brim of his hat in the older woman's direction.

"I will, Mrs. Briggen. I give you my word."

He glanced at Jessica as he turned the horses away from town. She looked exhausted and was still holding on to the canteen with her good hand. Wrapping an arm around her waist, Blake brought her toward him, letting her rest against him. Her body pressed against his, and it felt right.

Once they were out of the town's view, Blake stopped the

wagon. Jessica's head still rested on his shoulder. He took the canteen she still gripped and held it to her lips. "Jessica, I know you're thirsty. Drink for me."

Her eyes struggled to open, but she obeyed.

Screwing the lid back on, he set it aside. "Jessica, you need to rest. I have a blanket in the bed of the wagon for you."

"Let me stay with you," she whispered close to his ear. "I don't want to be alone anymore."

He ached. Her words spoke truth he didn't want to face himself. He didn't want to be alone, but for so long he'd been afraid to have his heart torn out by death.

Blake held her close, placing her head against his chest. Doubts about Cliff began to take form, but he pushed them aside. The warmth of her body seared through him. He needed her—today, tomorrow, and in his future—and down deep, he believed Jessica felt the same. She had become a balm for his wounds, and he started to feel again, live again, love again when he was with her.

As they continued to the Eastons' ranch, he whispered, "Marry me, Jess."

She smiled up at him. "Yes."

CHAPTER SIXTEEN

Barely able to see with the sun shining through the slits in her eyelids, Jessica lifted her throbbing hand to avoid the light and regretted the motion. She'd forgotten for a moment about going into town with Blake and Matthew, the doctor's visit, and … there was something else. She wasn't sure what it was, but it seemed important. If only she could remember, but the fire flaming from her hand snatched her breath.

She inhaled and pushed the covers off her. Her nightgown, drenched with sweat, stuck to her skin as she swung her legs over the edge of the bed. Her bare feet hit the floor, and she swayed. The room spun, and she collapsed onto the hard floor. She managed to grip the edge of the bed and get one foot underneath her before her strength vanished and she fell again.

Something banged and slammed within the room. "Oh, Jessica. Trent! Blake!"

Her teeth chattered. "R … Rosalind?"

"Yes, it's me." A hand covered her forehead. "Blake. Hurry. I found her on the floor."

Someone lifted her to the bed. A familiar scent of leather

and outdoors. "She's hot with fever." Blake's voice gave her comfort. "Send Pete or Nick for the doctor. I'm not leaving her."

Jessica swallowed, fighting to open her eyes. "Blake ..."

Fingers smoothed over her forehead.

"Yes, Jess. I'm here."

"My hand is on fire, and I'm so cold."

"I know, sweetheart. You're shivering. Let me go down the hall and get you my blankets and your medicine."

"You'll come back?"

"Always."

She tried to smile, but her eyes closed against her will.

Blake hurried into his room, swiped the blankets from his bed and the medicine from his dresser, and rushed back to Jessica. She'd fallen asleep again. He tore the damp blankets from the bed onto the floor. He lifted her, and her body shook as he held her tightly against him. Limp, damp hair stuck to her flushed cheeks.

"Jess, if you can hear me, I'm here." He placed her on the white sheets and covered her with his quilts. Leaning down, he kissed her heart-shaped face. "Please, Lord ..." His throat closed.

"Blake." Rosalind came into the room and gently touched his arm. "I'll take care of her until the doctor arrives."

"What happens if she doesn't wake up?"

"We'll pray she does. But know that God loves her more than you do."

"I'm in love with her." The admission sent tears to his eyes. He blinked hard and wiped the moisture away.

"Then you'll accept my help and let me tend to her needs."

He forced a nod. With a heavy heart, he backed away and through the door and walked toward the front door.

"How is she?"

He hadn't noticed Pete standing on the bottom step of the stairway until he spoke. "Alive. Who went for the doc?"

"Nick."

He pushed past him and headed to the barn. Once he'd closed the barn door, Blake fell to his knees and prayed.

After what seemed like hours, carriage wheels crunched in the yard. Doc was here, and he'd know soon enough of Jessica's health. It took all his strength not to rush up and stand over her bed, ask the questions that continually ran through his mind, and make deals with God if only He'd heal her. Instead, he shuffled from the barn to the fence and stared out into the darkness.

"Blake?"

"Over here."

Trent passed the barn and looked up into the evening sky. "How is she?"

"Last I was there, shivering with fever and soaked through."

His friend pointed into the sky. "Look at those stars. 'When I consider your heavens, the work of your fingers, the moon and the stars, which you set into place, what is man that you are mindful of him, the son of man that you care for him?' God cares for Jessica, Blake. Trust Him."

"I'm afraid He'll take her away like He took Abigail. If I hadn't rushed our marriage, she might still be alive. If I had listened to her parents and waited one more year … But I had loved her ever since we were children. I couldn't wait to make her my wife, to start our lives together."

"There was no way you could have known the future. All you can do is hope, pray, and trust in our Creator, leaving the rest to Him."

Blake drove his fingers through his hair. "I'm afraid I did the same with Jess as I did with Abigail."

"What do you mean?"

"I married Jess last night." Blake was glad he couldn't see his friend's face.

"You did what?" His voice rose. "I don't understand. How? When?"

"On the way back from town. She asked if she could stay with me because she didn't want to be alone. For the first time since we met, she opened herself up and trusted me with how she felt. I realized I had fallen in love and I never wanted to leave her side. I thought I'd never love again, yet this is nothing like anything I've ever experienced. Jess changed my heart."

Trent cleared his throat and paused before he spoke. "I knew she was special from the first time we met."

"And how's that?"

"You put a claim on her the moment you came from the barn and declared you were the one taking her home. I bet if you asked Matthew, he'd tell you the same thing."

"Too bad Pete didn't get the hint."

"He's young."

"They're almost the same age." Blake pushed off the fence and glanced back at the house.

"She married you, not Pete."

"It's killing me that I'm not up there with her."

"Then go. The rockin' chair is still in the room. You're more than welcome to use it." He chuckled. "As you remember, I spent many nights there myself."

"You're right. Thank you." Blake turned toward the house. Lights burned bright throughout, but it was the light from her room that was beckoning him like a beacon in the night.

Blake passed through the front door and immediately climbed the stairs to Jessica's room. The doc stood next to the bed, talking with Rosalind. Blake waited in the doorway.

Rosalind motioned him in. "Blake, the doctor was telling me her hand has an infection."

Doc gave Rosalind a jar similar to the one he'd had out when he'd seen Jess in his office. "Apply this several times a day. I've changed the bandage. I'll be back tomorrow to check on her."

Since Jessica was his responsibility, Blake wanted to take the jar and add it to the medicine Doc had given him earlier, but he thought better of it. He wanted to share the news of their marriage, but now wasn't the time. Jess was his main concern, and it would be better if he kept their marriage to himself until he had a chance to speak with her and they decided together. "Has she awakened?"

"No. Not yet." Doc closed his bag with a snap. "All we can do now is pray and wait." He turned to leave, and Rosalind walked him out, thanking him.

Blake planted a hand on the bed and leaned over Jessica. He wanted nothing more than to hold her close. Tell her how much he loved her and wanted to spend the rest of his life by her side.

He settled with taking in the sight of her. Her brown hair spread across the pillow, strands sticking to the side of her delicate face. "Jess, I need you to wake up. Did you know you have a pixie nose?" He kissed her nose and rested his cheek on her forehead. Sweat and heat pricked his skin. "Please ..." His prayer caught in his throat.

A solid knock pounded on the door behind him. "I came to see her."

Pete. Reining in his emotions, Blake took a deep breath and stood. He drew the blanket to Jessica's neck, completely covering her. "All right. Come in." He took a step back.

Pete walked to the bed and began to reach for her but stuffed his hands in his pockets. He sidestepped a few times, then glanced at Blake. Those hands weren't going to stay in those pockets for long.

Pete leaned over and began to whisper, "Jessica, can you hear me? It's Pete, and I …" His hands came out of his pockets. He touched the side of her face.

"Pete." Blake was about to tell the man a thing or two, but when he opened his mouth, Jessica moved.

Pete spoke first. "Can you hear me, Jessica? Will you open your eyes for me?"

For you? It should be me she opens her eyes for! Blake wanted to drag Pete out of the room, but he couldn't. She was responding to him, and no matter what, Blake had to be there. She had to know *he* was here.

Jessica's eyes wouldn't open, though a voice beckoned to her through the blackness. She felt constricted where she lay.

"Jess, be careful with your hand."

Her father called her Jess. She tried with all her might to open her eyes to see who was with her. Her mind clouded the more the light pierced her eyes, and she cringed, forcing them shut.

"Water." Was that her scratchy voice?

"I'll get it. Be right back."

She wanted to reach out to that voice, but someone lifted her fingers and intertwined them with theirs. "Will you try to open your eyes again? I'll wait right here until you do."

That voice wasn't the same as the one that had called her by her childhood name a moment ago. Her eyes fluttered open, and Pete smiled down at her.

"I was hoping I'd be the first person you'd see. How are you feeling?"

"I …" She licked her lips.

"Shhh. It's all right. I've got to head back to the bunkhouse, but I needed to make sure you were awake. We have much to talk about once you recover your strength."

"Are you ready for your water?" *Blake.*

Her sluggish eyes shifted to him as he hovered at the other side of the bed, water dripping from the glass in his hand. "Blake."

"Get better." Pete squeezed her fingers and laid her hand down. "See you soon."

She closed her eyes and licked her lips again.

"Jess," Blake said, bending closer. "Don't think about anything right now. I'm going to lift your head so you can drink."

A gentle hand slid behind her head and raised it slightly. She moaned and opened her eyes, and Blake gazed into them.

"Do you hurt a lot?"

She groaned when a cup lifted to her mouth, but she drank. The cool water felt heavenly as it coated her throat. When she finished drinking, he slowly placed her head back against the pillow. Her hand flamed. "Tired." Her words slurred. She closed her eyes.

"Rest now, Jess. I'm here. You're not alone."

She dreamed of soft kisses being placed against her temple.

The fever raged throughout the night, and there was nothing Blake could do but crawl into bed and hold her drenched, motionless body within his arms. He pressed countless kisses to her forehead and cheeks and started prayers he could never finish. Jess tore at the seams of his heart, and he was afraid of what would happen if they broke. He didn't want to go down this road again. Couldn't go down this road again. He promised God more than his words, his life. And he'd gladly give it to make her well.

"Jess ..." Like his prayers, his words faded into the nothingness. Movement against his chest caught his attention, and he held his breath. Had he imagined it?

"I'm here, Jess. Will you wake up?" *As you did for Pete?* A twinge of hurt found its way into his heart. He held her closer, her hair gathered under his neck, and kissed the top of her head. Shaking his head slightly erased his insecurities. After the ceremony, he'd carried her to the wagon, and as he'd laid her on Mrs. Briggen's blanket, Jess had whispered she loved him. "And I love you," he'd whispered in response.

Her body jerked, then stopped.

Blake loosened his hold and moved her hair from her face. He studied her breathing and her stilled body. Bells began to go off in his mind. She was too hot. "Dear Lord, please ..." He laid her on the bed, flat on her back, then rushed to light a candle. He hurried downstairs to the icebox, grabbed a block of ice and chipped away at it, added the chips to a bucket, then snatched a cloth from the counter. He filled the bucket with some water before taking it upstairs.

He found Jessica shaking uncontrollably. At her side, he set the bucket on the floor. All he could do now was wait, protect her from falling off the bed, and pray. This time Blake's words were a plea for Jessica to lie still. Instead her back arched and she moaned.

He laid his palm on her cheek. "Jess, I'm here."

She began to shake again.

He stepped back but continued to speak to her, hoping she'd somehow know he had kept, and would keep, his word and his vows. He'd love her. Protect her with his last breath and never leave her side, in health or in sickness.

Jessica's body arched, then rested against the sheets. Blake ran his hand over her forehead, feeling her sticky skin against his palm. He moved the rocking chair to the edge of the bed and sank onto it, reaching for the cold cloth in the bucket. He slid it across her mouth, cheeks, brow, and neck. He returned the cloth to the water before wiping her arms.

Blake glanced at her legs and inhaled a deep breath, noticing how his heart rate picked up. Yes, they were married, and it was in his rights to care for his sick wife, but he needed Rosalind to finish bathing her. There were some things he needed permission for, and touching his wife's legs was on that list somewhere. He palmed her cheek one last time and stood from the chair.

Blake knocked on Trent's bedroom door, and it didn't take long for him to answer. Trent greeted him with a yawn. "Everything all right?"

"Jessica's fever is raging. She had a seizure, but her body is resting now. I need Rosalind to change her clothes. She's soaked through."

"I'll get her right away."

Blake returned to Jessica's side and watched as her chest rose and fell. Several strands of hair matted to her ear. He leaned down, pushed them back, and kissed her warm lips. A gentle hand touched his shoulder.

"I'm not leaving her," he said.

"I didn't think you would."

Brows raised, Blake turned to Rosalind, and she explained, "Trent told me. He didn't think you would leave, so he thought it best I knew. What do you want me to do?"

Blake nodded. "I'd like it if you'd change her into dry clothes, then when you're done, we'll change her bedding."

"How's the fever? Trent said she had a seizure?"

"I bathed her face, neck, and arms in cold water. I think it helped, but I really don't know."

"Would you like me to finish bathing her?"

Blake nodded, then left the room.

Blake walked Doc outside to his carriage. "How much longer before her fever will break? It's been days."

"I'm not sure really, but it should be soon. We pray it will be soon, or we might have a problem on our hands worse than the fever and seizure combined."

A surge of fear and anxiety jolted his heart. He needed to thank him for tending to Jess, but neither Blake's mouth nor body seemed able to move.

Doc climbed into his buggy, then paused, eyeing him. "I'm trying to figure out the change in the room."

"What do you mean?"

"Well, Blake, I've only been a doctor for a short time, but normally the loved one of the family member stands closest to the injured person—in your case, Jessica. Yesterday, Rosalind acted as the loved one, taking charge and giving orders, but today, it seems you've taken on that role. Actually, Rosalind stood behind you most of the time and waited for your decision before acting. Why is that? What happened from yesterday to today?"

Blake glanced away. He hadn't noticed. He'd need to be more careful until he had a chance to talk to Jessica. Right now, he'd give the doc as much truth as he could until they announced their marriage. "Sometimes, when you realize you might lose someone, all you can do is give in and let the heart have its way."

Doc smiled, taking the reins. "I'll stop by tomorrow to check on your patient."

"I appreciate you coming out," Blake finally said.

Pete came to stand next to him as Doc headed toward town.

"What did he say? How's Jessica?"

If Blake wasn't sure about Pete's shooting abilities, he'd send him packing back to the bunkhouse with the other men, but he needed him. Jessica meant more to him than his pride. She meant more to him than his own life. He needed Pete. "She still has a fever, and he hopes it will break soon."

Pete released a long breath. "I know you have feelings for her, and so do I, but she won't marry either of us."

Okay, Pete had his attention. "And how do you know this?"

"Because I asked her to marry me, and she turned me down flat. Says men take what they want, and from what my aunt says, there have been several men who've tried to force her into marriage."

Men had tried to force her into marriage? His fists clenched. He didn't want to think about what could have happened. She was taken now, and everyone needed to know … as soon as she woke. He glanced back at the house. "No one will be forcing her to do anything again."

"Don't you know this woman? She doesn't need our help with anything." Pete strolled back into the barn.

And that was where Pete was wrong. Jessica might act like she didn't need anyone or anything, but when they'd left the doc's office, he'd seen clear through her. She trusted him, needed him, wanted him, and desired they have a life together. Even now it seemed she called to him.

He hurried up the steps to the house and let the door slam behind him.

As he entered Jessica's room, Rosalind looked up at him from where she knelt at the edge of the bed. "Her fever has broken."

Tears sprang to his eyes as he hurriedly knelt on the other side of the bed and touched her forehead. "It has." He hung his head, fighting back his emotions, thanking God in the process.

"Bla ... ke."

"I'm here," he whispered close to her ear. "I love you, Mrs. McKenny."

Her forehead scrunched together, and she struggled to open her eyes.

Blake pressed a kiss to her hairline, and she immediately relaxed. A smile played on her lips. He almost laughed.

"I'll change out the water and have Trent cut a few more ice chips." Rosalind rose and collected the bucket.

"Do you think the fever will return?" he asked, noticing Jess had fallen back to sleep.

"Yes, but it won't be much longer before it will leave her for good. Tomorrow, maybe. We can hope."

Blake reached over and took Jess's good hand and pressed it against his cheek. He kissed her fingertips and palm. *She'll finally be awake tomorrow?* He couldn't wait to start their lives together as husband and wife. Tomorrow, a new day, a new beginning.

CHAPTER SEVENTEEN

Jessica's arms seemed heavy. She was barely able to move her hand to her face and scratch an itch on her nose. Her hand fell to her chest with a thump. She opened her eyes and glanced around, trying to make out where she was.

It took her a few moments to recognize her quarters at the Eastons' ranch, but that's all she could recall. In the corner of the room, a creak drew her attention to a shadow moving toward her.

Her breaths came faster, and she gripped her blanket to her chest. The moon played with the shadow, turning it into a man. Not just any man. The sheriff.

"How are you feeling? Do you need anything? Would you like some water?" He knelt beside her and ran a finger down her jaw.

Why is he touching me? Unable to form words, she nodded.

Blake rose and left the room.

She closed her eyes and tried to push the fog out of her mind, but it didn't work. Something brushed her forehead. Her eyes flew open, and she gasped.

He chuckled. "It's only me."

Of course it's only you in my room at night.

One hand cupped the back of her head and lifted it slightly, then the other pressed a cup to her lips. She did what was expected. The cool water swished into her mouth, then slid down her throat. *Heavenly.* She sighed.

"Good? Do you want another sip?"

Where was her voice? Stolen by shock, that's where.

He gently placed her head back against the pillow and set the cup on the table beside the bed. "Do you need anything else?"

When she gave no answer, Blake lifted her chin and kissed the tip of her nose. "I'm going to sleep in my bed tonight because that rocking chair leaves a lot to be desired."

He said something else, but she couldn't think straight. Did he just *kiss* her? The door closed with a click.

She had to be dreaming. But why did it seem so real? And why did his small touches and gentle kiss feel so right?

It had been months since Blake had a restful night's sleep, so the moment his eyes opened the next morning, he threw the covers off and dressed. Joy filled his heart. Today was the start of his life with Jessica. *My wife.*

Blake stopped in front of the vanity by the door. Dark whiskers covered his jaw. He ran his hand over the rough surface. He needed a shave ... and a haircut. Nothing he could do about it now. His Stetson waited for him on the dresser, but he was staying close to home today. He didn't need it. All he needed was waiting for him in the next room.

Crossing the hall, he found Rosalind had already beaten him to Jessica. His wife met his gaze and sent his heart to gallopin'. Even with her hair askew and matted, she was breathtaking. "I thought I'd check on my patient," he said.

Rosalind pushed to her feet and came to him quickly. Worry marred her features. He looked over Rosalind's shoulder, and something passed over Jessica's eyes. She raised her blanket to her chin.

Rosalind pushed him into the hall and shut the door behind her. "Blake—"

"What's going on?"

She glanced at the door separating him from Jess. "I don't know how to tell you."

"Then just come out and say it. I want to be with Jessica. We have some things to discuss."

"And there's the problem. She asked me why you were in her room last night kissing her. I was taken aback by the questions, and I didn't answer. She's embarrassed. I don't think she remembers marrying you."

He stood motionless for a minute, staring at the closed door, and his mind flashed to his proposal, the wedding with Pastor Bligh presiding and Mrs. Bligh standing as their witness. The last four days as he cared for his wife, loving her with all that was within him—and she didn't remember any of it? Not even her vows to love him until death parted them?

Anger at himself for loving her—and fear that he might lose her—chafed his heart raw and bare. Although they'd never been physical, in those moments he'd lain next to her and breathed in the scent of her, he'd felt as if they were one.

He moved past Rosalind and grabbed the knob. She put her hand over his. "I know how you must feel—"

"You don't know how I feel," he snapped.

"I don't know, you're right, but Jessica is scared. She doesn't understand what happened, and she's so weak. I don't think she could handle the news she's married right now. Give her time. A few days. To rebuild her strength." Rosalind's eyes pleaded for him to listen.

His hand slipped from the doorknob. "Tell Trent I'm leaving." He turned back toward his room.

Rosalind followed close behind. "I don't want you to leave, Blake. Stay here. Jessica does need you." Her words slapped him.

"That's where you're wrong. I'm the one who needs her. Yet, she doesn't even know her husband exists." In his room, he opened a dresser drawer, pulled the marriage certificate from the drawer, and tossed it on the bed. "I only exist on paper." Blake stuffed a few of his things into a bag and grabbed his Stetson. "Mr. Vines is expecting two dozen of Jessica's little breads before church on Sunday. She needs to make sure she takes them there, or Mrs. Briggen will have my hide."

"Blake, please …"

He returned to the hallway and glanced at Jessica's room as he passed. He'd promised her he'd never leave, that she'd never be alone again. But what did it matter? She didn't remember his promises anyway.

By nightfall, Blake arrived at the hotel in Fort Worth in search of more information about the Cliff Gang. Laughter carried from a saloon across the way. Two women with gowns that left little to the imagination stood at the entrance, enticing men to enter. For most, the temptation was too much. But something else drew Blake, calling from inside to ease his hurt and the pain of so many years.

He dismounted. Pulling in a weary breath, he collected his rifle and bag from the saddle, then entered the hotel. Seats flanked the stairway as he approached the register. The gray-haired man behind the counter scribbled something on a sheet of paper.

"Do you have a room available for a few days?" Blake asked.

"Good thing you came in tonight. Tomorrow the town will be in an uproar." The clerk slid the register and a pen toward Blake. "Visitors are already pouring in, and there are only two rooms left."

Blake signed his name. "What's happening tomorrow?"

"We've had some trouble with robbers around here. They arrested one man, and they're transportin' him to our jail until the marshal comes to town. This is the most excitement we've had 'round these parts for some time. Can't wait to get a real look at him. Those *wanted* posters usually don't do a bit of justice." The clerk handed him the key. "Your room is on the second floor, fifth door on the right."

One? Captured? "It's a good thing I came in early then. Night." Blake tipped his hat and climbed the stairs. He opened the door to his room, set his stuff down, and headed back out with his rifle in hand. Striding down the street, he kept alert to the possibility of Cliff's gang coming to free their captured member—or kill him before he could talk. Blake passed the blacksmith's shop and the bank, then entered the sheriff's office, where his friend Mark Connors spoke to a room full of lawmen. Some of the men he'd met the last time he was in town.

Mark looked over at him from where he sat on the corner of the desk. "Blake! Heard about the capture? Hope you can stay and help. We need all the men we can get."

"Hadn't heard until I rode into town."

"Then you're just in time. Everyone, for those who don't know him, this is Blake McKenny, sheriff from the town of Graham."

Blake nodded to the men and leaned against the wall,

crossing his arms over his chest.

"Guy Stevens should arrive here around noon tomorrow." Mark stroked his beard and continued, "He's being transported by five armed men. Two will stay on as his guard, but that leaves the rest of us to secure the town and the jail from a mob. Does anyone have any questions?"

"When is the marshal set to arrive?" one of the men asked.

"In two weeks," Mark answered. "There will be a lot of new faces in town since word has gotten out Guy will be here. You need to memorize those faces." He pointed to *wanted* posters along the wall where Blake stood, then rose. "Any other questions?"

No one responded.

"Fine. We'll rotate shifts. Eighteen hours each. Three of you on a shift. We'll keep this up until the marshal arrives. When you boys are off, rest up. You'll need it." Mark strolled to Blake. "Good to see you. Can you stay?"

"I came to see if you found out anything, but I guess you have. Where did they capture Guy?"

"A saloon in Abilene. He had too much to drink and talked up a storm. Told details of their killings."

"How do you know what he said was true?"

"The deputy who captured him is here. Said he wanted to come along to testify against Guy and make sure he didn't escape. I admire a man like that, willing to give up everything for justice."

Blake strolled to the *wanted* posters and studied the men shown there. He'd never seen a picture of Scott Turner, but the other man next to him he recognized. "Mark, this picture here of Bryan Berkley. I've seen him. He and his brother, Cliff."

Mark's eyes widened. "When?"

"A stagecoach was robbed about three weeks ago. I came up

on them, but they got away."

"You … let them get away? Did they get the drop on you?"

"Not exactly. There was this woman on the stage. I was trying to protect her. I didn't realize who the robbers were at the time." Blake pointed. "Bryan and Cliff Berkley. Yep. These are the men who robbed the stage."

"And where was this?" Mark crossed his arms over his chest.

"Between here and Graham. I've replayed those moments in my mind many times. They knew the stage had a strong box."

"What happened to the girl?"

I married her. "She's still in Graham. Waiting for her horse to come in on the train."

"I wonder why they didn't take her. This gang is known for taking women from stages and selling them. Do you think she was in on it? The robbery?"

"No. I've spent time around her since the robbery." *Nights, loving her back to health. Whispering in her ear that I was thankful God brought her to me.* Blake's gaze fell to the floor. *Dear God, help me be right about Jess. But how is she involved with them?*

Mark gave a snort. "Have you now? Is she beautiful?"

"Very." The word slipped out before he could stop it, the same way he hadn't been able to stop thinking about her since he'd left.

Lines formed on Mark's forehead. "She's gotten to you. I'd be careful and keep my distance. She could be up to something. If you hear anything, report it back to me. We'll get these men, hopefully before someone else gets hurt." Mark set his hat on his head. "I've got to go make the rounds. When are you leaving?"

"After I speak with the deputy who captured Guy. I want to get as much information as possible."

"Good thinking. I'll set up a meeting for tomorrow at the diner. Let's say eight in the morning for breakfast. My treat. No arguments." With a firm nod, Mark strode out.

Jess was tied to this somehow. Her words came back to him.

I've met Cliff Berkley before. I realize now he was one of the robbers on the stage.

"Let her go!" her father yelled, pointing a gun toward her and her captor.

A metal blade pressed against her throat. Jessica trembled at that as much as the fear in her father's eyes.

"I'm taking her, Sheriff," Cliff roared in her ear, "and you ain't stopping me."

"Blake!" Jessica bolted upright, her breathing labored, her body clammy.

"Jessica. It's Rosalind. You're dreaming. Shhh. It's all right."

Her hand flew to her neck, and tears sprang to her eyes. She squeezed them shut.

"Shhh." Rosalind's hand rubbed her back in a circular motion, eventually soothing the horrid memories back to the corner of Jessica's mind.

CHAPTER EIGHTEEN

The next morning, just before eight, Blake entered the crowded restaurant, hoping Mark had been able to set up the meeting with the deputy who arrested Guy. He had more questions about the robbers, and there were only two people who had the keys to unlocking those answers, and Jessica wasn't talking.

Blake glanced around the dining area. Mark and another man sat at a table. His friend stood and waved him over.

"Blake, this is John Reed, the man I was telling you about," Mark said as he approached.

Blake nodded as he joined them at the table. "Blake McKenny, sheriff of Graham." After they shook hands, Blake measured the older man across from him—the firm set of his mouth, the keen look in his eye. "I've been looking forward to talking with you about Guy and anything else you can tell me about the robbers."

John lifted his water glass. "Mark mentioned you ran into the brothers, Cliff and Bryan." He drank and set the glass down.

Blake glanced at Mark. What else had he told him? "I did.

Too bad I didn't know who they were at the time. I'd certainly do things over." But how much would he have done differently? Did that include marrying Jessica? He lifted his own glass and downed his water.

After they placed their order, John talked about how Guy had drunk himself to jail. The more John spoke about the outlaws and what Guy said in a drunken stupor, the more disgusted Blake became, knowing women and children were being sold into slavery. According to John, some of them had been found and rescued.

When the waitress placed their food on the table, John looked from Mark to Blake. "There's something I find interesting." He shoveled a forkful of eggs into his mouth, then a strip of bacon.

Blake waited while he chewed.

"The outlaws," John said around his mouthful, "they're looking for a certain woman."

Blake tensed. "A woman? What's so special about the one they're looking for?"

"I don't know. Guy didn't say. But if we could find her, we'd find them."

Mark turned to Blake. "What about the woman you mentioned to me yesterday? Do you think there's a connection?"

John looked between them again. "What woman?"

"There's a woman from Oklahoma visiting Graham." Blake took a breath. "She was on the stage when it was robbed."

"If I remember correctly, you said a very beautiful woman." Mark chuckled. "John, I've known this man for five years, and not once has he ever commented on a woman's looks. I might have to ride out to Graham to see her myself."

John sat back in his chair and crossed his arms. "All I know about her looks is she has stormy eyes. Sometimes gray, at times darker. Guy made a comment about them."

Blake worked to keep his voice calm, though he felt anything but. "I'll keep that in mind." He cocked a brow. "What else did he say?"

John wiped his mouth with a napkin. "She was Cliff's girl."

Blake couldn't breathe. His blood ran cold through his veins.

The waitress brought the bill, and Mark glanced at it, then rose and took money from his pocket. "Never seen a woman with eyes like that. Blake, I hate to cut this short, but I'm on duty, and John has agreed to help keep an eye on Guy today. Are you hanging around town? Want to see him for yourself?"

Blake stood, gripping the table for support and suddenly craving the numbing effects the saloon offered. He swallowed the emotions surfacing in his throat before he spoke. "Have to get back. My deputies need to know what I've found out. Most importantly, three men are still out there."

John held out his hand, and Blake shook it. "Great meeting you, Blake. Hopefully next time will be under better circumstances."

"Let's hope." Mark patted Blake on the shoulder as they walked out of the restaurant. "Tell the boys I said hello."

Blake tipped his hat and stuffed his hands into his pockets, heading toward the hotel. He felt miles away from Graham—from Jessica, the woman with stormy eyes he'd fallen in love with so quickly.

He pulled his hand out of his pocket to grab the hotel's door, and the room key tumbled to the ground. He bent to pick it up, and when he stood, a woman leaned against the doorframe of the hotel. She twisted a strand of golden hair around her finger. His eyes bounced from her low cut dress to her eyes and stayed there.

"Excuse me." He tried to walk past.

She stepped directly in front of him and tilted her head. "Too bad you don't live here. Maybe I can make you change your mind about living in Graham."

His eyes narrowed. "How do you know I live in Graham?"

"You're too serious, Sheriff." She touched his arm. "But I can help you relax."

Blake moved away, gritting his teeth. "You must have a reason for stopping me."

"That can wait. I'm having fun."

Blake pushed by her and entered the hotel.

"Wait!" Her voice rose to a high pitch.

He stopped and turned. "I'm listening."

"They paid me. I'm to give you the message."

He glanced around. "Who paid you?"

"Some men at the saloon. They told me to tell you Cliff wants his girl back. If you aren't willing to set her free, they'll come get her themselves."

Blake stepped closer. "What men? Show me." He dragged her by the arm from the hotel to the saloon window. "Where are they?"

"I don't see them."

"Are you sure?"

She held out her hand. "Money talks, sugar."

Blake took out his wallet and pressed a bill into her palm.

She smiled. "I'm not sure who they were, but one was called Bryan."

"And?"

"That's all, sugar. Now, if you'll let me go—unless you've changed your mind and are ready to relax."

Blake turned and walked away, his mind spinning. He had to get home. Mark was right. Jessica was involved with Cliff's gang, but not the way they'd thought. They were connected in some way, and he planned to find out how.

Blake walked to the hotel as casually as possible, then sprinted to his room. He locked the room door behind him, threw everything in his bag, and felt for his Colt on his belt.

Oklahoma.

Dark, stormy eyes.

"Jessica ... how are you involved?" he exhaled. "Dear God, have I made a mess of things? I seem to do that from time to time."

She was Cliff's girl.

Blake opened the door and took a step into the hallway. "Help me, Lord. I can't do this on my own."

Rosalind wouldn't allow Jessica to help in the kitchen, so Jessica took the two children to pick flowers before dark. She pulled them in a contraption with wheels that Trent had made, but the more she walked, the more the flower basket on her wrist rubbed into her skin. Too bad there wasn't room to place the basket inside with the children. It had been two days since she'd had a fever, and carrying the basket was tiring enough. Never mind pulling the wagon.

When they made it to the patch of sunflowers Rosalind told her they'd find, she lifted the children out and then sat on the ground as the little ones ran off. Exhaustion pulled at her limbs like quicksand. She wasn't sure she'd make it back when it was time to take them home.

The children wobbled as they ran between the flowers, some as large as ten feet high, with the pollen dusting down to tint Steph's dress yellow. Their laughter rose into the wind and blew straight to her heart. She got to her feet and collected her knife to cut flowers for a bouquet. "Steph and Timothy, go pick the flowers you want, and I'll cut them down."

Timothy pointed to the one he was standing next to. Jessica struggled to cut the stalk with her good hand, but after several attempts, she'd done it. She instructed him to place it in the wagon instead of the small basket she brought since the flowers wouldn't fit. He ran in the direction she indicated. "Steph, did you find one?"

Steph looked up at a few and finally picked a shorter sunflower. Jessica knelt, cut it, and placed it in her hand. Steph smiled. "Pwetty."

Jessica giggled at the two-year-old. "Yes, it is. Go place it in the basket with your brother's."

She nodded and went on her way.

They picked flowers, one at a time, until each child had five. Then with the sunflowers collected and placed in the basket, Jessica announced it was time to head home. The sun had already fallen to eye level.

With her good hand, she lifted them back into the little wagon, supporting them with the injured one. She cringed at the pain even that use brought, but slid the empty basket onto her arm, then pulled the children toward the house with slow, steady steps.

Jessica wasn't halfway there when twilight descended and Blake's tall, handsome form cut through the field toward them. She wished she were strong enough to pick up speed and walk the children to him, but her steps slowed. Her body was weak, and she couldn't go any farther without his help. She stopped as he neared. "Will you take the children back to the house?"

"Are you all right?"

She nodded. "I'm tired is all."

Blake walked by her to the children, who were trying to climb out of the wagon, and scooped them back in. "Hold on, kids." He rolled them near her and held out his hand. "Basket." His voice was curt.

She extended the basket, and he palmed it and walked on, taking everything but her to the house. Jessica sat on the ground, amazed, as Blake disappeared into the night.

He's back.

Her body relaxed at the thought, and peace surrounded her as she planted her good hand on the ground and leaned into it, closing her eyes. If she could rest for a minute, maybe she'd make it back. How could a simple task drain her so?

Her arm gave out, and though she told herself she had to get up, it was useless. She lay down in the grass and closed her eyes.

Blake cupped his mouth with both hands and yelled into the darkness, heading toward where he'd left Jessica. "Jessica! Where are you?"

Why had he expected her to follow him to the house? When she hadn't, pride stopped him from going to help her home. It was obvious she was weak. She'd been so pale, tugging the children to the house.

"Jessica! Answer me!"

He fisted his hands. What had he been thinking? She'd been bedridden with fever two days ago, and from what Rosalind told him, this was her first time out of the house. And he'd left her out in the fields because of his pride, in the dark, alone, aware that a killer was after her.

"Please, Jessica! Answer me!"

"Here … I'm here," she called out.

He squinted in the dark at a form sitting in the grass. Jessica? She was still where he'd left her an hour ago? He'd never forgive himself if she got sick again from his negligence.

He hurried over and lifted her up into his arms. Relief poured over him as her arms wrapped around his neck. Maybe she thought he'd drop her, but whatever the reason, he cherished the warmth of her bare arms on his skin, her head on his shoulder. He nuzzled her hair, inhaling the earthy scent of sunflowers that clung to her skin. The yearning to tell her about their marriage pressed him with each step as he carried her to the house.

She had no idea what she did to him. Physically, she amazed him. Desires he thought had died with his wife came back to life when he neared her. Emotionally, she frightened him. What would happen when she found out they'd wed? Would she accept him? His love? His devotion? His heart?

But then there was his greatest fear. How was Jessica involved with a wanted man?

When they reached the house, Blake carried her upstairs and gently placed her on her bed, then slipped her shoes off and tucked her under the blankets. Moonlight filtered through the window, allowing him to see a sweet smile crest her lips before he shut the door behind him.

Trent and Rosalind met Blake at the bottom of the stairway and followed him to the parlor, where he sank heavily into a chair.

Rosalind was the first to speak as she and Trent sat across from him on the sofa. "Where was she? Why didn't she come in?"

"I found her where I left her. She's worn out. I should have gone back for her right away."

"How are you?" Trent asked, concern in his expression. "Rosalind told me what happened before you left."

Blake took off his Stetson and ran his fingers around the brim. "Honestly, I'm not sure. And the more I investigate the robberies, the more Jessica seems to be involved somehow."

Trent sat on the edge of the seat. "How?"

"Well, Matthew got her to admit she had met Cliff Berkley, the ringleader."

"How did they meet?" Trent asked.

"She never said, but my trip to Fort Worth has brought a lot more questions, and I fear the answers. I don't believe Jessica is part of their operation, but she's involved someway."

Rosalind chuckled. "You can't be serious."

"I don't know." Blake met their gazes. "I married her, and I have no idea about her past. While I was in Fort Worth, a woman from the saloon came to the hotel with a message for me. A threat, really. She told me Cliff wanted his girl back, and that if I wasn't willing to set her free, they'd come get her."

Trent stood and paced. "They know she's in Graham, which means they've seen her. They've been in town. But I don't think they know about your marriage because they said *set her free.*"

"Blake's prisoner," Rosalind added.

"My thoughts precisely. What they don't realize is I'm never letting her go. Not unless I have proof she's involved in their schemes somehow." Blake pushed aside the idea and rose to his feet. "They caught one of the robbers, and he's in Fort Worth until the marshal arrives. If the other robbers are already here in town, we need to be on the lookout for them. There's three still on the loose."

"And if the outlaws know Jessica is here at the ranch, we need to be prepared. I'll tell the cowhands to be aware of anyone on the property. I'll have two other men in the barn with Pete."

Blake nodded. "I'll tell Pete what's going on."

If only he knew himself.

CHAPTER NINETEEN

Blake strolled into the night as the screen door slammed behind him. He rubbed the back of his sore neck. Sleep hadn't come easy last night with the threat hanging over his head. Tomorrow, he'd sit Jessica down for a long talk, whether she wanted to or not, and find out once and for all how she knew Cliff. It was the only way to protect her, because he wasn't giving her up without a fight.

Blake swung the barn door open. A small light shone in the back where a cot normally rested against a wood plank. "Pete, we need to talk."

"Come on back."

Pete lay on the cot, one hand behind his head, the other holding a Bible. "Whatcha need?"

"Your help. Came to talk." He glanced at the worn Bible. "Where are you reading?"

"The story of Jesus and the little children. How God gathered them in his arms when others looked down on them. Jessica reminded me the other day about God's love for us—His creation."

Blake gaped. "Jessica? She reminded you of this?"

Pete set his Bible on his stomach. "She's quite a woman. The way she cares about Tom's kids, makin' them her little breads and sharin' Christ with them. I couldn't have said it better."

Blake ran his fingers through his hair. Jessica was sharing Christ. To the kids of the man who did her wrong by overcharging her for a horse. And then there was a killer searching her out. Blake's account of Jessica was in complete contrast.

Pete chuckled. "I surprised you. I can see it in your face, Sheriff. To be honest, she surprised me. What brings ya out?"

"I wanted to speak with you about what I learned while I was in Fort Worth. The short version is they caught one of the four robbers. One of the men is in the Fort Worth jail. The marshal is said to be coming in shortly."

"*Four* robbers? I thought there were only two."

"The information I received a few weeks ago was wrong. With only two posters, there was no reason to doubt. Thankfully, one robber's been caught, so we're only looking for three."

Pete nodded, closing his Bible. "I can handle that."

"I hope so, because there's more, and it needs to stay between us."

The cowboy's eyes bored into him. "I give you my word."

"I'm expectin' trouble. Two men from the bunkhouse will be keeping you company in the barn for a while. You'll be in charge."

Pete sat up on the cot. "I take it Trent and Rosalind know. Does Matthew?"

"He doesn't, but Sunday I'm taking everyone to church. I'll speak to him then." Blake strode to his trunk by the barn doors and pulled out a towel and a bar of soap. "I'm heading to the creek. Keep an eye on the house."

"Will do, but what is it you're not telling me?"

Blake stuffed his things in his saddle bag.

"Blake."

He let out a long breath. "Jessica is involved somehow. They're looking for her, and they know she's here on the ranch as my prisoner."

His eyes widened. "Our Jessica?"

Blake ground his teeth. She wasn't *our* Jessica. She was his and his alone.

When Blake remained silent, Pete continued, "It has to be a mistake. I've been with Jessica, and she's no outlaw. She's a caring, loving Christian woman. Her father was a lawman. She wouldn't go against the way she was raised. Neither would I …"

A lawman? Blake had thought he worked with horses. Why hadn't she ever mentioned it?

"What's on your mind?" Pete pressed. "Ya look like—"

"Keep an eye on the house," Blake repeated. He strolled to his horse, climbed up, and rode from the barn. A bath should ease the mounting tension in his shoulders.

It wasn't long before twilight fell, and warm water surrounded him as he sank into the deepest part of the creek. Heavenly. He took in the twinkling stars, the slight breeze against his skin, and the toad croaking in the evening.

So Jessica's father was a lawman. Had her father taught her how to ride? It would explain so much. If Blake had his guess, he was sure she'd be able to shoot that gun she carried, maybe even give him a run for his money.

He felt his smile fade. No matter if she could shoot, Jessica was in danger.

He slammed his eyes shut against memories of the night his wife died, and a vision of Scripture came to mind.

A woman with hair and eyes like the night, pressed within a crowd, suffering in torment for something she couldn't control no matter how much she tried. Twelve years of bleeding. Twelve years of the pain and disgrace of her past branding her. But she had something Blake did not. Strong faith. She wanted to reach out and touch Jesus, because she knew if she did, the healing would come.

Words whispered within the warm breeze. *Go in peace and be freed from your suffering.*

Blake sensed God's presence as clearly as if he could reach out and touch the hem of Jesus's cloak. Yes, Blake was much like the woman, desiring to be healed, except it wasn't his blood but his wife's—twelve years ago tomorrow. Would he ever be freed from the guilt of not being able to protect her? Tormented by the things he couldn't control? Could he ever know peace?

His muscles tensed with each breath. *God, please free me.*

He sank under the water, a passing thought of Jessica floating through his mind once again. She might never love him, but he'd rather die trying to protect her than have her be alone in this world.

Climbing out onto the rocks lining the creek, his wrinkled fingers snagged his towel. Blake dried himself off, dressed, then draped the wet cloth around his neck. As he traveled back to the house, he listened to the wind, but neither God nor His Word were in it, only the image of the woman reaching out to touch Jesus.

By the time Blake reached his bed, the house was quiet. He stared at the ceiling. "Dear God ... "

He stilled.

Listening.

A noise came from the hall. He hurried out of the bed and slipped on his clothes. He grabbed his Colt and walked down the hallway. The noise turned into whimpers. Then through the fear ringing in his ears, Jessica yelled, "Blake! Help!"

Blake threw open the door and rushed in. Jessica was alone and was sitting up in bed. Her eyes were closed. He realized with a start that she was still asleep.

His fear eased, and he watched her as he laid his gun on the nightstand.

"She did the same thing last night," Rosalind spoke over his shoulder. "It took me over ten minutes to get her to wake up. She's calling out for you, Blake. Comfort your wife."

He knelt by the bed and took Jessica's hand, and she responded with a fierce grip he didn't know a woman could have, especially one who could barely walk from exhaustion. Rosalind had told him Jessica was slowly regaining her strength, and her grip said she had.

The bedroom door clicked behind him.

"Jessica," he whispered, wiping her tears with his free hand. She shrilled, "Blake!"

He sat on the bed and held her hands. "I'm here, Jess."

"Help!"

"How can I help you?"

"Please."

Helpless, Blake collected her against him.

She gripped his shirt with one hand as she whimpered, then mumbled something. Her hand slipped from his shirt, and her head rested heavily against his chest. Blake relaxed, allowing himself the joy of holding her, of feeling the warmth radiating from her skin and the softness of her hair. It had been days since he'd felt the warmth of her against his arms. How he'd missed it, missed her. He felt complete as a man and worthy to love again, knowing she needed him.

Blake closed his eyes at the thought of this evening and

where his mind took him. The memories had come anew, like time had stood still when his wife had died. Freedom came with a cost, but hadn't he paid enough over the years?

He pressed Jessica closer. *Why did God give you to me only for me to fail you?*

Blake's eyes eventually drooped closed, but a light snore from Jessica woke him, making him smile. There would be too many questions if Jessica awoke to find him sitting on her bed, yet there was no other place he'd rather be than holding her.

He laid her head on the pillow and drew the quilt to her shoulders. His fingers ached to trail down her soft cheek, but he left for his room before he threw caution out the window and stayed.

Jessica awoke refreshed—and happy. She couldn't understand why, yet relished it as she almost skipped down the stairway to the living room. She stopped by the window as the sun began to make an appearance.

"Sunday," she murmured, then filled her lungs with air. Today she'd go to town with a basket full of baked goods for Mr. Vines, and then attend church. Yes, that had to be the reason for her mood: anticipating her day. She struggled to stuff her thoughts of Blake and how wonderful it had felt when he'd carried her into the house after she'd fallen asleep near the sunflowers. Or how glad she was he returned to the ranch, for no one could tell her a time he'd return.

"Good morning, Jessica." Rosalind stood alongside her. "Looking for something or maybe someone?"

"No." Jessica shot her a look. Had she said his name out loud? She hoped not. "I think I'll collect the eggs. Would you like me to make breakfast? My breads will be on the menu."

Rosalind gave her a tired smile. "I'd be grateful."

"If there's anything I can do to help out more now that I'm getting well, please say so. After all, I came to work." She scooped up the basket by the front door and turned back to Rosalind. "I'll start breakfast shortly."

The screen door squeaked and closed behind her with a bang she was becoming used to. She made her way to the barn, eager for Blake to be there. As she entered, a ping of regret settled within her stomach at seeing Trent, Blake, and Pete seated on stools, milking the cows.

"Well, hello, Miss Jessica." Pete's grin spread across his face, causing her to smile in return. All three men looked at her now, but Blake was the first to turn away and refocus on the job at hand.

Why did it bother her that Blake wasn't interested in her? Yes, he'd said she was beautiful, but his trying to push her into Pete's arms? Arms she could never see herself in. Yet when she'd dreamed last night, she'd pictured Blake's strong arms holding her.

"Good morning, Jessica," Trent said as milk filled the bucket.

"Good morning. Looks like you have everything under control in here."

Pete stopped milking and sat up straight. "You're welcome to join us."

"Don't mind Pete." Trent chuckled. "I think between the three of us, we'll have everything done quickly."

"Good, then. I told Rosalind I'd cook this morning, so bring your appetites. I'm heading out to collect the eggs."

Pete said something in return, but it was Blake whom she wished would speak—a word, anything—but nothing passed through his lips. Not even a glance in her direction as she turned to leave.

Disappointment followed her to the chicken coop. She didn't concern herself with the roosters or the hens, who didn't seem to want to move, as she collected the eggs. She counted them, then struggled to count them again.

Think, Jessica!

Blake captivated her thoughts and tied her stomach in knots. She couldn't even count eggs! With a huff, she secured the fence, checked it twice, then reentered the house. Steph, sat in a chair while her mother took out pans from a cabinet.

"Rosalind, I can find my way around the kitchen." If her mind wasn't elsewhere. "Is Timothy still asleep?"

"He is."

"Then go rest."

"But you might need my help. Steph will keep you busy, not to mention cooking at the same time."

Jessica planted her hand on her hips. "I'll have you know I ran an orphanage in Oklahoma, and little ones were always at my ankles. There were twenty-seven in all. One or two here will make no difference in the least."

Rosalind's eyes grew wide. "How did you manage all those children? I'm exhausted with two young ones."

"Oh, I had help, but my father's support and his belief in me was my driving force. He always said I could do anything a man could, and better. Being the sheriff's daughter didn't hurt much either. He treated me like a princess but showed me how to live by his words and actions." Jessica glanced at the basket she was still carrying and set it on the counter, then recounted the eggs. "Will eighteen be enough for breakfast?"

"Plenty." Rosalind lifted a small cup to her daughter's lips. "So where is your father now? Still in Oklahoma?"

Jessica took a long breath. "No. He died a little over a year ago. Been traveling ever since."

Rosalind met her gaze. "Oh, I'm sorry. I didn't mean—"

"It's all right." She shrugged, trying to hide her emotions. "I usually don't talk about what happened or about my father much. It brings up memories I'd rather not ... remember."

"Then may I ask you about the orphanage?"

Jessica swallowed past the lump in her throat and began the search for flour and lard to make biscuits. "Not much to tell. When my father died, I left everything behind." She spun to search another cabinet.

Blake stood in the doorway, watching her. Was that pain she saw in his eyes?

Rosalind scooped Steph from the chair. "I think I'll take her upstairs and get her ready for church." Her gaze landed on Blake with a smile. "I'm glad you're here. Will you help Jessica find the rest of her ingredients for her little breads? We're heading upstairs for a bit." She disappeared into the living room.

"I didn't hear you come in." Jessica avoided his stare, although she felt his gaze straight to her toes. She yanked open another cabinet door, revealing a clear jar with *flour* etched in the glass. "Just what I was looking for."

"What can I help you find?"

She set the jar on the table in the middle of the kitchen. "Rosalind made the dough already. You can set it here." She returned to the cabinet where she had found the cinnamon and grabbed the canister of sugar.

With all the ingredients on the table, Rosalind began to make her little breads.

Blake left the room for a few minutes, then came back with a portion of meat. "Would you like me to slice the ham or cut it into chunks for the eggs?"

She met his blue-eyed gaze and forgot the question for a

moment. "Um … whatever you'd like." She refocused on the dough, giving it a few light punches and regathering her thoughts so she could get through what she needed to say. "Blake, I want to thank you for helping me into the house yesterday. I feel a bit embarrassed about you having to lift me from the ground, but if you hadn't come for me—"

"I should have come sooner."

Her fingers stilled in the dough. Her pulse raced as it did the day by the cemetery when he'd wiped her tears. When she'd found him in her room, running a finger down her jaw and pressing a kiss on her nose. She had asked Rosalind why Blake was there, but she'd never received an answer. She almost asked him now. Instead, she added a pinch of sugar to the dough. "Well, whenever you came, thank you."

Silence settled around them as she formed dough balls on the table with her good hand and carefully trimmed the breads into shapes while Blake cut ham slices. It wasn't an uncomfortable silence as they worked together, preparing several trays of her breads, sliding them into the oven, scrambling the eggs, and frying the ham on the stove. Time seemed to pass much more quickly than she'd expected.

"I'll set the table." Blake slid a handful of plates out of the cabinets and smiled at her as he passed.

Her heart skipped a beat. She couldn't allow these feelings she was beginning to have for Blake to take root.

Uproot them. Yes, today on the way to town, she'd keep her distance. That's what she needed to do, what her mind told her to do.

But her heart continually searched him out, yearned for his touch, much like when she'd found him in her room. If she were honest with herself, she wanted Blake to be the man in her life— and the truth scared her. She could never love a lawman. He would die trying to protect her, and in return, she would have killed another man she loved.

Love? Wait. She couldn't possibly ... not so quickly. But as Blake withdrew a pan from the stove and their eyes met, her heart whispered, *Yes, that quickly.*

CHAPTER TWENTY

The sun beamed down on Blake's shoulders, and heat penetrated his Stetson as he hitched the wagon. He couldn't wait for fall and cooler temperatures—for more than one reason. He'd finally buy the land Abigail and he had dreamed about. Would Jessica share the same dream of breeding and training horses? He'd have to give up being sheriff, but he'd be able to do what he loved best—spend time with his horses.

Maybe during their trip to church they'd have an opportunity to talk, a chance he hadn't taken advantage of this morning. Instead, he'd enjoyed working alongside Jessica in companionable silence.

The screen door shut with a bang, and Blake glanced up to see Jessica coming down the steps in a brown dress that had seen better days. She carried a basket full of little breads, and happiness edged the smile on her face.

"Ready?" Blake took the basket from her and set it on the wagon bench.

"I think I am." She glanced back at the house. "I hope I'm not leaving anything."

Her hair was tied back with a light blue ribbon that allowed it to hang down over her shoulders. He was tempted to touch the ribbon but held himself in place. Jessica looked beautiful in anything she wore—breathtaking, really—but would she prefer a dress to match the ribbons? Color, instead of the dark clothes she carried in her trunk? "Do you have a Bible?"

"Oh, thank you!" She lifted her dress slightly and rushed back into the house.

Grinning to himself, he turned to the wagon and secured the basket under the bench seat. Trent and Jessica both came out of the house. "Is everyone ready?" Blake asked Trent as he neared.

Jessica was the first to reach him at the wagon. "Rosalind doesn't feel well."

Worry lines stretched across Trent's face, though he tried to hide it. "You all go ahead. We're going to town to see the doctor. How about lunch after church? It might encourage Rosalind to eat a bit more than she has in the last two days."

She hadn't been eating? Blake hadn't noticed, except for this morning at the breakfast table when she'd moved her food around her plate. But besides this morning, why would he? He'd been too preoccupied with his own wife. Guilt ate at him because he would have noticed before Jessica came into his life. "I'll be praying. Do you want us to go with you?"

"Thank you, but we'll be fine. We'll see you both." Trent strolled up the steps to the house.

Jessica gripped the wagon with her good hand. "I wonder what was on his mind just now."

"Let me help you." Blake took her waist and lifted her to the seat. "Concern. Love for his wife." He walked to the other side of the wagon and climbed up next to her. "It's what happens when you become husband and wife."

Blake took the reins and set the wagon off toward town.

He'd meant what he said with Abigail and now Jessica, but there was a wall of questions standing in his way to Jessica. About their marriage and secrets that needed to be shared about Cliff.

The drive was quiet, too quiet for his liking, as Jessica looked out over the land. He pointed to a row of trees nearing town. "Since we're close to town and have plenty of time, do you want to stop?"

She shrugged. "Sure."

He steered the horses to the shade and set the brake. Her mouth opened when he turned to her but then shut quickly. "Did you want to say something?"

Jessica fingered the hem of her sleeve. "More like a question I've been thinking about on the way."

He chuckled. "Well, I've never seen you hold your tongue with me, so don't start now."

Her hands stilled, and she met his gaze. "All right. Earlier when you spoke of a man having a wife, it sounded as if you knew. Are you married?"

Dear Lord, how do I answer her question? I'm married to you? Blake glanced down at her bare ring finger and her slender hands. He wanted to reach out and hold them within his own, to feel the warmth of her again. "I was once, to a woman named Abigail. We were childhood sweethearts, and I had always loved her, wanted to marry her from the first moment I saw her at a church gathering. I was older by three years, so it almost did me in waiting for her to turn sixteen."

"So you married."

His lips turned upward at the thought of Abigail in her wedding gown. It took her a year to make her gown, and it was worth the wait seeing it on her as she walked down the aisle. "She was everything I had ever wanted." He glanced out over the land. "Abigail was killed six months after we were married.

Two men broke into our home in the middle of the night and robbed us. I was busy fighting off one man, who had our entire savings, when another one … shot Abigail. When I realized what had happened, I left off fighting to find her. She was on the floor, shot in the chest. I tried to help her, but I was hit on the back of the head and everything went black. I woke up hours later to find my wife dead, lying next to me." He met her gaze, and tears shone in her eyes.

She cupped his scarred cheek, as if knowing he'd received the scar that night. The heaviness and pain from the memories fled when she touched him. With no will to stop himself, he kissed her wrist as it brushed against his mouth.

Tears brimmed in Jessica's eyes. She didn't want to think of the pain Blake must have endured, waking to his wife's lifeless body. The loneliness he must have felt for the woman he'd waited for all his life, who'd left him so early, so young.

She cupped his cheek, covering part of his scar and meeting his teary gaze. He held her hand against his face and pressed his mouth to her wrist. The warmth from his lips seared her skin.

She should move. Couldn't move. "I'm sorry for your loss."

"I was lost without her. So many times I've replayed those moments, wishing I could have stopped her death in some way."

She broke eye contact. She understood those feelings well. If only she would have listened to her father and not gone to the orphanage as he asked. "I felt the same way once." Sorrow filled her heart, and her mind yelled at her to stop thinking, stop feeling.

"Jessica, please don't pull away. Let me in."

Jessica met his gaze again and wiped her face with the back of her hand. Why was it when he looked at her, when they were together, it was as if he opened the windows of her soul and drove out the darkness and fear she cowered in?

"Will you tell me about your father? I heard you speak of him this morning with Rosalind. You said he was the sheriff where you lived? I thought he was a horseman."

She slipped her hand free from his and sat upright. The windows in her soul slammed shut, and darkness settled back in. "I think we should go. I'd like to get the little breads to the store before the service."

"We have time, and I would like to know about the man who fathered such a tenderhearted woman."

She couldn't discuss her father with him. It was too hard, too painful. What good would it do anyway? She'd leave town soon enough and never see Blake again. "Why would you possibly want to know about me, or hold my hand, when you begged me to marry Pete?"

"I was a fool, Jessica. Convinced myself I wanted the best for you, and I thought ..."

"Pete was what was best for me? Why the change?" She regretted the question the moment the words slipped from her lips.

He ran a finger down her cheek, and her breath caught. She gripped the bench to steady herself.

His eyes darkened with emotion. "I've fallen in—"

"Don't." She rose quickly, afraid of what he'd say next, and hopped down from the wagon. This couldn't be happening. How she felt when they were together. She didn't want to love this man or accept his love in return.

Blake followed her. His hands slid over her shoulders. "I didn't mean for it to happen. I didn't want it to happen. I tried to push you away. I was wrong to do that to you, to us. I'm sorry."

She shook her head. "You can't."

He turned her to face him, raising her chin to meet his eyes. "I can and I do. It's too late for me to turn back now. I'm in love with you, Jessica."

"Well, I'm not in love with you." The lie stung her tongue. She turned around, afraid he'd witness the truth. She bit her lip, focusing on the physical pain, not the pain in her heart. She'd carry what she felt, hide it, bury it.

"Why can't you love me, Jess? Are you in love with someone else? Cliff Berkley, perhaps?"

It wasn't just the mention of Cliff's name that made her sick, but the insinuation she was involved with the man that brought nausea to her stomach. The memories of the stench of alcohol on his breath, his lips against hers, his fingers around her throat, and the promises he made as he groped her were engraved within her soul. She would never escape, she realized, and his words were coming to fruition. *You're no longer daddy's girl but mine.*

Dear God, please help me. She began to tremble.

Blake touched her arm, jarring her back to the present. "Jessica, you're shaking."

She yanked her arm away. "Don't! How dare you imply … that I would … what type of woman do you think I am?" She marched the few steps to the wagon and climbed in, released the brake, and took the reins. With the snap of her wrist, she sent the horses into motion.

"Oh, no you don't. You're not leaving me here." Blake grabbed the nearest horse's harness, slowing the team to a stop. "We're going to hash this out right here and now." He climbed into the wagon.

"I have nothing to say to you." She crossed her shaking arms over her chest, her eyes focusing on the back of the horse's rear end.

"Are you involved with Cliff Berkley? And why didn't he

take you the day of the robbery and sell you like the other women?"

"No. And ... I don't know."

"Then why does Cliff call you his girl?"

Jessica met his gaze, and terror gripped her. "Please, Blake, leave this alone. Release me from my month as your prisoner. I will leave Graham, and you'll never have to see or think of me again."

"I can't do that, Jessica."

"Yes, you can. It's really rather easy. Just say the word, and I'll be gone."

"I've fallen in love with you, and I'm tired of trying to hide it."

She shook her head. "You can't. I can't."

"Are you married?"

"No."

"Are you in love with someone else?"

"No."

"Jess," he whispered, lifting her hand to his mouth. He kissed her knuckles.

She shivered against his touch. "Please don't."

"I feared the worst when you went looking for my horses and Legend returned without you. It pained me when I saw what one of my horses had done to your hand. I knew then I loved you and I never wanted another day without you by my side."

"Blake, I can't ... I can't love you. I don't even trust you."

"Then we're both in agreement. I don't trust myself when I'm with you." He lifted her chin and lowered his mouth, capturing her lips. Then pressing his hand to the small of her back, he brought her close.

She moaned in frustration and pleasure, the rightness of the moment. Blake wasn't what she needed—but he was everything she'd ever wanted. She placed her hands on his chest and gently pushed herself from his arms.

His gaze studied her, searching.

"I can't love you," she said quickly, perhaps too quickly, giving herself away. Her heart mourned for them, for what might have been.

His eyes softened, as if he were deaf to her words but privy to the beating of her heart. He wiped her cheek, brushing away the single tear that had slid down her face without permission. "Is it that you can't, or you won't?"

His touch set her nerves on end. "I cannot. I will not."

Blake's face was void of emotion, but within her, she mourned the love she so desperately wanted. She loved him. But she loved him enough to give him up. Cliff would find her soon, if he hadn't already.

"I think we should be on our way. We don't want to be late." He lifted the reins and set them into motion.

She nodded, turning her face to the sun, wanting to feel its heat instead of the ache within her heart.

By the time they reached town, the streets were crowded. They parked in front of the general store. With only a few minutes to spare before the service started, she hurried to grab the basket and climb down, but Blake was at her side of the wagon, holding out a hand to assist her.

She hesitated. "Why are you being kind to me?"

"Would you expect me to treat you any differently after I've just shared my heart? I want to take care of you, Jessica. To love you for the rest of our lives." He took hold of her waist and set her feet on the ground, then handed her the basket. "We can talk more on our way back to the ranch."

She ran her hand down her dress. With a breath, she took a few steps toward the general store. Blake strolled by her side. He walked tall, shoulders back, stride sure.

"Howdy, Sheriff. Ma'am." A man she'd never met stopped on the boardwalk and tipped his hat as they neared.

"Mornin', Jerry. How's the leg?" Blake asked as they slowed their steps.

The man grinned and palmed his knee. "Headin' to church now. The wife and kids beat me there."

Blake gave a warm smile. "Good, because from what I hear, those boys of yours are claimin' they'll win next year's sack race."

"Not if I can help it. It's the reason I decided to walk into town. They took the wagon with their ma." Jerry looked between Blake and Jessica. "You comin' to the service?"

"We'll see you shortly."

"Ma'am." The man tipped his hat and slowly crossed their path to the church.

"Is he all right? What happened to his knee?"

"Fell off his horse. He was showing off for his boys." He glanced at her hand but said not a word. Neither did she.

Another man tipped his hat at the sheriff from the street.

Blake nodded. "Mornin', Harry."

It was obvious the town loved their sheriff, respected him along with everyone at the ranch. Pride soared as they entered the general store.

"Hello." Mr. Vines smiled at them. "Hope you have your breads."

"Yes, sir. Two dozen." She set the basket on the counter.

He lifted the cloth. "Perfect. Can you make another two dozen for next Sunday? Word's gotten around. I've had a few customers asking about them."

"How wonderful." She smiled up at Blake, who winked back. "I'd be happy to. Thank you."

"You're welcome. And here's the money from your last batch."

Jessica accepted the few coins he slid across the counter.

"You both have a good day," he said.

"Thank you. We will." Blake placed his hand on her back and led her outside. "Before we leave town, if you'd like to purchase something, you can."

"Actually, I'd like to go to the livery to see about my horse. It should be here next week, but I want to let Tom know where I'm staying so he can send word when it arrives."

Blake grew silent. Did he think she would change her mind and stay because he loved her? It was the best reason to leave.

"When my horse comes on the train, and you release me, I'm leaving."

His hand fell, and his jaw twitched. She sensed his controlled movements as he placed a gentle hand on her back and steered her across the street.

Once they entered the church, Blake greeted anyone and everyone who strode within arm's length of them and included her in his conversations. He led her to a bench, then proceeded to follow her down it as they took their seats.

She rested her hands in her lap and discreetly glanced at Blake out of the corner of her eye, pretending to look across the church.

He inhaled a long breath and released it as he turned to her. "Why are you in such a hurry to leave Graham? Have you not enjoyed the town and its fine people?"

Was he referring to himself as "fine people"? Blake McKenny was better than fine, he was perfect. Handsome in every aspect of the word, and with brown hair she wanted to run her fingers through. It wasn't only his looks, but his heart, which was as big as her father's. And when he walked alongside her, she felt proud to be in his company.

But the longer she stayed, the longer she put others at risk.

"I'm leaving, Sheriff, and there's nothing you can say to stop me." The words hurt, but it was for the best. She had to leave—tonight perhaps, when no one expected it.

CHAPTER TWENTY-ONE

"And look who just came out of the restaurant with that sheriff. Do we want to take her now?"

Cliff glanced at his brother, then around at the busy streets. They'd been in town for a few hours, and no one knew who they were yet. He wanted to keep it that way. It wouldn't be easy to take her, and he didn't want to make a mistake.

"It looks like they're not alone." Bryan pointed, watching another couple walk alongside them. "Let's lag behind and follow. If we get a chance to get closer, then we'll nab her. Let's split up. You take the buildings behind the doc's office, and I'll take the right flank."

His brother nodded, then headed off in the direction he was told.

Cliff stood still at the corner of the building. Jessica pointed to the livery, then wiped her face with a cloth. The couples stood near the boardwalk for a few moments before parting ways. When their backs were turned, he followed.

Jessica was the prettiest little thing he ever did see, and if it weren't for her father, they'd be together. He thought back to the stage they'd robbed. It wasn't supposed to be carryin' passengers, only the strong box, so it surprised him when the stranger pulled the little filly out from the stage. He chuckled, remembering the look in the man's eyes when Jessica stuck the gun in his back. Too bad he was the town's sheriff and she got herself on the wrong side of the law.

Stealing, Cliff had heard. Not Jessica. It was a mistake for sure, but it landed her as a prisoner and stopped him from taking what he wanted. Oh, he'd get a much higher price for sellin' Jessica to a brothel than he'd gotten from sellin' the others, but he wanted her for himself, always had growing up.

Being the poor orphan boy nobody wanted, he hadn't stood a chance with someone like Jessica. But it was her, always her, who had rescued him from the school bullies. She'd said she understood how he'd felt when he'd lost his family in the fire since her own ma had gone and died.

Her father never understood Cliff though. Never liked their friendship as kids, always telling him to walk the straight and narrow, keeping them apart, but Cliff saw her at school and at the orphanage when she came to visit as a little girl. Even at a young age she was drawn there, and that's how he knew she'd come that day. He'd only had to wait. Her father just didn't understand. He shouldn't have gotten in the way.

Just as Jessica waved to the Eastons as their wagon passed, the hair on the back of Blake's neck stood up. He glanced over at Tom's sons, who stood throwing stones behind the livery. Trent had told Blake on several occasions God had given him an unnatural ability to sniff out trouble, and each time Blake had laughed.

He wasn't laughing now.

He was certain he and Jess were being watched, but by whom?

Matthew ambled by the cemetery and strolled up to the boardwalk by the general store. He smiled and tipped his hat in their direction. Blake raised his hand, palm out, a silent command to stop, even though they continued to walk to the front of the livery. Matthew's eyes narrowed, then he entered the general store.

"Tom," Blake called as his eyes adjusted to the darkness inside the livery.

Tom tossed his rag on an old three-legged wooden chair propped against one of the doors. "What can I do ye for, Sheriff? Miss Thompson."

"Nothing for me, but Miss Thompson wants to speak with you about her horse."

"Well, lass. I'm not givin' back ye money, if that's why ye bringin' the sheriff. Him and I already—"

Jessica huffed and placed her hands on her hips.

Blake took a step forward, unsettled by the way Tom had taken advantage of her before. He wasn't going to allow him to do it again. Jessica threw an arm against his chest, stopping him. Blake swallowed a laugh as she eyed him. Oh, how he loved this woman and her spunk.

"She's a pushy little thing," he said. "You better watch it, Tom."

"Mr. O'Connor, I'm not here about the money. I'm here to let you know I'm staying with the Eastons. As soon as my horse comes in, I need you to ride out and deliver him."

"As long as you got the money."

"I do. Next week, right?"

"As far as I know. Nothin' changed."

"Good." Jessica forced a smile, and Blake could see the

wheels spinning in that pretty head of hers. He had the distinct feeling he needed to tell her they were married before it was too late. He glanced at the general store. First, he needed to talk to Matthew.

"You ready?" He placed a hand on the small of her back. "I need to visit the general store before we head back."

She glanced at him quickly before saying, "Thank you, Mr. O'Connor."

"Good day to ye both."

Blake tipped his hat and escorted her across the street.

"Weren't we just here?" She looked at him.

"Yes, but I need to speak with Matthew." The bell rang as they entered the general store.

Matthew met them by the barrels of potatoes. "Hello, Miss Thompson. Blake. Just the man I wanted to see."

Blake turned to Jessica.

She waved her hand. "Take your time."

He smiled his thanks, and he and Matthew walked to the corner window of the store and stared out.

"What did you see?" Matthew asked, leaning his Henry rifle against his leg.

"It wasn't what I saw, but felt. We were being watched. Did you see anyone? Anything unusual?"

"Nope, can't say I did."

"Keep a look out. I came from Fort Worth yesterday. There are four robbers, not two. Mark has one who was arrested in Abilene. He'll be there until the marshal arrives."

When Matthew remained quiet, Blake turned to him. "What's on your mind?"

"I'm concerned. I know you care for Jessica, but I want you to be careful. In my gut, I know she's tied to this somehow."

Blake took a breath and continued to stare out the store

window, watching a brown bird land on the boardwalk, then peck at the wood. "Cliff knows she's here in Graham, staying at the ranch."

Matthew remained silent for several moments. "I'm coming back with you."

"But I need you here."

"Send Pete. He's good. Or a couple other men. I'm not going to let you fight this alone and risk your life for a woman you barely know."

"I'd risk my life for her … she's my wife."

Matthew's eyes widened as he met Blake's gaze. "When? Where was I when this happened?" His voice rose.

"Shhh." Blake glanced over his shoulder. Jessica fingered a bolt of cloth near the register. "She doesn't know. I thought she did. At the time she did." Blake ran his fingers through his hair. "The day we took her to the doctor. I think the fever from her injury caused her to forget."

"You married her then?"

"After we left." He shrugged. "I'm in love with her. I asked. She said yes, and we married. Have the marriage certificate, but no one knows but Trent and Rosalind. Please keep it that way."

"When do you plan to tell her?"

"I tried a few times. She doesn't realize I know about Cliff and that he's looking for her. She won't talk to me, but I know he scares her. I think she's planning on leaving town. I can't let her go."

"Do you think she'll stay, knowing you're married?"

"I can hope and pray."

Matthew ran a hand over his face. "I'm coming back to the ranch with you as soon as I tell Jake I'm heading out. I'm not going to let you be a sittin' animal ready to be picked off by a wanted man."

"All right. Maybe with you at the ranch you can run interference between Pete and me where Jessica's concerned. On our honeymoon night, while her fever raged, he touched her face and was holding her hands. I almost knocked him out cold."

"Are you boys done playing? I'm ready to head back." Jessica's voice sounded from behind them.

Blake turned to her, warmth climbing his neck. Hopefully, she hadn't heard a word they said. When nothing about her expression indicated she had, he widened his eyes at Matthew and exhaled a heavy breath of relief.

The moment they left the store and stepped out on the boardwalk, Blake's skin crawled. Matthew stepped closer to Jessica, as if also sensing trouble. She glanced between them but said nothing until they entered the sheriff's office.

She spun to Blake, her hands shaking. "He's here. Cliff is here. I know he's here."

Blake wanted to tuck her in his arms and reassure her she was safe, but he couldn't. Doubt crept in his mind. *You couldn't keep Abigail safe.* "He is. He found out you're staying at the ranch."

Her face paled, and her hand flew to her throat, like it had when they'd come to town to see the doctor.

"Tell me about him, Jess. How come he calls you his girl?"

Blake caught a glimpse of Matthew staring at him. He didn't care what his friend thought. In his heart he knew Jessica wasn't Cliff's girl. Not with the way her body trembled at each mention of him. She looked as if she were about to collapse.

He wrapped his arm around her shoulders, and she leaned heavily against him. "Come sit."

As he led her to a chair, Jake came through the door and took in the scene before him. He quietly propped a chair against the front door and sat, effectively blocking the entrance.

Blake knelt before her, holding her sweaty palms within his hands. "How do you know Cliff?"

She avoided his gaze, her head hanging low. "His family moved to the town where I lived in Oklahoma. We were in grade school together. There was a terrible fire that killed both his parents, leaving his brother, Bryan, and him to fend for themselves. They were mere boys and sent to the orphanage. They were picked on at school for not having a mother or a father." She swallowed and met his gaze. "I couldn't let the children pick on them, so I stood up for them, became their friend. I was ten when I started visiting them in the orphanage."

"You did a wonderful thing, Jess."

"Several years later, Cliff got into a fight with one of the kids from school. It was pretty bad, and my dad was called. He put Cliff in jail to try to set him straight, because he was getting into a lot of trouble by then. Dad would try to tell him he needed to walk the straight and narrow, but that day it backfired. Cliff threatened my dad. Before Cliff left town, he came to see me, told me he'd come back when he made something of himself. He kissed my cheek, called me his girl, and rushed off. I'd never been his girl."

Jessica put her head in her hands. Tears pricked her eyes, and she bit back a sob.

"Jess, tell us about the orphanage." Blake's tender voice drew her gaze. He wiped her tears with his thumb. She clung to the strength she felt in his touch and continued. "I loved going to the orphanage," she whispered. She caught a glimpse of Matthew moving closer. She'd forgotten there were others in the room. She took a deep breath. "I had been helping after school for several years, mostly with schoolwork, but I'd cook or clean from time to time. When I turned sixteen, I was asked to help run the home. Have ever since. That is until ..."

"What happened last year? The reason you've been on the move? Did Cliff come back?"

She touched her neck. Her heart pounded in her chest.

"He did, didn't he?"

"Yes." She bit her lip and wiped her face with the back of her hand. "He was waiting for me at the orphanage. Dad told me not to go. I didn't understand why, but the kids needed me. I wasn't going to be gone long. When Dad found out I'd left, he came looking for me." She shook her head.

"Did Cliff hurt you ... force you ..."

She met his gaze, understanding taking form. "He would have, if my father hadn't stopped him. He tried to kidnap me, held a knife to my throat. If only I'd listened to my father and not gone to the orphanage, he'd still be alive. I killed my father."

She began to sob.

Blake collected her in his arms. "Listen to me, Jessica. You didn't kill your father. Cliff did. You are not responsible for his death."

"I didn't listen. I should have listened."

Blake lifted her into his arms and carried her from the room, to another smaller one. When her tears finally ran dry, soft whispers floated to her ears. "I'm here, Jess. You're not alone."

She peeked up at him through her wet lashes. His blue eyes, turned dark, studied her, roaming her neck, her face, drinking her in. Warmth seeped through her, but it was his words that held her there. And why did it seem so natural to be in his arms, listening to his voice, as if she'd heard it a hundred times before?

She lifted her hand to Blake's cheek. His whispered words continued to wrap around her heart. He searched her eyes. Her breath hitched at how close their lips were, only inches apart. She wanted to lean forward and kiss the man … she loved. She loved him, but she wouldn't. The memory from their last kiss would be painful enough when she left. She'd leave tonight before she put Blake in harm's way. She'd stop by the boardinghouse to say goodbye. Word would get around quickly that she'd left town, and if Cliff was in ear shot, he'd follow her.

Blake would be safe. No one else would die because of her.

CHAPTER TWENTY-TWO

Something passed over Jessica's eyes, and it frightened Blake. What was it he'd seen? She pulled away, and the beat of his heart doubled. "I'm not letting you go," he spit out. He had to tell her they were married before it was too late.

Please, Lord, help me.

She rose from his lap and stared at him, a brow arched. "Why would you say that to me? Will you not release me after my month's time?"

Was it the right thing to do knowing Cliff was after her? Regardless, he had to keep his word. Would it be their undoing? Their lives?

Blake stood beside her. "I'm releasing you."

Jessica blinked twice. "Really? Releasing me? Like, free to go?"

His heart tightened as he forced the words past his lips. "You are free, no longer my prisoner."

She folded her arms across her chest. "You're confusing me, Sheriff. I'm free to go, but you're not letting me go? Which is it?"

"Against my better judgment, I release you as my prisoner, since I now have a better understanding as to why you were in my room."

Moisture filled her eyes once again. "Thank you. Will you take me back to the ranch so I may collect my things?"

Blake couldn't speak. She was indeed leaving. Leaving him. He nodded.

When they exited the sheriff's office, they found Jake sitting in the wagon and Matthew holding the reins to Jake's horse.

Matthew handed the reins to Blake. "We thought it would be better if you could ride. I'll be alongside you. Jake will follow us to the ranch. We should be back before the rain hits."

Blake looked at the graying skies, then switched the reins to his left hand, holding out his right to Jessica. She accepted his hand and climbed up into the saddle. He slid behind her and wrapped an arm around her waist. He needed her close, to feel her next to him.

Please, Lord ... I love her. The thought ripped through his chest. The nights he'd held her within his arms, praying for her recovery and chasing away her nightmares, seared his mind. He thought only of her as they rode and how their time together seemed too short. He wanted a lifetime with Jessica. He pulled her closer.

She covered his hand with hers.

As they neared the ranch, Blake slowed his horse and waited until Matthew rode alongside them. "Give us a few minutes," he said.

Matthew nodded, then went on ahead.

Though they were alone now, neither of them spoke. If she was concerned about a repeat of their earlier roadside conversation and kiss, she didn't show it. He kissed the top of her head and spanned his fingers over her stomach.

"We need to talk," he finally said. No matter how much she protested, she loved him. He'd felt it before on their wedding day and when she'd called out to him at nights through her tears. Even now, with the way she leaned her head against him and let out a soft moan. He rested his cheek against her hair. "Please don't go."

"Blake, I can't stay."

"Is there anything I can say to stop you?"

"No. I'm sorry." She slowly sat up, avoiding any further contact.

When they reached the barn, Jessica slid from the saddle, and without a word, hurried toward the house.

He had to tell her the truth before it was too late. As she climbed the porch steps, he called after her, "We're married, Jessica."

She stilled as her foot touched the top step, then stood there, frozen, before eventually turning around. Her gaze narrowed at him. "That's impossible. I would remember my own wedding."

"It's not impossible."

"If you're trying to keep me here, it won't work." Saying a quick prayer, he dismounted from the horse and neared where she stood. "You're my wife. I have a certificate to prove it."

She crossed her arms against her chest. "When did this supposed marriage take place? I don't believe you. Why wouldn't I remember?"

"The day I took you to the doctor—"

Her arms slid to her sides. "I was angry. You took that as love?"

"It was after. On the way home, you told me you never wanted to be alone. That you didn't want me to leave you. That you loved me."

She shook her head. "I would not have … I … I never wanted to marry—not after what Cliff did—or the other men who tried to force me to be their wife." Her voice faded as she looked away. Seconds ticked by before her pained gaze found his. "I have to hand it to you, Sheriff. You're smarter than the others. You waited until I was most vulnerable."

"Jessica." Blake's long strides ate up the distance between them, but she backed away and held out her hand.

"Don't. Don't touch me." She fled into the house.

Blake stared after her. How could she not remember anything? Think he'd force her into something like marriage?

He turned at the sound of wagon wheels rolling down the hill. Jake waved at him, but he didn't respond. Matthew came out of the barn just then, meeting his gaze. He'd heard everything, Blake was sure.

The wagon rolled into the yard, and Jake set the brake and hopped down.

"I'll tend to the horses." Matthew took the horses' reins from the wagon. "I sent Pete and the boys to the bunkhouse to round up some men to head to town. See what they can find."

Blake nodded. It was all he could do to contain the pain her words had caused. He strode into the barn and paced, glimpsing the tree branches he'd cut down for Jessica. He'd make those atlatls for Tom's boys.

After instructing the cowhands how to secure the town, he sent them away with Jake. Blake returned to the barn and began working on the atlatls. Between stripping the bark and carving, he kept his hands busy and his feet from taking him to Jessica's room to try to explain about their marriage. What did it matter anyway? It was only a matter of time before she left him.

The wind blew at the hem of Jessica's dress and her hands shook as she waited outside in the shadows of the house for Pete. Where was he? Her heart tightened within her chest.

She'd overheard Matthew tell the deputy and Blake about finding men to secure the town, but how long did it take for Pete to return from the bunkhouse? Had she missed him? Dinner had already passed, and there was still no sign of him.

The sky was growing darker by the hour. Traveling by night was out of the question, but she needed to see the preacher, and knowing Cliff was terrified of storms, she was certain he was holed up in a room or barn somewhere.

But she couldn't stop thinking about Blake's betrayal, and how it multiplied by the second. She'd trusted him like no other man except her father, and look where it had gotten her.

Married?

Jessica caught a glimpse of Pete headed down the hill toward the barn.

She ran toward him, yelling his name for all she was worth against the wind. "Pete!"

He slowed and craned his neck, searching. He must have seen her because he turned his horse around and rode to where she stood.

The horse's hooves hadn't stopped before she called out, "Pete, lend me your horse."

His smile faded. "What?"

Could he not hear her? "I need to ride. To feel the wind against my face. Just for a bit."

"It'll be dark soon." He glanced up. "It looks like rain."

"I know. I'll be back soon. Before dark."

Pete looked to the house and back. "I don't know."

"Please, Pete." Moisture filled her eyes. She couldn't be married. She had to know for certain. Needed more than to see a slip of paper.

He climbed down and searched her gaze. "I'm not sure what's going on, but do you want to tell me about it?"

"I can't."

"Jessica." His voice softened as he handed her the reins.

"Please don't tell anyone I went, especially Blake."

"So this has to do with Blake?"

She climbed into the saddle. "Thank you." She turned the horse and galloped up the hill, away from Blake and Pete to find the truth.

By the time she arrived in town, the wind had begun to howl and the rain blurred her sight. She narrowed her focus, not on the church but next door, on the saloon's swaying lanterns, to guide her way. Laughter billowed out of the building as she neared.

She hurried past it, and at reaching the church, Jessica quickly dismounted and tied the reins to the hitching post. She ran under the covered porch and knocked. Another gust of wind pounded the rain against her already half-soaked body. She pulled her jacket tighter in an attempt to protect what little of her was still dry and hammered the door with her fist.

No answer. Perhaps he didn't live here. She scurried to the back of the church and found another walkway, directing her to an attached building. A flower bed and garden greeted her on each side as she neared. She pounded on the door, and a moment later it swung open, revealing the pastor and his wife. A bewildered look skirted their features before recognition settled on the man's features. "Mrs. McKenny. How may we help you?"

Jessica's breath left her. *Mrs. McKenny.*

"Samuel, can't you see she's soaked through?" Mrs. Bligh scooted past her husband, took Jessica's arm, and ushered her into the kitchen. "Please, sit here while I get you a towel."

"I don't mean to impose."

"Nonsense." She waved her off and turned to her husband. "Make her some tea or coffee. We don't want her to catch a chill. I'll be right back."

Jessica watched as the older woman hurried off, giving her time alone with the parson. "Mr. Bligh." She turned to him. "Please don't worry about coffee or tea. I came to speak with you. It's regarding my ... marriage."

He smiled. "Oh, yes, I can't remember the last time I've seen two young people so open about their need for each other. Not out of duty, mind you, but out of love. It was an honor to join your lives together."

Jessica swallowed at his words, heat rising to her cheeks. "Parson, I have questions."

"I see. It's not every day we have visitors, especially during a storm." He dragged his chair out from the table and sat. "I guess whatever it is you're seeking must be important."

"It is."

Mrs. Bligh took that moment to reappear, carrying a towel and quilt. "Here." She handed Jessica the towel and draped the quilt across her lap. "I don't want you to catch a chill. Blake would be worried sick."

Blake. Insufferable man! And yet, the idea that the pastor and his wife believed Blake had cared for, even loved her, was stunning. As was them knowing her feelings of love for him, even when she fought to admit them herself. However, it was obvious that she and Blake had come here, but had they truly wed? She was beginning to doubt her sanity.

"You were saying?" Pastor Bligh prodded, his gaze searching.

Jessica wasn't sure where to begin, or how to relieve the questions that seemed to cross the pastor's features.

She dried off her arms and face before settling the towel

with the quilt in her lap. "I've come because … well … I can't recall marrying Blake."

Husband and wife glanced at each other. Mrs. Bligh frowned and lowered to a chair next to her husband. "You don't remember?"

"I'm afraid not. I didn't learn of it until today."

"Today!" The pastor boomed. He stood quickly and took a turn around the small kitchen. "I don't understand. The ceremony was weeks ago."

"It seems I became ill with fever the night of our wedding, a septic infection from my hand injury. I was mostly unconscious for four days."

"Then once you became well?"

"He never said a word. Not until today, when I told him I planned to leave town."

"Oh, dear." Mrs. Bligh's widening gaze followed her pacing husband. "Samuel."

"I know, Beatrice. I know." Mr. Bligh reclaimed his chair. "Mrs. McKenny—"

"Jessica, please."

"Jessica. I want you to know that you are indeed married to Blake. Beatrice and I were with you both from the moment you walked in, to the moment you walked out. I performed the ceremony, and you both signed the marriage license."

"There was a marriage license?"

"Of course, dear. Have you not seen it?"

"No." She looked to her hands on the fabric. "He'd mentioned it, but I hadn't. All I remember was that I was ill with fever and Rosalind cared for me." *So did Blake,* her heart whispered. Jessica shuffled in her seat. A memory came to light. Could she tell them? Would they think poorly of her? "There was this one night though."

"Yes." Mrs. Bligh leaned in.

She swallowed and pressed on. "I awoke in the night to find Blake in a rocking chair in my room. He, um, kissed me, said a few things I can't remember, then left. The next morning, I told Rosalind what happened. She spoke to him about the incident."

"What did he say?"

"We never spoke. He left for Fort Worth."

"He was crushed," Mrs. Bligh whispered, but Jessica didn't miss it. The older woman looked to her husband. "What do we do now, Samuel?"

"The words they spoke, their vows to each other and before God … they're united in holy matrimony."

"But I never wanted to marry," Jessica said quickly.

Mr. Bligh looked to her, remorse in his eyes. "I'm sorry, Jessica, but you're married. To Blake. Even before you left, you said you were thankful to us for marrying you both."

"I can't remember," Jessica whispered, trying to understand, even more confused than before. Would she thank them for something she didn't want? "What about an annulment?"

The couple glanced at each other again. Worry knitted Mrs. Bligh's brows, but it was Mr. Bligh who answered first. "Have you spoken to Blake about this?"

"Well, no, but I'd like to know how I can get our marriage annulled."

"Annulment isn't something I'm familiar with, but might I suggest speaking with Blake? Perhaps you can talk things out, give each other a chance, and make this marriage work."

There were only two things that Jessica knew at this moment: Cliff was after her, and he would kill anyone who got in his way. Her stomach churned at the thought. No. No matter her feelings for Blake, he wouldn't die because of her.

Jessica slowly stood, handing the quilt and towel back to

Mrs. Bligh. "I should be going."

Mrs. Bligh followed on Jessica's heels to the door. "Please speak to Blake about your feelings. He's a good man. He'll listen. Trust him."

"Beatrice," Mr. Bligh said as they reached the door. "Give us a minute."

Mrs. Bligh nodded. "Bye, dear. Our home is always open. Don't be a stranger." She patted Jessica's hands and left them.

Mr. Bligh watched his wife leave, then turned to Jessica. "I know this is hard to hear, but Blake loves you. I've never seen him as happy as he was standing in my living room, holding your hands, and committing his life to you. And what I witnessed in you was much of the same. At that moment, you loved each other. Isn't that worth fighting for?"

She wanted to say yes, and almost opened her mouth to agree, but bit the inside of her cheek instead.

Mr. Bligh pulled the door open, and she noticed the rain had stopped.

"We'll be praying for you both, Jessica," he said.

"Thank you, Mr. Bligh." She nodded and headed toward her horse. She had one more stop to make, though darkness would soon be closing in. She had to see Doc Adams.

Small pings sounded from the barn roof, and dime-size hail flew inside, bringing Trent with it. "It's getting bad out there." He shook his head, shaking off pieces of ice.

"Yep," Blake said.

"What happened? You've been overly quiet."

Blake brushed Legend's side, inhaling a deep breath. "We saw Tom today. Jessica's horse will be here next week. I told Jessica we're married." It was all he could do to keep his tangled-up thoughts from lynching his heart.

Silence filled the barn. "I see. How did she take the news?"

"She was angry, hurt, and many other things."

"That explains why she avoided you at dinner and why she seemed riled up when I saw her running up the hill to tell Pete something."

Blake paused. His jaw clenched, and he swiped the bristles down the horse's legs, then dumped the brush in a bucket. "I told her I couldn't let her leave, especially with Cliff coming after her. I couldn't let her leave me."

"What are you going to do about Cliff's gang?"

Blake faced Trent. "I have no idea."

A crack of thunder ripped through the barn, and lightning lit the concern on Trent's face.

For the first time in his life, Blake had no plan to follow, and his life and marriage was an utter mess. Everything revolved around his wife. "I'll be going to town in the mornin'," he said. "Do you need anything?"

"Not from town. We'll be headed to Fort Worth in a couple of days to help the Hadleys with their move. While I'm there, I'll pick up a gift I bought for Rosalind. You'll be here for her birthday dinner next month, right? It's still a surprise, and she has no idea Oliver, Catherine, and Lilly will be there."

Lilly. How he missed Oliver's little girl, her love of horses and peppermint sticks. Their rides across the property and her many questions, all fueling his desire for family. One that he might never have.

He grabbed the bucket and hooked it to the peg. "I bet Lilly's grown a lot since we've seen her last. I wouldn't miss seeing them again."

"Good."

Blake leaned against the barn wall. "So how does it feel to

have baby number three … or maybe four on the way?"

Trent chuckled. "Excited. Nervous. But definitely excited. And congratulations on your marriage, now that it's out in the open. Don't lose hope, my friend. God has a way of working things out for the good of those who love him. Remember that."

Pete rushed into the barn. "Blake! I knew better with the sky being so dark, but … she was upset at you when she left."

Blake's pulse quickened as he straightened. "Where is she?"

"Jessica asked to borrow my horse … she's out there in this storm."

Blake grabbed his saddle, flung it onto his horse, and tightened the straps. "I can't believe you let her go—again—out in this weather."

"She looked like she'd been crying. She said she needed to go for a ride and would be back before dark. She's always kept her word."

Blake's hand stilled. Had he done this? Pushed her away so that she'd go out in a storm? He'd seen the anger and hurt in her eyes. It was him. Deep within his core, he knew, and now because of him, another woman could lose her life.

"I'm going with you." Trent saddled his horse.

Blake rode out before Trent and met raging winds head on. He bent his head and looked side to side. He could barely see the ground in front of his horse.

Lord, help me find her.

Jessica lifted her gaze to where the clouds met the land and wiped the rain from her face as she rode back to the ranch. The pastor wouldn't lie. Even his shocked expression answered lingering questions. And Doc Adams said the medicine he'd given her for her hand could cause her to not remember much afterward. He'd never mentioned that fact to Blake.

Blake hadn't known.

He was as innocent in all that had taken place as was she, but Blake had laid his heart on the line for her. She, on the other hand, hadn't known she was giving her heart away. Should she take Doc Adams's offer to help her with the annulment, since she hadn't been in her right mind when she'd married?

The pastor's words came back to her. *I know this is hard to hear, but Blake loves you. I've never seen him as happy as he was standing in my living room, holding your hand, and committing his life to you. And what I witnessed in you was much of the same. At that moment, you loved each other. Isn't that worth fighting for?*

Wasn't it?

Blake was a good man, a man she could trust, as others had mentioned. And he loved her.

What was she to do now? How would Blake feel knowing why she couldn't remember their wedding? Knowing that she'd never meant to say she loved him, needed him. Even if it would be a lie to deny it.

The wind whipped past her. The smell of dirt, hay, and rain mingled in the air, and she inhaled a deep breath. In the distance, clouds and darkness spread across the flat land. She was riding headlong into the storm. A gray sheet of rain nearly obscured the path ahead.

She pushed the horse harder as the rain drenched her in a matter of seconds. It was becoming increasingly dark with the sun now hidden by the storm, but she wouldn't break her promise to Pete. He had never betrayed her, nor lied to get his way, even when he'd asked her to marry. Neither had Blake, regardless of what she'd first thought.

A bolt of lightning sparked through the sky, revealing angry clouds. A reflection of how she'd felt going into town, but now, the fire in her belly had turned to sorrow. She couldn't love Blake, shouldn't, but still her heart leapt at the parson's repetition of her thanks for him marrying her and Blake. Suddenly, as if she were back at the parson's house, with Blake, her hand in his, thanking the Blighs. It was as if her soul and heart remembered and stirred the memory to her thoughts.

No. *She* remembered.

Another resounding clap shook her in the saddle. The storm quickly rolled on top of her. Lightning split the air before her, blackening a bush to her right. She began to slow their pace, but it was too late. A shot crackled through the air, and the horse reared. She tightened her grip on the wet reins, and pain seared her injured hand. Her fingers slipped.

"Trent, wait! Do you hear that?" Blake squinted against the rain as he scanned the trail ahead. Nothing was there but the pounding of the storm and ... He closed his eyes and listened. A horse neighed in the distance. "It sounds like—"

"That's Pete's horse!"

Blake's chest squeezed as he caught sight of the horse on the ground. There was no rider.

He and Trent raced to the horse, calling it by name. Blake flung a leg over the saddle and scanned the ground around it. Had Jessica been thrown and was lying unconscious somewhere?

Jess, where are you?

The rain slackened to a drizzle.

"I see her!" Trent called. "Fifty yards to your right."

Fear gnawed his insides as Blake ran to her crumpled form.

As he and Trent approached, Jessica shifted, her shoulders

rising as if she were trying to push herself up.

"Are you all right?" Trent called.

"I'm fine. Embarrassed."

"Good to hear. I'm going to check on Pete's horse."

Blake skidded to a halt beside her, relieved. "Are you hurt?" he asked, noting that her foot was twisted in an odd way. He knelt and reached toward it.

"Don't! Please." She held out her hand, as if to ward him off. Fear flashed in her eyes as she tried to scoot away.

He paused for a moment. "We're married. I will always take care of you."

"But I don't remember saying vows, pledging my love. What about after?" Her voice cracked, and she turned her head away. "You know."

He understood what she meant. He needed to ease her mind that there'd been no physical contact, except for him caring for her while she'd been deathly ill. "After we were married, you came down with fever, and … well … nothing happened. I assure you."

It was too dark for him to see her face or gauge her reaction, but when he lifted the hem of her dress above her ankle, she smacked his arm. Undeterred, he gently took off her boot.

"What are you doing?" she demanded. "I'm fine. Ouch!" "I'd never intentionally hurt you, but wounds have to be dealt with. I need to check to make sure nothing is broken." He took her slender ankle in both hands. "Does this hurt?" He probed and gently rotated her ankle.

She gave a sharp gasp.

He leaned back on his heels.

Jessica yanked at the hem of her dress and flicked it over her ankle. "Is it broken?"

"I believe you twisted your ankle. We need to get you to the house." He bent to lift her, but she pushed his shoulder away.

"I can get up on my own. I'm more than capable of taking care of myself." She managed to stand, and then limped off toward the house, which was still a hundred yards away.

"Why are you being so stubborn? Jessica, stop. Do you want to hurt your ankle worse?"

She continued for the house, and his blood boiled.

"You're the most cantankerous woman I've ever met." Blake caught up to her and scooped her up from behind. She gasped but flung her arm around his neck.

"Put me down. I can walk."

"I'm taking you to the house. You're wet through, and I will not allow you to catch another fever if I can stop it. You about sent me to an early grave last time you were ill, not responding to anything I did or said. All I could do was to hold you and pray."

All I could do was to hold you and pray.

Jessica replayed Blake's words as he walked past the barn, entered through the back door of the house, and carried her upstairs to her room.

He set her down on the edge of her bed, then went to her dresser and pulled out a few things, including the yellow cotton dress Rosalind had given her the day she went to the doctor. The way he confidently drew things out indicated he knew which drawers her things where in. Heat rose to the back of her neck.

Blake had been so attentive since he'd carried her from the sunflower patch. How close he stood to her in town today, the small touches to her back, the declaration of his love and his kiss under the tree.

She fought to breathe. "That's why you were in my room

the night I awoke from my fever. You were caring for me?" Which meant the dress he held was her wedding dress.

"Yes and yes." He set the folded clothes gingerly in her lap. "I have never seen a lovelier woman than you in this dress." He gave her a meaningful look and left the room.

Long after the door closed behind Blake, she sat there staring after him.

Finally rousing herself, she struggled to undress and then clothe herself without putting much pressure on her foot. A yellow ribbon draped across a flowered ceramic bowl on the vanity. She touched the thick thread and brought it to her nose. A hint of the outdoors lingered in it.

Jessica rearranged the ribbon on the vanity. She glanced at her hand, which was still bandaged, then flexed her fingers and palm, recalling the rope slicing through her skin and how Blake insisted on helping her. At first, she'd believed he cared out of responsibility, as she was his prisoner, and out of duty, since it was his horse that had caused the injury, but now … had he loved her then?

CHAPTER TWENTY-THREE

Rosalind frowned when Jessica entered the kitchen and hobbled to the table, where she sat feeding Steph. "Trent told me you rode off on Pete's horse in this storm. Are you all right?"

Jessica lowered herself into the chair. "Are we talking about my ankle or my heart?"

She shrugged. "Both."

"We're married."

"I was a bit surprised myself—not that you don't make a fine couple—but it came as a shock." She smiled.

"You knew?" Heat rose to Jessica's cheeks. "Am I the only one who didn't know we married?" Oh, and Pete? She pressed her hands to her face. She'd hurt her friend.

"Only Trent and I knew, but there was no point in talking to you about your marriage because your fever raged for days."

Was her fever so high nothing happened between them, as Blake had said?

As if reading her thoughts, Rosalind, her gaze understanding, said, "While you were ill, Blake and I took care of you, but there were times when he stepped out of the room. Although you were married, he felt he needed your permission to attend you in … certain circumstances. Nothing physical happened between you. Blake is as honest and trustworthy as men come." Rosalind leaned over and touched her hand. "He wouldn't have married you if he didn't love you."

"But I don't know him." Jessica looked to her folded hands in her lap. "I was only trying to travel across the country to find peace, freedom. Instead, I married a total stranger."

"Maybe God had other plans. A plan to give you a hope and a future. One that included a man who was devoted enough to stay by your side during sickness, and even after, when the nightmares took over."

Jessica hadn't had nightmares since her father first died, since … Could Cliff having found her be the cause of them? She leaned forward and whispered, "Nightmares?"

"Yes, you should have seen him. Each time you called out to him to help you—"

"I called out for him?"

"I tried to comfort you, but it seemed Blake was the only one who could. He devoted himself to you, loving you, praying for you, and holding you close when you wouldn't awake from your dreams. But now you're better, and your nightmares have stopped." She broke another piece of biscuit for Steph. "I know this is hard to take in. Talk to Blake. Work this out."

"I've heard that a lot lately, but I don't know if I can. Blake and I, I can't explain it." How could she explain it when she didn't know how to talk to Blake about anything? When she tried, the tension between them drove them apart.

"You can count on him, Jessica. You know, he's a lot like Trent. Maybe that's why I hit it off so well with Blake when I first arrived on the ranch."

"Blue eyes you can get lost in?"

"That too." Rosalind chuckled. "Yes, they're both cowboys—tough, willing to live on the edge for their life and land. But within, they're kind and gentle. They're passionate for their women, and God is their driving force. You surprised him, Jessica. You stole Blake's heart, and he wasn't willing to let you go."

Steph threw pieces of her biscuit to the floor, and Jessica collected them and took them to the trash, then returned to the table. "I'm sure you can understand I'm a bit overwhelmed by all this. I never planned to marry, and this is hard for me to accept. Blake isn't the type of man I'd ever marry." She fingered Steph's small curls, and the sweet child rewarded her with a smile.

"And what type of man is that? One who loves you and is willing to do whatever it takes to protect you? Because you need to know, Blake is that man."

She knew that type. "A lawman like my father. He died because of me. Protecting me. I can't let that happen again."

Rosalind just stared at her, and if her wide eyes were any indication, Jessica understood the shock. Her heart still hadn't recovered.

"I'm sorry," she murmured. "I didn't know. Was he protecting you from Cliff?"

Jessica chewed on her lip. She'd said too much, but maybe it was time she confided in people who cared about her and whom she cared about in return. She lowered to a chair. "Yes. Cliff tried to kidnap me, but my father stopped him by giving up his life. And now Cliff is after me once again."

Rosalind nodded as if she understood. "God used Trent and his family to rescue me from an abusive man. He brought them into my life just when I needed them. I can't help feeling that

God brought you here for a reason. Maybe to give you the life He's had prepared for you all along. Maybe Graham is the place for you to find that peace and freedom you were looking for."

God's plan. The thought reminded her of how much she missed her father. Their nightly chats on the porch, where God felt so real it seemed as though He sat with them in the moonlight. Wetness filled her eyes, and she stood. "I think I'll get some ice for my ankle."

"All right. I can take a hint. But know I'm praying for you and for Blake."

Maneuvering to the ice box, Jessica was near the back door when it swung open, startling her into losing her balance. A strong arm caught her, steading her. The scent of horse, wind, and rain invaded her senses.

She didn't need to look to know who it was who held her, yet she gazed up into Blake's deep blue eyes anyway. His brown hair had turned a bit darker from the rain, and it clung to his forehead. He held her there for a moment longer, and Rosalind's words came to mind. *You can count on him. ... The way he feels about you is obvious to those who know him. He loves you, Jessica.*

A chair scraped the floor, and she pulled away, but Blake didn't let go. Rosalind ambled out of the kitchen with Steph on her hip.

"Jess," her name came out as a whisper, and her heart quickened. His hands ran down her arms. She told herself to move, but the lovely feel of his touch locked her in place.

She licked her dry lips and watched as his gaze fell to her mouth and lingered. "Thank you for looking for me. I—"

The back door to the kitchen opened and almost hit them when Pete entered with two other cowboys. Pete eyed them for a moment, and his jaw tightened. She took a step toward the icebox, biting her lip to hide the throbbing pain in her ankle and the physical desire to be near the man she'd obviously married.

The other cowboys headed into the living room, but Pete, he came to stand by her and Blake. "You shouldn't be walking on that foot." Pete held out his arm for her to use as a crutch. "Let me walk you to the couch while Blake chips you some ice to put on your ankle."

Blake groaned, but he started for the icebox.

She hesitated. Should she accept Pete's offered hand now that she was married to Blake?

"I can carry you if you'd like?"

No, she wouldn't allow Pete to carry her, but she wasn't sure what to say, let alone how to act. He was her friend, always had been, so why did she suddenly feel like she was betraying Blake?

"I can walk," she finally replied as she took a step toward the couch, but Pete held her elbow and assisted her the rest of the way. She lowered to the cushions.

Pete yanked off his Stetson and hung it by the front door. His gaze turned toward the kitchen, then to her. "I wanted to talk to you, Jessica." He sat beside her and took her hand within his.

She pulled away. A flashback sprung to her mind: hands capturing hers, Pete's voice. But his words had eluded her. "Did you visit me while I was ill?" she asked.

A wide smile lifted his lips. "You remember. Yes, I came to see you."

"Actually, there isn't much I can recall from when I was feverish."

"But you remembered me." He reached over and squeezed her hand. "I think that's a wonderful sign."

Blake strolled into the living room with a cloth and a bowl of ice and stopped in front of them. She pulled her hand from Pete's, but Blake's expression turned cold, like the ice he carried.

"Here." He jammed the bowl into Pete's hands. "I'm needed in the barn. I'll be back in a minute." Blake walked out of the house, letting the door slam behind him.

Pete scooped ice from the bowl with his hand and set the ice in the center of the cloth. "This should help. Lift your leg onto the couch."

Jessica did as Pete asked, but when he lifted the hem of her dress and placed the ice on her swollen ankle, she blushed. "Pete, this isn't proper." She recovered her ankle and ice.

"If we were courting, it would be."

"But we're not. We're friends."

He gazed into her eyes. His Adam's apple bobbled when he swallowed. "I want to change that. I want to marry you, Jessica. I know I wasn't in love with you when we first met—I only wanted a wife—but when you made the treats for Tom's boys and you spoke of our Lord, I knew right then and there I loved you."

Jessica shook her head. This couldn't be happening. Pete was asking her to marry him when she'd only just found out a short time ago she was already married? *No, this definitely isn't happening.* "Pete, there's something I need to—"

"I don't have much to offer you now, but I can purchase some land outside of town, where we can build a home and raise a family."

"Pete, please, listen to me."

He collected her hand once again, but this time she stood. The cloth fell to the wood, scattering ice across the floor.

"I have to tell you something, and you have to listen."

Pete rose and moved a strand of hair from her face, tucking it behind her ear. He cupped her cheek. "As long as it's yes."

"I suggest you unhand my wife," Blake boomed.

Jessica jumped and felt as if her heart flew right out of her chest. She hadn't heard anyone enter the house.

Shock marred Pete's features, and his hand fell. "You married Blake?" He took a step back, pain filling his piercing gaze. "When were you planning to tell me?"

"I was trying to tell you, but you wouldn't let me."

"And you waited until now? After I proposed?"

The accusation, the betrayal in his tone, broke Jessica's heart. How would he ever trust her again? She cherished Pete's friendship, but now what would become of it? She turned to look at Blake for help. He ran his fingers through his hair but said nothing to defend her when clearly she'd been clueless about their marriage as well. She stepped toward Pete, swallowing the throbbing jolts shooting up her ankle. "I'm sorry, Pete. Truly I am."

"Sorry isn't good enough." Pete stormed out of the house through the kitchen, leaving his Stetson on the hook.

Jessica looked to the ice by her feet. "I hurt him."

"Do you love him?"

She glanced up at Blake. An emotion she couldn't name crossed his features. "No. I've made it clear from the start I wouldn't marry him, but I also made it clear I wasn't marrying anyone. And now you say we're married … that you love me, but Pete has always been there for me. He was my only friend when I came to town. He thinks I lied to him, and I can see why he's hurt."

"I'll talk to him, Jess. I'll explain."

She nodded. "Thank you. I'm still trying to wrap my mind around it myself."

Blake knelt, picked up the ice, and rewrapped it in the cloth. "You should stay off your ankle for at least tonight."

He held out the cloth, but she ignored it and sat, propping her foot up on the couch. Blake slid the ice onto the swollen area and pulled the hem of her dress over it, but in the process, the pad of his thumb traced her skin. Tingles raced up her leg. Her breath caught, and she marveled at how fast her pulse quickened.

Blake rose and turned to leave.

She felt odd, lightheaded somehow, and she didn't want him to go. "Will you talk with him now?" she blurted as he reached the door.

He stilled, his back toward her.

Jessica studied him from across the room. Without his Stetson, his hair was a mess, tousled every which way, and the muscles of his arms and shoulders were evident under his damp shirt. She breathed in, filling her lungs to suppress wayward thoughts of those arms holding her throughout the night.

"I'll talk to Pete." He turned to her. "But for the record, I wouldn't change how we were married. For the first time since we'd met, you trusted me, and down deep, so help me, I believe you love me." The door closed gently behind him.

From the couch, Jessica pulled the curtains back and watched as Blake strolled out into the rain. She trusted him all right—to leave her in this godforsaken world alone, loving him for the rest of her life.

Rain continued to fall as Blake walked into the barn and removed his slicker. He wiped his face with his hand as one of the stalls opened and Pete walked out. "Pete, I think we need to talk."

Pete ignored him and continued through the barn.

Blake ground his teeth and forced himself to take a calming breath and follow him to the hay bales. "I promised Jessica we'd talk, so I'm here to talk."

Pete spun around, his expression angry and hurt. "How could you marry her? You knew how I felt. And she told me she didn't want to marry anyone. She lied to me and married you. I thought she and I were friends. I thought *you* and I were friends. I'm a fool."

Blake ran his fingers through his wet hair. "No, Pete. She didn't lie or deceive you. She only just found out we were married. We married on the day I took her to see Doc."

Pete took a step toward him. "Wait, you're telling me she doesn't remember marrying you?"

Blake inhaled a deep breath, then exhaled. "She doesn't remember anything. I think it might have been the fever that caused her to forget."

Pete burned him with a look. "Did she even say yes?"

When Blake didn't answer quick enough, Pete hauled back and threw a punch to his face, causing him to stumble a few steps.

Blake palmed his cheek and worked his jaw, meeting Pete's angry glare. "Fine. I deserved that, but Jessica did say yes—and a few other things besides—and her signature is on our marriage license."

Pete's hands balled into fists. "So help me, if you've hurt her. If you're lying …"

The open threat didn't bother Blake; it reassured him Pete was the one man who would protect his wife if he wasn't around. "I would never hurt her, but there are men who will try. I need your help to protect Jessica."

"She might not be my wife, but I love her. I'd do anything for her."

Blake nodded. "I know."

CHAPTER TWENTY-FOUR

Jessica caught a glimpse of Blake by the barn as she waved her goodbyes to Trent, Rosalind, and the children from the porch. Blake had tried to persuade them to wait until the Cliff Gang was captured, but Trent had said God was their protector. Nevertheless, Matthew insisted on going, saying something about family living in Fort Worth, so Trent agreed. Jessica was still concerned, knowing what Cliff was capable of, but Rosalind assured her that with Trent and Matthew along, they'd be safe.

Finishing a prayer for her friend and for safety for the family as they met the Hadleys' train and assisted them in their move to Fort Worth, Jessica hollered to Blake, "What time would you like me to prepare dinner?"

"There's no need. The new cook Trent hired will cook for the men. I'll be eating at the bunkhouse."

She bobbed her head and holler back, "All right." She turned, disappointment filling her as she climbed the stairs to the empty house. The screen door banged against the wood. She stood restless in the middle of the living room when an idea came to mind. Blake said there was a marriage license.

She took to the stairs and entered Blake's room. The furnishings were sparse, as in her room, but she could see herself here with him, which would be a terrible mistake since she was still considering an annulment.

She went to his dresser and scanned each drawer's contents until she reached the bottom one. There, in an otherwise empty drawer, was a document. She withdrew the slip of paper, her mind racing at the implications. She flipped it over, and it was indeed their marriage license. An overwhelming sense of fear and joy mingled within her heart at the sight of her signature neatly written next to Blake's manly script.

What was she to do now? This was the final proof she'd needed. They were married to each other.

She'd never expected to be married, but here she was, and loneliness settled somewhere in her chest. If she were honest with herself, she didn't want an annulment. She wanted to take Mr. and Mrs. Bligh's advice and talk with Blake, but he had barely spoken to her at all since Pete gave him a busted lip. Why had Blake married her if he didn't want her?

Thoughts of her father pressed on her mind, and she wished to hold him again, to draw from his strength. She missed the quiet nights when they'd sat on the porch and prayed, prayed for the townspeople and the orphans. She needed his prayers now.

What would her father say about her being married? No matter how much she wanted to leave town and never turn back, she and Blake were bound together, in sickness and in health. Her father once said marriage was sacred, but he never mentioned anything about being lonely. He never mentioned husband and wife living separately, but maybe it was best she left. They could still be married, but Blake would be safe. She could return after Cliff was captured.

Her stomach growled. There was no point in cooking when

she was the only one eating. Jessica smiled, thinking of Mrs. Briggen. She could go to town and see Mrs. Briggen and help her with supper. How she'd missed her.

She entered her room, then readied herself for the two-mile-long trek. She packed extra clothes in case she needed to ride through tonight's storm. She hated riding through the rain, especially after the other night, but it was the only way, since Cliff was afraid of storms.

With purposeful steps, Jessica hurried to the barn and entered Legend's stall. Blake had insisted she ride him if she planned to go anywhere. Too bad she hadn't the night of the storm. If she had, she was sure she wouldn't have fallen off and sprained her ankle. Thankfully, it had almost healed.

After saddling Legend, Jessica climbed up and headed out to tell Blake where she was going, but after a full quarter-hour searching, neither Blake nor Pete could be found. Should she ride out to the bunkhouse to tell them? She patted her gun hidden at her side and turned Legend toward town instead.

She caught sight of a figure riding toward her from the bunkhouse. Her pulse rose at the thought of Blake. A moment ticked by before she realized her error. It was Johnny, a cowhand she'd seen with Pete a time or two. "Hi." She waved, grabbing his attention. "Have you seen Blake or Pete?"

"Blake is riding the land. Pete is in town. Is there something I can do?"

Should she ask? She'd be back before anyone would notice she was gone. Besides, dark clouds were already forming. Cliff wouldn't be out in this storm. Yet. "Do you mind riding to town with me, then finding Pete to give him a message?"

He looked to the sky. "What's the message?"

"That I'll be visiting with Mrs. Briggen. If he could come by after he's finished with his duties in town, I'll need an escort back to the ranch." Plus, it would give them time to talk. Even though Blake said he'd spoken to him, Pete had been avoiding her.

He nodded.

"Then let us be on our way before this storm hits."

Jessica tied Legend to the post in front of the boardinghouse and watched as Johnny continued to the sheriff's office. "Thank you, Lord," she whispered.

She hadn't realized how nervous she'd become when the storm hadn't hit as she'd expected. Leaving the ranch and Blake's protection might have been a mistake, but she'd continued to ride, grateful for Johnny's presence.

Adrenaline raced her heart as she finally stepped through the doorway of the boardinghouse. The aroma of roast wavered in the air. "Mrs. Briggen?" Jessica moved into the kitchen.

"Jessica, dear." Mrs. Briggen turned to her with wide eyes. "I didn't know you were coming! Good to see you! Now grab your apron and come stir." She nodded toward the waiting pots on the stove.

Chuckling, Jessica shook her head and snatched the work apron from the hook by the door. She slid it over her head and joined Mrs. Briggen. "I hope this means I can still keep the leftover dough for my little breads?" She smiled.

"Anything. You know Mr. Briggen won't be down for some time." Mrs. Briggen threw an arm around Jessica's shoulders. "Have you decided to come back to stay? I've missed you around here. Wasn't the same once you left."

"I'm still staying at the Easton ranch, but I thought I'd come for a visit. I've missed you, and I know how busy you are at certain times of the day."

"I'm glad you're here." Mrs. Briggen went to the oven and slid out a roast and began cutting thin slices. "How's your hand? Better I take it?"

"It is." Jessica stared down for the first time at the mush she moved around the pot. Did Mrs. Briggen know about her marriage to Blake? "How did you know about my hand?"

"Blake brought you here after the doctor tended to you. Don't you remember? I brought a blanket out to you and told you to come back and visit, and you said you would."

She did recall something about a blanket. Blake's handsome face came to mind. He was helping her onto the blanket … in the wagon.

"You're staying, aren't you? For dinner, at least?"

"I thought you'd never ask." She gave the spoon to Mrs. Briggen, then went to the cabinets and collected the ingredients for her little breads and began mixing the dough. When the dough was ready, she grabbed a knife and rounded the edges to make shapes.

After placing the last tray into the oven, Jessica rested her hip against the counter, wiping her hands on the apron. "Anything else I can do?"

"Say you'll come back tomorrow. Better yet, stay the night. It will be much too late for you to ride back to the Eastons'."

"I hope not. I sent word to Pete that I was here and asked if he'd ride back to the ranch with me."

"Is Blake still keeping you as his prisoner?"

For life. "I didn't know you knew."

"Oh, he came by here and told me what happened. I said he was crazy to think you'd steal anything and insisted he release you. But when he told me Pete was there, watching over you, I let it go. Until now. Any hope of you and my nephew getting married?"

Jessica took a breath, wondering how much she should say, if she should say anything at all.

Mrs. Briggen frowned. "I take that as a no."

"Sorry, Mrs. Briggen." Jessica pushed off the counter. Maybe now the wedding bells the older woman heard would finally still. Although they did ring, just not to the man Mrs. Briggen wanted.

Jessica took one of the trays of little breads and piled the others on it, but set eight to the side on a plate. "When I come back tomorrow, I'll take these to the livery for Tom's boys."

"Fine. Now you sit and eat." With the wooden spoon in her hand, she pointed to the table. "You're nothing but skin and bones. Don't they feed you at the ranch?"

"Not as good as you." Jessica smiled.

"Just what I like to hear."

Mr. Briggen hurried through the kitchen door and collected a tray and began plopping food on the plates his wife spread out on the counter. Like clockwork, Mrs. Briggen cooked and dished out the food while her husband waited to the last minute to serve.

Jessica missed them and the boardinghouse. The constant busyness and the feeling she were needed, that she belonged. At the ranch, Rosalind said she could help cook or help with other things around the house, then rarely allowed her to lift a finger. Jessica felt out of place, but at the boardinghouse, she just pitched in and helped. In a way, when she was here, she felt like she was back at the orphanage, where people came together to care for one another, giving them a home for as long as they needed it.

She wanted that, a place to call her own, where people came together and shared their lives day in and day out. If she were honest with herself, she wanted this type of life with Blake.

No, an annulment wasn't what she wanted.

A plan began to form. Maybe while Rosalind and Trent were away, and if Blake agreed, she could stay at the boardinghouse, he at the ranch.

She envisioned Blake's handsome face crumpling at the idea. She'd hurt him. Though they weren't husband and wife in the normal sense of the word, and probably never would be—

She closed her eyes against the hurt, when a memory of her husband's arms around her took hold. The feeling had been foreign at first, and she'd shook with fever. Soft words of love were being whispered close to her ear. It was Blake's arms, his words, and they almost felt tangible now. Within the middle of her chest, her heart tore.

"Jessica?" Mrs. Briggen stroked her hair.

She swallowed hard and looked away.

The kitchen door swung open and banged against the wall. Mrs. Briggen jumped.

"I just heard. Where's—" Pete stopped midstep, meeting Jessica's gaze. "What are you doing here? You should be at the ranch."

His voice came out harsh. Maybe it was the fact she'd wounded him, but she flinched at his words.

Mrs. Briggen shook her stubby finger at his chest. "Don't you come in here talking to a woman with that tone, do you hear me?"

"I deserve it, Mrs. Briggen," Jessica said. "I slighted him."

Mrs. Briggen frowned, turning to her. "How, dear?"

"I ... I married Blake." The more she admitted the truth, the more real it seemed.

Mrs. Briggen gasped. "The sheriff? You married the sheriff? When? And I wasn't invited to the wedding?" Hurt flashed in her eyes.

"It was the day he collected my things, the day you gave him your blanket. I barely remember anything after the doctor tended to my hand." She looked up at them both and prayed they'd understand. "I was hurt and angry at Blake when I found out, so I spoke with Mr. and Mrs. Bligh, then went to visit Doc Adams. No one realized the doctor had given me medication for pain that could cause me to forget. He never mentioned this to Blake when he picked me up. Blake didn't know, and Mr. and Mrs. Bligh said we both seemed so happy." She looked to her hands. "I could have the marriage annulled, but after knowing the truth, I can't. I'm sorry, Pete. Mrs. Briggen."

A nerve pulsed in Pete's jaw, and she counted out the seconds before his body visibly relaxed and he finally spoke. "I'm sorry too, Jessica. I wish things would have been different."

"Me too, dear." Mrs. Briggen wiped her eyes. "You know how much I love you like my own." She strolled back to the stove.

Jessica looked down at her plate, then back at Pete. "Will you have supper with me?"

Pete swiped his hat from his head and ran his finger along the brim. "I'm not sure it's a good idea. We need to get you back to the ranch. Besides, Nick's with me. We've picked up a few more supplies for the shootin' contest."

"Sit." Mrs. Briggen pushed her nephew to the table and placed a plate down with a thud. "You're friends. Talk. Eat. When Nick comes in, I'll fix him a plate. Now sit." She pointed, and her fierce look sent Pete dropping into a chair.

Jessica almost giggled, seeing what Pete might have been like as a young boy caught in mischief. He faced her now, and she tried to hide her smile.

Instead of showing anger or disappointment, Pete smiled back. "I learned a long time ago it's not worth resisting." He set his hat on the table and lifted his fork. "We better say grace. I'm starved."

As he finished the prayer, Nick walked into the kitchen. "Perfect timing." He pulled out a chair between them and sat.

Pete smiled at her and stabbed the chunk of roast on his plate. "Eat up."

Thankful for their friendship and answered prayers, she stabbed her own meat.

Blake ran from the house back to the barn, grinding his teeth. Where was Jessica? He shouldn't have told Pete to head into town to buy supplies for the Women's Day of Shooting. He hadn't meant to be so long riding the fences, but he'd seen one section of the fence down, and as he'd investigated, he'd discovered it had been cut. When he yanked open Legend's stall, Blake's eyes widened. His horse was gone.

He saddled Bucky and walked him out of the barn, then lifted his Stetson above his brow, wiping his forehead with his sleeve.

"Everything all right, Sheriff? You seemed a bit panicked a moment ago," one of the cowhands said, leaning over the horn of his saddle, brows dipped slightly in the center of his forehead.

"I need you to stay at the house." Blake swung a leg over his saddle and took up the reins. "You remember the woman staying here with the Eastons, Jessica? If she rides up, keep her here until I return."

"And how do I keep a woman from leavin' if she don't wanna stay?"

Blake wished he knew. "Hog tie her if you have to."

The cowhand's eyes crinkled at the corners, and any other time Blake would have laughed. Not today.

Blake rode out behind the house, where Trent had planted a

sunflower patch for Rosalind, hoping Jessica was there. He thought about the last time he was here with her, she'd seemed so weak and much too pale. He'd let pride stand in the way of helping the woman he loved, and allowed what he'd learned in Fort Worth to cloud his judgment. Now he'd been hurt to think she didn't want him or their marriage, and because of his pride, he'd avoided her, even though he ached to hold her, to love her the way a man loved his wife.

She'd rejected him twice, once after he kissed her, then the day she found out they were husband and wife. No longer would he let his pride stop him from loving her, even if she didn't love him in return. Even if she walked out of his life and never looked back, he'd love her regardless.

Blake glanced around, seeing no one. "Jessica!" he shouted. When no answer came, the sour taste in Blake's mouth grew. An unexplained fear drove him to pray. "Lord, your word says you are our shield. Protect my wife … and my life."

CHAPTER TWENTY-FIVE

Cliff entered the Easton ranch through the fence they'd cut yesterday. He waved his brother over and pointed to the longhorns in the distance. "What do you think? Run 'em off or just shoot 'em?"

"We can use 'em as target practice. Get ready for that women's shootin' day everyone's talkin' about. If your plan works, we won't even need to fire our guns."

"Don't fool yourself. Guy's in jail, and the sheriff knows we want Jessica. You keep that Colt by your side at all times." Cliff eyed his surroundings. "Let's get the layout of the land first. We need to be prepared for next week."

Bryan nodded and pulled his hat over his eyes. "You first."

Cliff rode through the longhorns, careful not to cause a stampede. He wanted to live long and die in the arms of his woman, not have a painful death at the mercy of some bulls. He'd been thinkin' some about death. Not that he'd tell his brother, but it was a naggin' thought that wouldn't leave him. He'd thought his life would have been different. He was a wealthy man now, but regret seemed to hit him hard at times, the times he seemed to need Jessica more. She was special, and soon he'd have her. She'd make him a better man.

How far they rode Cliff wasn't sure, but they came across several large shooting targets. Bryan took out his gun and aimed.

"Put it away," Cliff said. "If we shoot these targets, they'll know we were here, deep into their property. I've heard they have some of the best gunslingers as cowhands, and I don't feel like a shootout tonight. Besides, now we know where they've planned the competition. Everything is coming together."

"Yep. I'll get one good look at Jessica when she goes to the general store with her breads, then it won't be long before we take her."

"I know you're tired of waiting, but the men need a few more days to get ready. This Women's Day of Shootin' plan is genius."

Cliff drew in a long breath as pride filled his chest. Yes, he was tired of waiting for Jessica, but he had no choice. Why the sheriff had to get in the way he didn't know, but Cliff would make him pay like Jessica's father had ... with his life.

"Come on." Cliff steered his horse back the way they'd come. "Let's kill us some horns at a safe distance, then be on our way."

Gunfire sounded in the distance.

Blake quickened his pace across the property toward the shots. As he neared the section of land where the fence had been cut, the sound of steers bellowing and the thundering of hooves closed in on him. His eyes widened.

Stampede.

He was in front of hundreds of steers. There was no time to move alongside. He grabbed his gun and shot into the air to redirect them, but it was too late. He swung his horse around.

The steers barreled at him, and there was no escaping.

His life was in God's hands.

Shots echoed in the darkening sky.

Jessica's heart jolted and looked toward the ranch, although she, Nick, and Pete were still too far off for it to be seen.

"Jessica!" Pete pulled the reins, slowing the wagon to a stop. She followed quickly. "Trade with Nick. Hurry."

She did what she was told and slid next to Pete.

Pete grabbed her hand and squeezed. "Hold on." He whipped the reins. "Yah!"

Nick pointed to something on Jessica's right side. She couldn't see much from where she sat on the bench of the wagon, wishing she was back on Legend for more height. Pete took the reins with his left hand and grabbed his Colt with his right.

A cold shiver crawled up Jessica's spine, a physical sense of … *him*.

Cliff.

Her breath caught. She slid her hand into her pocket and wrapped her fingers around the butt of her pistol. Two men appeared through the darkening haze and rode toward them. "They're coming."

Nick rode Legend to her side, she supposed as a barrier of protection, blocking her view. Within moments, they'd be face-to-face.

The tree from the Easton property rose within the darkness like a grim shadow of death.

Pete slowed the horses to an abrupt stop, hoisted his gun, and aimed.

"Nick! Pete!" a voice called.

Pete's arm fell to his lap, and he hung his head and let out an exasperated breath. Nick slid the shotgun back into the saddle holster, but Jessica wasn't so inclined to release her grip on her gun.

They slowed. Whoever these men were, it was obvious Pete knew them, but the hairs on her arms rose. She still couldn't see anything where she sat.

"Nick, I want back on Legend." Her brisk tone left little room for discussion, especially since she'd already clambered down from the wagon.

Now in Legend's saddle, she glanced around while the men said something about Blake. "What happened?" she asked.

"There's been an accident. Blake's horse went down."

"Yah!" She pushed Legend into a run toward the ranch. "God, please take care of Blake."

She turned cold as she topped the hill. Someone was watching her, she was sure. She glanced over her shoulder from where she'd come. Two riders sat off toward the east.

She looked back at the ranch, where Blake stood motionless near the barn. *He's alive.* A lantern revealed that his clothes were stuck to his chest, and as Jessica neared, it looked like blood doing the sticking. She reached him and dismounted. Emotions she couldn't control assaulted her as she cupped Blake's cheek. His eyes closed.

"You're covered in blood. Are you hurt?" She cradled his face with both hands, looking him over. "Blake, please say something. Are you hurt?"

"The blood isn't mine. Someone cut through the fence and shot the longhorns. Killed six, but after the stampede, several others didn't fare much better."

"Stampede?" Her hands fell. He could have been killed.

A shadow of sadness settled on his features. "I lost one of

my horses. The one you lassoed."

"Oh, Blake, I'm sorry. I know how much your horses mean to you."

"Not as much as you, Jess. Nothing means as much as you." He lifted his hand to her cheek and ran a finger along her jaw.

They stood there, silent, the unspoken words between them unbearable. She might have lost him today, and it scared her. She loved him. He needed to know.

Jessica opened her mouth, but the sound of the wagon pulling up the drive stopped her. Blake's fingers slid down her arm as Pete jumped from the bench and Nick followed close behind. His touch left.

"What happened?" Pete asked as Nick slowed his steps as he met them. "We heard the shots."

"I'm not sure," Blake said. "I was looking for Jessica in the sunflower patch when the shots went off. By the time I made it to that side of the pasture, the stampede had already started, and I got caught in the middle."

Jessica hurt for him and his loss. "I'm thankful you're all right."

Blake nodded and gave her a faint smile before looking to Nick. "I need you to head out to the bunkhouse and round up the men. We have a long night ahead of us." Then he turned to Pete. "I need you to stay with Jessica. Find Johnny. Nick will stay with you both after he gets the men. Stay in the house and lock the doors."

"Is there anything I can do?" Jessica asked.

"Stay put." He pressed a soft kiss to her forehead, then walked away, taking her heart with him.

The candle Jessica had lit in her room earlier in the evening had all but burned the last of the wax by the time Blake returned. She moved from the window and opened the hall door as male voices met her ears. Her heart pounded as she waited for Blake to appear. A creak startled her, and Blake stepped from the stairs, carrying his boots.

She straightened from the doorframe. "Hi." Her voice came out raspy to her own hearing.

"It's late. Could you not sleep?" He set his boots on the floorboards near her door. The smell of fresh soap fluttered in the air at his movements.

She shook her head and let out a sigh. There was much she wanted to say, but where did she begin?

He searched her eyes.

She hesitated. The need to apologize, to see him safely upstairs, had held her waiting for him all night. She wasn't used to opening her heart and leaving herself vulnerable to anyone, especially Blake. It gave her pause, but she had much on her mind. "I'm sorry for leaving today," she said, taking the first step, as hard as it was.

"I wouldn't have known if Johnny hadn't told me, but I'm thankful he accompanied you to Mrs. Briggen's."

"I should have waited until I found you, but I didn't think it mattered."

"Everything about you matters to me."

"Sometimes it's hard to tell. You've barely spoken to me the last few days, unless I spoke to you first."

She was trying then, as she was now, to find her footing in this unexpected marriage. One she had planned to cast aside until she'd crested the hill and found Blake soaked in blood. Her heart had almost stopped, and at the memory, tears threated.

He took a step closer. "Jess." The pad of his thumb grazed the corner of her mouth as it trailed along her jaw, stilling the blood-soaked image of earlier. Now that same man stood before her alive, and well, and oh so close. "I've let my pride get in the way. Will you forgive me?"

"There's much to forgive," she whispered against his touch, knowing how she'd planned to leave. Her own pride, fear, and selfishness had almost driven her to make choices she'd never be able to take back. "I have to tell you something."

"I'm listening." Yet his caresses hadn't stopped.

"The night of the storm, when I hurt my ankle, I'd gone to see the Blighs. I needed to find out about our marriage. They assured me we were indeed married. I asked about getting our marriage annulled."

His hand stilled, then slid to his side. In the dim candlelight, she couldn't name the emotions that flicked across his handsome face. "What did they say?"

"I should speak with you and try to work things out, but as I left, I went to see Doc Adams. I'd been thinking about why I couldn't remember something so important as being married."

"He wouldn't know we married after we left."

"I realize, but I asked him about the medicine he gave me only hours before the ceremony. He explained that it could cause me to be a little loopy and then forget."

"Jess"—he shook his head, eyes imploring her to believe him—"I had no idea. None."

"I know. The doctor told me he never said a word to you."

"I thought you forgot because your fever raged for days on end." The bridge of his forehead creased, and he took a step back. "You were searching for a reason to annul our marriage? It seems you found one." He looked away. "Our marriage was a farce. The words you said to me in the wagon, your vows, it was the medicine talking. And here I was thinking that you truly loved me, even if you couldn't remember, that a part of you held on to us, no matter how small."

"Blake, please."

He lifted his boots from the floor and walked to his room but stopped in the doorway. "I'll give you time, but I won't fight you on this if you want our marriage annulled. I won't stand in your way."

Jessica stood cold, still, afraid to move. If she did, surely her heart would shatter.

Chapter Twenty-Six

After tending to the chores, instructing the men to finish making the targets, and speaking to the two cowhands who'd come from town, Blake watched the last two men he'd sent out to protect the perimeter of the house ride up. Nothing he did prevented his mind from swirling with emotions from yesterday. His horse was dead, along with fifteen longhorns. His marriage to Jessica would soon be over, and the pain, anger, and disappointment from her words cut deeper than the scar on his face had ever gone. The worst yet, Jessica's life was still in jeopardy. No matter what had happened last night, or how soon she planned to annul their marriage, he loved his wife and would do anything in his power to keep her safe.

He decided Jessica's idea of staying with Mrs. Briggen would be for the best. He'd have more control over the small area and be able to protect Jessica and his town at the same time. Blake was certain Cliff was hiding close by and would do anything to get to Jessica, but what Cliff didn't know was that he'd have to go through him first.

"Time to switch up?" one of the cowhands asked, coming

from the house.

Blake finished readying Legend for their trip to town. "Yep, and let that new cook fix you something good. Then rest up. Next week is the women's shootin' contest. You'll need your energy."

"Maybe I can find me a single gal," the youngest cowhand said, pumping his brows.

"Not if you act like that." Blake chuckled as the men mounted and peeled away toward the bunkhouse.

"Blake."

He turned to Pete and Nick as they came from the barn, horses trailing behind them.

"You ready?" he asked.

"An hour ago." Pete smiled, but it faded as he looked at something over Blake's shoulder. He dropped his gaze, and he yanked the tie down strap too hard while Nick slid his shotgun into the saddle.

Blake turned to see what had caught Pete's attention. Jessica stood on the porch. She'd bound her hair up in a bun at the back of her neck, leaving small ringlets hanging close to her face. Her dark eyes seemed to lighten in the sun.

He swallowed against the lump in his throat and the ache in his chest. She'd never worn her hair like a schoolmarm, but it suited her just fine.

Jessica descended the steps from the house and found him still gawking. "Can you take this for me?"

Blake hadn't noticed the carrying case she held. He nodded, took the brown bag, and tied it to the saddle, giving it a few shakes to test the hold. It was awkward but should make it in one piece.

"I have something for you." He strolled to the barn, where he'd hidden the atlatls, gathered them up, tucked them under his arm, and strolled to where Jessica now waited by Legend.

The smile she gave him turned his insides upside down. She held out her hand, and he placed one in her palm. She eyed it carefully, admiring his work while he admired her. He was lost to know what to do, but prayed for a miracle in their marriage. He wasn't willing to let her go no matter how defeated he'd been the night before.

"I can't believe you carved them," she said. "Tom's boys will love them as much as I do."

"Boss," Nick called. "We'll head out a ways and wait for you."

Blake nodded, watching Pete turn away. Saying a quick prayer for Pete and himself, he turned his attention back to Jessica. "I'm glad you like them."

"They're perfect." She handed it back, then reached out and touched his face, stilling him.

His eyes slid closed at her touch, and he palmed her hand against his face. "Jess."

"I don't want an annulment."

He gazed into her eyes, trying not to pull her closer. "But yesterday?"

"Well, at first I did, but then I realized I was indeed in love with you. It wasn't a farce. I guess the medicine gave me the freedom to take a leap when I never would have before."

"What are you saying?"

"I want this marriage. I want us."

He waited in anticipation for her kiss. What would it feel like? Soft like on their wedding day, hesitant like under the trees, or sweeter than he remembered? But when she made no move to kiss him, Blake stepped close and leaned down, nose to nose. "Are you going to kiss me, woman, before I die of starvation?"

She giggled and wrapped her arms around his neck, pulling his lips against hers. A mixture of soap and a light rose scent invaded his senses. He touched the wisps of her hair, capturing her face within his palm, and her lips parted in response. He deepened the kiss and felt alive in places he'd never known existed, and his heart pounded in response.

He moved back, searching her eyes. Fire raged inside her orbs, like the fire she lit within him. Her chest rose and fell, and he pressed his hand against her heart as she tried to catch her breath. She leaned in and caressed his lips so sweetly.

The softness of her mouth, the beating of her heart. This moment was forever etched in his mind.

Jessica and Blake rode their horses down Main Street, while Pete and Nick veered toward the general store. She rather liked having Blake by her side as they rode through town, pride once again filling her. He sent her one of his handsome smiles, reminding her of the kiss they'd shared. Heat rose to her cheeks. She felt it clear to her toes.

Jessica slowed her horse at the boardinghouse. "She must be cooking. I thought I could smell her pies as we came around the general store." She slid off Legend and tethered him to the post.

Blake had already dismounted. "I know what you mean. My mouth started watering. I might just have to sneak in the kitchen and grab me a piece."

"Wouldn't that be considered stealing?" She raised a brow, eyeing him. "Be kinda shameful to have the sheriff under arrest in his own town for stealing pies." Suppressing her laughter, she pushed through the boardinghouse door.

Blake smiled. "You think that's big news. Just you wait until everyone finds out we're married." Blake followed close behind, her bag clinched in his fist. "Did you tell Mrs. Briggen about our marriage?"

"I did. Yesterday."

"Then most people already know." Blake shoved the kitchen door open and held it for Jessica to pass.

Mrs. Briggen held a spoon in one hand and rested a large bowl against her chest with the other. She paused at seeing them. "I didn't think you were coming." She looked at Blake, not batting an eye.

Jessica felt sorry for him for a moment, unsure what Mrs. Briggen might say.

"You will take good care of my Jessica. Do you hear me, Blake?"

"Yes, ma'am. I wouldn't have it any other way." He turned his attention to her. "I'll go put our things in your room since the deputies are using my old room."

"I'll have no such thing!" Mrs. Briggen set her bowl down with a thump, then wiped her hands on her apron. "Come with me." She pushed through the kitchen door and climbed the stairs.

Jessica looked over her shoulder at him and shrugged. She didn't know where they were going, but Mrs. Briggen left little option but to obey. They followed her to the end of the hall, where she now stood at a corner room.

"Here we are. No need to thank me. Just help with dinner every night, and that's thanks enough." She patted Jessica's cheek as she turned and headed back the way they'd come.

Blake palmed the door and swung it open, and they stepped inside a space that was the size of three of her rooms put together. She never knew a room this lovely existed in the boardinghouse.

"It's beautiful," Jessica said, running a finger along a plush couch. Its floral pattern matched that of a corner armchair. "I can't believe it has a small sitting area." There wasn't much but the couch and a rocking chair, but it was cozy. Toward the back of the room sat the bed and two small dressers, which flanked the back walls, a window between them. "An actual window." With gauzy drapes blowing in the slight breeze. She exhaled, plunking down on the bed as her fingers felt their way along the fabric of the wedding ring quilt.

She stilled. *The bed. Their bed.* She stared at the quilt like she'd never seen one before. She couldn't help herself. It was what she wanted, to share Blake's bed—and he was her husband, after all—but still, the thought brought butterflies to her stomach.

Jessica quickly stood and walked to the window and ran a fingertip along the edge, staring out over the town, seeing nothing. Blake's legs brushed against the back of her brown skirt.

"It's beautiful, isn't it?" He stood so close his breath tickled her ear. Pride swelled in his voice, the same she'd heard many times in her father's.

"My father loved his town, and it showed in his voice. I hear it in your voice too. He said he couldn't imagine doing anything else. Will you always sheriff a town?"

"Does it worry you?"

Her eyes focused across the way on the sheriff's office. "I promised myself I'd never love another lawman. Then I promised myself I'd never marry. I think I've broken too many promises, don't you?"

"You're worried."

"I'm scared."

He kissed the back of her head. "Don't be. I'll protect you."

"You don't understand. I'm scared to give myself to you, to love you with all my heart, body, and soul. Then, if I were to lose you, I don't know how I'd handle it. When I saw you at the barn yesterday, all bloody …"

Blake's arms wrapped her waist, tucking her against his

chest. "Will you ride with me this afternoon? I'd like to show you something."

She turned her head up to him. "It might not be safe."

"No one will know we're gone."

"How's that?"

"I have my ways." He kissed the tip of her nose, sliding his arms from her. "There's a few things I need to tend to before we leave. I'll be back to get you." He turned and left without a backward glance.

She looked out the window, then when he appeared, followed his steps to the sheriff's office. He turned in the doorway, meeting her gaze straight on, tipped his hat, and disappeared into the office.

Shaking her head, she grinned. She loved him and he knew it, but as she looked at the bed once again, was she ready? No matter how much she wanted to be Blake's wife in every sense of the word, her heart screamed in protest at the thought of giving it all, then losing it, losing him.

Jessica slid her hand into her pocket, her fingers wrapping around the butt of her Colt.

I'll protect you. Blake's words.

She laid the gun on the bed and wished she'd had a gun when Cliff came after her, after her father. Now he was coming after her and Blake. She was tired of hiding, and she could no longer run. She had responsibilities to another now, and she'd never walk away from him.

Jessica could still hear Matthew's hearty chuckle the day Blake drove her to town to see Doc about her hand. *One thing you need to know is the Eastons' are a God-fearing family. I'm not sure how Blake feels about this, but I believe God brought us here.*

Was it God who brought her here? For the first time, she

was starting to believe it was true. Her father had said more times than she could remember that the Lord would direct her path. Did God lead her to Blake for him to be killed like her father, in front of her eyes? No, God wasn't an unjust God, no matter how terrible life seemed at times.

Jessica glanced around the room, fingering the metal of her gun. She lifted the weapon and checked the bullets. Half loaded. She rarely loaded a bullet in each chamber.

Matthew also said the men who came to the Easton ranch were handy with a gun. Maybe God would use her since she had an uncanny way with a weapon. She wasn't a man, but she could shoot like one. Her lips rose into a grin. *Better than most.*

Blake stepped in the doorway of the sheriff's office and glanced back at their room. Jessica stared down, and his heart leapt. He tipped his hat toward her and strolled inside, closing the door behind him. "Jake, I need your horse for about an hour."

"Sure, but where are you going?"

"I want to take my wife to where I plan to build our home." He sat behind the desk and opened the top drawer, then pulled out the land deed he'd held on to for months. It was time.

"Do you think that's a good decision with those outlaws on the loose?"

Blake's gaze roamed his desk. "I'm sure about only two things—my heavenly Father's love and the love I have for my wife. And, well, I guess one more." He lifted a stack of files, then newspapers, to discover the tip of a pen poking out from under a napkin. He nabbed it, then set everything back down. He scribed his signature on the line of the deed. "I'm finally going to buy my land."

"It's about time."

He rose to his feet and stuffed the deed into his pocket. "We'll take your horse and exit like we did the night I took Jessica to the ranch as my prisoner."

Jake's wide smile showed straight white teeth. "And look how that turned out for ya. She was nothing like you expected."

"Nothing at all." Blake chuckled, but it faded too quickly. "There's a lot that's happened on the ranch. I'll fill you in when I get back. All I want to do is take my wife out of town for a bit and dream, just the two of us."

"I'll have the horse ready."

An hour later, Blake knocked on the closed door of his and Jessica's room. Jessica opened it and moved aside for him to enter.

Blake closed the door with the back of his boot and followed her into the room. "You have to find out who it is before you open the door."

"I knew it was you." She continued to walk away from him. When she rounded the bed, she stuffed something in her pocket.

Blake grabbed her hand. "Jessica."

She gave him a slight smile. His eyes bored into her for understanding as he pulled her close. "I watched you coming from the street. But I'll ask next time."

He was tempted to lean down and gently caress her soft lips with his own, but if they planned to go, they needed to leave now. "We better go, or we won't have enough time." He placed a hand on the small of her back and directed her to the sheriff's office.

She glanced up at him, and her mouth rose in a beautiful smile. "Where are you taking me, Sheriff?"

"To our future."

Chapter Twenty-Seven

Had she not known better, Jessica would have thought they were being chased, at least judging by how hard Blake pushed the horse. But soon enough, he slowed and lightened his hold around her waist. Not that she minded, of course, so long as he held her. He walked the horse across the open land.

She was accustomed to seeing flat country and sparse trees in Texas. This was no different, until he leaned close to her ear and pointed to a stand of trees she'd not noticed before. "See those maple trees?"

She nodded. He didn't say more but drew closer to her. The trees resembled a hedge, shielding the view from the other side. "Did you plant them, the trees I mean?" she asked.

"No, but someone did. It's the only place around with so many hardwoods. You should see them in the fall." Blake slowed to a stop, dismounted, then wrapped the reins around one of the smaller trees. Blake intertwined his fingers through hers once she slid from the saddle. "I want to show you something," he said, eyes twinkling.

After several yards, her anticipation rose, as did the ground.

The trickling sound of water reached her ears. "There's a creek?"

"Yes, and a watering hole within the property." He pointed ahead. "Do you see it?"

She shielded her eyes from the sun with her hand and scanned the area. The land wasn't as flat where they stood. Instead, it dipped and rose. In one of those dips stood a large barn. In another, a stream of water cut through the ground and traveled farther than she could see. She drew a deep breath. "Of all the places I've traveled, this one speaks to me. This is breathtaking."

A slight breeze lifted the ends of her hair, and Blake tucked a loose strand behind her ear. "I brought you here because earlier you asked me if I'd always sheriff a town. I believe that a husband and wife should make decisions together, so I guess it depends on what we agree on."

"We're going to decide together? About you being sheriff?"

"Not only that, but where we'll live." His focus returned to the tree line. "Abby and I had talked about buying land and building a home. After her death, I moved to Graham. I scouted out this land and started making small improvements. I promised myself I would buy it to keep my word to Abby, but things are different now." He faced her. "If I bought this land, it wouldn't be because of the past, but for us and our future. I want to build *our* home here and raise *our* children on this land. I want to give up being Graham's sheriff."

Hope stole her breath. "What else will you do?"

"Ranch. Raise horses. Breed the stock I have at Trent's."

"I love horses, you know."

"I do." He pulled her into his arms. "What do you say? Would you like to live here, raise horses, have a family, and teach our children about God, in a home we'll build together with love and passion?"

"Passion, huh?" She smiled, wrapping her arms around his neck.

"Yes, Mrs. McKenny … passion." His hand climbed to the back of her neck, and warmth seared her skin from his touch. His fingers wound into her hair, holding her possessively against his chest. She sighed when his lips found hers. A fierce yearning lit her belly as his kisses, full of promises of things yet to come, searched her mouth and face.

Her pulse raced, and she gasped for air.

He moaned, trailing kisses down her neck. "Yes, Mrs. McKenny." His breaths labored against her ear. "God … ordained … passion."

It took them several moments to compose themselves, knowing their time here was coming to an end. But before the intimate moment had passed, she kissed him soundly on the mouth, feeling his grin beneath her lips. She pulled back and returned the smile. "You're happy."

"I am. Everything is perfect." He returned her kiss before taking her hand and leading them back toward the horses. "I want to show you one more thing."

He walked her to the edge of the tree line and pointed to where a single hardwood stood before the open land begun. "See that tree there? The one all by its lonesome?"

She squinted, finding the tree. "Yes."

"A little over a month ago, I was resting at that very spot when your carriage barreled across the plains. And might I say, even despite the gun stuck in my back, I'm thankful to God you rode into my life." He pressed a kiss to her temple.

She was about to speak when hooves pounded in the distance. Blake turned and pushed her behind him. He reached for his gun as a rider galloped toward town. "We should head back."

He scanned the area. Once he deemed the rider alone, they headed back to Graham, his arm holding her firmly to his chest.

When they arrived at the sheriff's office, Blake opened the back door and ushered her in. A man a little taller than Blake stood in front of Jake, his back to them. His dark, wavy hair twisted at the corners of his white collar.

At seeing them, Jake stood from the desk. The stranger turned, and he, too, wore a star over his heart. His eyes narrowed. In the next moment, a smile lit his face. "Definitely like a storm, raging with questions too." The man strode to Blake, and they shook hands. "You planning to introduce me?"

Jessica had no idea what he was referring to, but in the same moment, Blake slipped an arm around her waist. "Mark, I'd like you to meet my wife, Mrs. Jessica McKenny. Jessica, this here is the Fort Worth sheriff, Mark Connors."

"Nice to meet you," she said.

Mark yanked his Stetson from his dark curls and bowed slightly. "Believe me, the pleasure is all mine." He looked her over from head to toe. "Beautiful for sure. Small, ain't she? No mistaking the eyes."

She glanced back at Blake for a little help. Was he just going to let this man ogle her and do nothing about it? She took a step back.

"Sorry, ma'am. No offense, but the last time Blake came to town, you were a topic of conversation."

"Really?"

Blake cleared his throat. "Yes, well. That's all settled."

"It seems so. When you mentioned her, a spark flared in your eyes. I knew you were hooked." He turned his attention back to her. "Mrs. McKenny, never has this man talked about women in all the years I've known him, so when I mentioned you might be caught up with Cliff, Blake here didn't say your name, but didn't forget to mention you're beautiful … Yep, a goner for sure." Mark glanced out the window. "Does he know she's here?"

Since the moment she'd walked into the sheriff's office, she'd been ogled, been the center of gossip, and now was spoken about as if she wasn't there. "Are you always this straightforward, Mr. Connors?"

The corner of his mouth lifted into a sly smile. "Yes, ma'am. No reason to beat around the bush."

Jake handed Blake a worn piece of paper. "I found this knifed to the door after walkin' the town. Pete and Nick were with me."

Blake released her and held the missive high and out of view. "Yes, Cliff knows she's here."

Jessica wanted to see the message and almost complained, until Jake returned from the desk with the Bowie knife that had once been held to her throat. As if the cut to her neck still bled, she pressed her hand against the area and shivered.

"Here's the knife." Jake handed it to Mark.

Mark ran a hand over his mustache. "The marshal should be in Fort Worth on Saturday. He was delayed because another one of the Cliff Gang members was captured. Three of my deputies will be traveling with the marshal as they carry the wanted men to Houston to stand trial for their crimes. They'll be comin' through Graham. I came to warn you to be on the lookout for the other members of the gang, but it seems they're already here. I can send two more deputies to leave in town for as long as they're needed."

Jessica spoke up. "Saturday? We're having the women's shooting contest on the Easton ranch. Everyone from town will be there."

Blake glanced at her from the corner of his eye, then folded the paper and stuffed it in his pocket. "Someone was on the Easton ranch two days ago. Cut through the fence and started a stampede. Killed over a dozen head, my horse, and almost buried me in the process."

"I'm certain I saw Cliff in the distance." She looked to the pocket he'd slid the note into and almost asked to read it, but her husband's astonished look was the first emotion he'd shown since Jake had handed him the letter, so she decided to wait until they were alone.

"When did you see him?" Blake's brows dipped even further. "Why didn't you tell me?"

"I was with Pete and Nick coming back from town. I had this fear something wasn't right. When we reached the top of the hill before the ranch, I looked over my shoulder and saw two riders in the east."

"But you aren't sure since you didn't see him clearly. Only the horses?" Mark asked.

"I've always had this reaction to Cliff. Every time he'd stare my way, my blood would run cold and the hair on my arms rise. It was the same when the stage was robbed, but I dismissed it because I was too distracted by Blake. I had the same reaction yesterday. The rider was Cliff."

"I'll send extra men with the marshal when they travel through town on Saturday. They'll stay a few days, then when you're tired of 'em, send 'em back."

Everyone skirted the truth as if it were a purple bull standing in the room ready to charge. Cliff and his brother were here, and the rest of the gang would be in Graham on Saturday while the entire town was attending the Women's Day of Shooting.

Cliff was coming for her.

After taking Jessica back to the boardinghouse to help Mrs. Briggen with dinner, Blake headed to the land office. This should have been one of the happiest moments of his life, but the note knifed to the door had sliced him with razor sharpness straight to his core. Anger toward Cliff and protectiveness over Jessica simmered as he approached the land office. Who cared that the note stabbed to the door was meant for him? He wasn't intimidated by threats toward him—those he could handle—but when they were directed at his town, that was another matter altogether. Cliff was coming for Jessica and would use any means possible to get to her, even killing innocent people in the process.

Blake strode into the land office, fighting to steel his emotions, as he was known to do, as he'd done in his office after Jake handed him the knifed message. But now that he was away from Jessica's and the others' stares, he wasn't sure he could manage.

Sam greeted him with a smile. "What can I do for you, Sheriff?"

He inhaled a forced breath and controlled the tenor of his voice. "I think it's time I claimed that parcel of land."

"Took you long enough." The man rested his arm on the desk and yanked a pen from one of the drawers. "Still going to raise horses?"

"Only the best in Texas." Blake smiled, even though he felt anything but joyous. From his pocket he took out the land deed he'd signed earlier.

Sam opened a ledger on the desk, then scribed the information Blake had written from one document to the other. "Since you're filing an application for your homestead, and you've been doing improvements on the land for five years, just pay the cost for the one hundred and sixty acres."

Blake patted his pant pocket where he'd placed the money, excitement finally beginning to fill him. "Been ready."

"Then that will be two dollars filing fee plus the cost of the one hundred and sixty acres, which will run you this figure here." He spun the paper around and rapped a bony finger on the sum.

"Thanks, Sam." Blake withdrew the money and counted it out.

"Good for you, son."

They both signed on the line, and Sam set his pen down. "I'll let you know when the deed title comes from the General Land Office in Washington, DC."

"Appreciate it, Sam. You have a good afternoon." He tipped his hat and strolled out into the sun, feeling its warmth. God's warmth and love, for He was pouring out blessing, covering him in His grace.

Yet concern for Cliff's capture, grew and doubt once again found its way into his veins. The message stabbed to the door was clear. Cliff was coming. Would Blake be able to protect Jessica? Would he fail her as he'd failed Abby? His steps grew heavy when he caught a glimpse of Pete and Nick walking with Jake. He moved in their direction, meeting them in front of the livery.

"Everything is quiet." Jake was the first to speak. "We're headed to see Tom."

"Yep," Nick chuckled. "See when that mail-order bride of his is comin' to town. Pete here is thinkin' of orderin' him one too."

Pete looked Blake in the eye. "Since I no longer have any prospects, I need me a woman. Someone to love."

Nick patted Pete on the shoulder. "Come on. Times a-wastin'."

Jake moved to Blake's side as they watched the cowhands

amble off. "I take it Pete's holding up all right. I know he was sweet on Jessica."

Blake pulled the bandana from his pocket and wiped his face, lifting his Stetson above his brow. "He'll be all right. All I got on my mind is Cliff and his gang being here on Saturday. I know the same thoughts are running through Jessica's mind, although neither of us are speaking of it yet. It's giving me time to pray before we have a chance to talk."

"Did you get the parcel of land?"

Blake's heart lifted a notch. "Yep."

"How are you going to celebrate? Have some ice cream down at the restaurant?"

"That sounds nice, but Jessica and I plan to have a quiet night at the boardinghouse." Not only for her safety, but because there was no celebration compared to what the night ahead promised them.

"You got me there. I wouldn't know what to do without Missy. Takes care of the kids, waits for me by the door when I get home, warms my bed at night. The good Lord knew what He was doing creating women."

Blake chuckled. "That He did. I'll see you tomorrow first thing to relieve you."

"No complaints here."

Blake ambled his way down the street. It was funny how two men could want such different things. Yes, he wanted Jessica to be a mother to their children, and she'd be a loving mother he was sure, but he also wanted a partner. Someone he could run ideas and thoughts by, and then receive hers in return. He could picture Jessica at their ranch helping him care for the horses, breaking in a horse or two.

A picture of Jessica riding across the field on the hunt for his runaway horse came to mind. The way her hair blew thick in the wind, the strength in her tanned arms, and the straightness of her back as she swung the lasso through the air. His mouth went dry. He had himself a wild filly. No other woman had ever set his heart on fire and blood boiling at the same time. Not once, but three times since she'd walked into his life. He chuckled. She was perfect for him. *Thank you, Lord, for knowing what I need before I do. I'd be missin' out on a lifetime of love and happiness if it wasn't for You.*

A woman's scream pierced the air.

Jess.

He raced down the street and barreled through the boardinghouse door.

CHAPTER TWENTY-EIGHT

As Jessica spun at Mrs. Briggen's scream, Blake rushed through the kitchen door with his pistol in hand. Panic glossed his eyes, and his face was as white as death when their gazes met. It took them a second before either of them knelt beside Mrs. Briggen, lying prone on the floor. Water pooled near where she'd fallen. White ceramic pieces that were once a bowl lay scattered all over the kitchen. Her eyes opened and her face pinched in pain.

Jessica brushed her hand across Mrs. Briggen's forehead, moving strands of gray hair from the woman's face. "Mrs. Briggen, what happened? Did you slip?"

She struggled to sit upright. Blake lifted her, supporting her back as she rose to a sitting position. Her face contorted.

"Are you hurt?" Jessica asked.

When she didn't answer, Blake asked again. "Are you all right?"

Mrs. Briggen pointed a finger at him. "Only my pride. Now get me up from this floor."

Blake obeyed while Jessica lifted broken dish pieces from

the ground and grabbed a cloth from the counter to dry the floor. "Did you slip?"

"I told myself to clean up the mess, but I wanted to grab the pot first to wash the vegetables. Now look at what I've done." Mrs. Briggen bent to pick up a large piece but moaned and placed a hand along her side.

"Would you like me to call the doctor?" Blake gently placed a hand on her elbow. "Maybe sit down?"

"Now don't you go fussin'. I've got a meal to cook." Her forehead wrinkled as she walked back to where the vegetables lay on the counter.

Jessica and Blake followed. "I'll take care of dinner, Mrs. Briggen. Go upstairs and rest."

She waved Jessica off. "Nonsense. I'm fine."

"Mrs. Briggen." Jessica sounded stern to her own ears, although she suppressed a smile at the woman's stubborn streak—one much like her own. Perhaps it was their kindred spirits that caused them to appreciate each other's company. "Did you not allow Blake and me to move into the room upstairs rent-free with the agreement that I would help you cook the evening meals?" One brow raised, she eyed the woman for a long moment.

Mrs. Briggen glared at Blake. "You will not leave her to cook the entire meal, then appear at the last minute. Do I make myself clear?"

Blake gave her a lopsided grin. "Yes, ma'am."

The woman eyed them both, her gaze jumping from one to the other. "Fine. You may escort me to my room, Sheriff."

Jessica stifled a smile as she bent to the floor, then placed the rest of the broken pieces of ceramic in her apron. She didn't look at Blake or Mrs. Briggen as he led her by the elbow through the kitchen door. The older woman would surely have bruises tomorrow, but tonight's dinner would be perfect. She'd make Mrs. Briggen proud.

After throwing the ceramic in the trash, she mopped the floor and tackled peeling the potatoes.

Blake came in, dug through the cabinets until finding another white pot, then placed the fresh carrots in the pot. "I'm not much good at rolling out dough or pounding out circles. I'm better at using a knife, so when I'm finished with these vegetables, I'll take over the peeling and cutting." He took a knife from the drawer and sliced the carrots.

Jessica started on the dough. "What did Mr. Briggen say when you entered the room and explained what had happened?"

"He didn't say much of anything but took her other elbow and led her to a chair. I excused myself, but before leaving, I told them if they needed anything to let us know. We'll take dinner up to their room when it's finished."

"Do you think she will be all right? I know she'll be bruised."

"I'm sure she will."

"Why do you say that?"

"She gave me an earful on the way to the room. Told me how she'd wanted Pete to marry you, but you weren't interested in him and I'd better take care of you. She's very fond of you. Has been from the first moment she met you. She even told me to buy your little breads the first time you took them to the general store."

Jessica paused in kneading the dough. "She didn't! She asked you to buy them?"

"They really are good, you know. Sweet. Buttery. Almost melt in your mouth."

She tilted her head, hands back to kneading the dough. "Did you and Doc really flip a coin to see who would buy the last little bread?"

"We sure did. It was the best investment I've ever made."
He grinned. "Until today."

She folded the dough over, took an empty can from the
table, and used it to cut out circles. "Did you get the land?"

"I did." His eyes sparkled with excitement and an emotion
she couldn't name.

She forced herself to continue cutting out circles from the
dough instead of gawking at the handsome man before her.

"I'm excited about our future, Jess." He paused and looked
to her, his voice light, expectant. "I can't wait to start building
our lives together."

This is really happening? Anticipation shot up her spine.
She was really going to have a life with this man. Maybe if she
could remember their wedding, it wouldn't feel so foreign, but
as it was, thinking of their future brought an unexpected thrill.

"Speaking of our future," she said, setting the circles on a
tray. "I know how much you like the Easton ranch, but do you
think we could live here until the house is built? That is, if Mrs.
Briggen will allow us to stay on."

He stopped peeling and set his knife down. "You don't care
for the ranch?"

"Oh, I love being out there, the open air, being around the
horses, but I miss being here. Actually, I miss Mrs. Briggen.
Since I came to Graham, she's been so kind and supportive,
giving me a job, then pushing me to sell my little breads to the
general store. I couldn't have done it without her encouragement.
I miss her, and I feel needed here. Wanted, really. Like this is my
home."

His brows dipped. "Was it a mistake to buy the land?"

"No. Of course not." She abandoned her biscuits and went
to him. "When we have our own place, I can do as I please and

not feel in the way. Here, I'm comfortable. I feel useful. I know Rosalind wanted me to help with the cooking, but every time I offered, she didn't want me to lift a finger. She treats me more like a guest, and with me being around, she might overexert herself. She really doesn't need more to do with her pregnancy." Jessica didn't know if she was making any sense, not with the way he remained quiet. Nor did he move. Had she said something wrong? Could she not express her opinion? Did it matter what she thought?

"Would you like for me to ask if we may stay on until our home is built? Would that please you?"

She wrapped her arms around his neck. "It would please me very much."

He began pushing her away. "Then I will ask her right this minute."

She giggled, resisting his effort to move away. "I think we can wait until later."

Blake's hands slid down her arms to the small of her back. His kiss was gentle, loving as he brushed his lips against hers. He held her close. "I was just telling the Lord earlier how I was thankful to have a wife to share my thoughts and ideas with. I wanted you to feel the same with me. Thank you for telling me how you felt. Thank you for your trust. It means a great deal." He kissed her cheek, his breath soft against her face.

"I think we need to get back to work, especially if we plan to stay here," she whispered, knowing there wasn't another place she'd rather be than in his arms.

"True."

She returned to her pans of biscuits and placed them in the oven. "Since we're being open and discussing things, when do you think you'll give up the badge?"

"After the structures on the property are built. It will give the town plenty of time to hire a new sheriff."

"When do you plan to tell the town?"

"I'm not sure, but it will be after the Cliff Gang is caught and sent to jail. I've sworn to uphold justice and protect this town, and I need to keep my word, even if ..."

"It means your life." She understood. It was the same pledge her father had made, and he'd never walk away at a time like this. But she wanted Blake to love her more than his job, his town. To love her enough to live.

"Jessica?"

She blinked back the moisture in her eyes and turned her back to him. "Yes." She couldn't face him. Her tears were hers and hers alone. She wanted to trust him with everything, but she couldn't, not yet. Fear and death had a way of holding a person's heart captive, and right now, its tentacles were alive and well. Blake could die protecting her like her father had, then she'd spend the rest of her life loving two men who were dead and buried.

"Are you all right?"

She didn't answer.

"I love this town, Jess. I love the people. I know this is hard, but God will take care of us. I don't claim to know the mind of God, but I do know your father saved you from Cliff. I also know God had a purpose for sending you here, although I'm not sure what that purpose is entirely, but I know I've found my helpmate. A wife to cherish. A wife to love with all that is within me, and that wife is you. You are my gift from God."

Tears rolled down her cheeks. She sniffed.

"You're crying?" He turned her around. His brows dipped, and he opened his mouth to speak, but she held up her hand.

"Happy tears."

He collected her in his arms and kissed her forehead.

"Happy tears are good, right?"

"They are."

"Good, because we have to get back to work. Mrs. Briggen would have my hide if dinner didn't get done," he said.

She pulled gently from his arms, but he held her there a moment longer. She looked up at him. "Everything all right?"

"I just remembered I need to let Jake know Mark's staying on for the night."

Jessica stiffened at hearing the news. "Why is he not heading back? Are you expecting trouble tonight?"

"No. No trouble. I had hoped …" Blake fingered the wisps of her hair, and his eyes fell to her lips. "I thought …"

Instantly, her shoulders relaxed, and she took notice of the way his cheeks were growing red. Understanding taking hold, she felt the heat of his gaze and swallowed. "Will you be long?" Her voice edged with nervousness.

"I'll be back before dinner."

She nodded, unsure of herself. Blake had been married before, but she …

He drew her close and pressed his mouth to her ear. "No pressure, Jess. I've missed you in my arms as we've slept."

Her eyes slid closed, and she mentally took stock of the moment, the feel of his hand pressed to her back, the way they were standing so close, his promised words. She wanted this, wanted a family with this man. She pulled back slightly and cupped his cheek with the scar. This was a new beginning for them. Husband and wife. A life she planned to cherish for the rest of her days. "Hurry back."

Blake left the boardinghouse, but his mind and heart were still with Jess. He'd let Jake and Mark know he was officially done for the day. Tomorrow he wanted to go over the plans for the Women's Day of Shooting at the Eastons' and find out if Mark had an idea when Guy should be arriving. They could be as prepared as possible, but that planning was for tomorrow.

As he neared the office, angry voices rose to meet him through its open window.

"Are they in town now?"

"Are we safe?"

"Will there be a hangin'?"

"When will the marshal arrive?"

Blake pressed into the small office, where men and women hovered like a pack of wolves, pinning his deputy to the desk chair. Mark, on the other hand, stood near the open window. If Blake were a betting man, he'd lay money on his friend planning to toss a few people out onto the boardwalk.

Mark saw him as he neared and shot him an exasperated look.

"What's going on here?" Blake looked to the town's newest parents, Phil and Sarah Patterson. Dark circles still hung beneath Mrs. Patterson's eyes, but the exhaustion must be contagious, as Phil hadn't fared any better, by the looks of him.

"Sheriff, we have the right to know what's going on." Phil slipped an arm around his wife's shoulders and drew her close. "There's been talk."

Obvious by everyone standing in my small quarters. "What have you heard?"

Voices rang out once again.

"Please, one at a time." He moved through the crowd to his desk, listening to one, two questions. Taking off his hat, Blake looked to Jake. "Make your rounds." He set his Stetson on a stack of papers.

Jake tipped his head and headed out the way he came.

With two more questions pelting him, Blake leaned against the edge of the desk, trying to portray a sense of ease, though he was anything but.

"Well?"

"Yes," Blake said, "it's true. A member of the Cliff Gang has been captured, and the marshal is bringing him through town. But there's been another capture." He looked to his friend. "For those of you who don't know Mark, he's the sheriff in Fort Worth. I'll let him share more."

Mark nodded and shifted his weight, standing taller. "Two men of the Cliff Gang have been captured. The second man is on his way to Fort Worth now and should be arriving the same time as the marshal."

Tom O'Connor stood from against the wall. "I don't plan to go to the Eastons' for the women's shootin' because of me boys, though they're wantin' to go." His burly arms folded across his chest. "Who will be protecting the town? I can wield a sledgehammer, as ye know."

Blake grinned. Tom could handle his own, probably the entire town of Graham—if only he'd carry a gun. "Mark and I will be in town while Jake, Matthew, Pete, and Nick are at the ranch. Mark will have five deputies traveling with the marshal. Two or three will stay on here until I feel the town is secure."

Cynthia from the quilting group asked, "And why do we need the extra men if the criminals have left town?"

Mark glanced his way, but Blake wasn't going to cause a stampede of fear worse than the one he'd experienced only days ago. No, it was best to keep Cliff and his brother's appearance to themselves. "There's still two men from the gang on the loose. I'm not taking any chances."

Cynthia visibly relaxed her stance and took a long breath.

"Thank you, Blake, for all you do for us. I've been worried sick since I heard. With Paul serving in the army, it's just me and the girls. I've been awfully concerned."

For the next hour, Blake answered each question individually, and by the time he made his way back to the boardinghouse, he was mentally and physically exhausted. Dinner was forgotten until he stepped into the building and the aroma of food made his stomach rumble. He hurried through the kitchen door as Jess was taking biscuits from the oven.

She turned to him and smiled. "I thought Mrs. Briggen told you being late was unacceptable."

He was still learning the complexity of this beautiful woman in front of him, but she seemed happy. "Maybe I'm more like Mr. Briggen than I expected." He heard her chuckle as he reached for another tray of bread and slid it into the oven. "How can I help?"

"I'll set a biscuit on each plate. Would you mind serving them?"

He quickly found a large tray and had set several plates on it when the kitchen door swung open. Mr. Briggen said not a word as he took the tray from Blake and went back out the door.

Blake looked to Jess, who looked to where Mr. Briggen had been. "What do you think?"

"I think Mrs. Briggen is still running the kitchen." She chuckled again and turned to add biscuits to several pre-made plates.

It wasn't until hours later, when the boardinghouse and most of the town of Graham was sound asleep, that Blake held his wife in his arms as she smiled sweetly at him.

"What?" he murmured, running his fingers along her bare arm.

"I'm not sure how it happened or why, but from the moment

I saw you at the graveyard, mourning, it was as if the dam I'd used to keep hold of every feeling and emotion I'd been hiding, broke. And when you looked into my eyes at that moment, I felt such a strong connection to you. It confused and scared me, but no matter how much I tried to fight it, it only grew. Day by day, I was falling in love with you. I didn't want to, but I did. I love you."

"Thank you for letting me love you in return."

CHAPTER TWENTY-NINE

"I can't believe the Women's Day of Shooting is tomorrow." Jessica lay in bed, enjoying the sight of her husband buttoning his shirt and the crooked smile he gave her. He winked, and her heart fluttered.

Finishing with his last button, he sat on the bed and drew her near, kissing the skin of her inner wrist. She closed her eyes and inhaled a lazy breath, slow, lingering, much like her husband's mouth on the soft flesh of her arm.

"I wouldn't mind being locked up here with you from now until eternity."

Oh, how she'd prefer just a few more days, but Blake was needed back at the sheriff's office. Jake was a good man, capable, but Mark was leaving today to head back to Fort Worth, and Blake wanted to run through their detailed plan one final time.

He moved her hair back behind her ear and whispered, "Have you thought more 'bout going to the ranch until the Women's Day of Shooting is over? Leaving the day after?"

She'd thought about it. Whether she liked the idea was

another story. She loved it here, but Blake had made several valid points, especially about putting some distance between her and the Cliff Gang when they entered town. "How do you expect me to think? You're too much of a distraction."

His kissed the nape of her neck. "Not too much. Are you sure you're listening?"

"Trying."

He knew what he was doing to her. "I love you, Jess. I want you to be safe." He slowly stood from the bed and headed for the door, palming his hat from the dresser. He settled it on his head with both hands before looking at her. "I'll be back. Be ready with an answer, all right? And, please, don't head for the general store without me. Are you making a double batch of little breads?"

Jessica understood his need for an answer so he could secure whatever place she decided to stay. She would trust his judgment, regardless, unlike she had with her father. She would stay put for her protection and for Blake's. "I'll go," she finally agreed.

He rewarded her with that grin of his that turned her insides to mush and set her heart to racing, a grin she'd do anything to see time and time again.

"And yes. Since this is my last batch for a few weeks while everything settles with ..." She avoided the name, but it did nothing to stop the grin on her husband's face from fading. She pressed on. "I think Mr. Vines would appreciate the extra."

Tomorrow seemed to loom in the balance of their new life together, and there was nothing Jessica could do to stop it. Blake hadn't even broached the sound of the name that weighed heavily on their minds. His heart was burdened, though he wouldn't admit it.

"I'll be back as soon as I can."

She'd be waiting.

Wishing he were still with Jess, Blake pushed through the boardinghouse door and headed across the street to his office. A cluster of women from the church quilters group stepped onto the boardwalk and turned in his direction.

"Sheriff!" Margaret waved a stout hand, a yellowed handkerchief clenched between her fingers. She began dotting her brow and neck. Six other ladies followed close behind.

He tipped his hat. "Howdy, ladies. Looking as lovely as ever. What can I help you with this fine mornin'?"

Margaret's hand landed on her hip, and her smiled faded fast—Blake was in trouble. "For you, it's a fine morning. We just learned of your wedding to Miss Jessica Thompson. Sheriff, we had no idea. We thought Pete planned to marry her. Their quilt is almost complete."

Blake couldn't say it bothered him one bit. He almost glanced up at the boardinghouse to see if Jess was there at the window. "Well, ladies, all I can tell you is Miss Thompson is now Mrs. McKenny, and I couldn't be happier." He should have known word would get around fast. Mrs. Briggen was probably the one who'd started the gossip mill. He wondered what else she'd told them. Nothing, he hoped.

"See, I told you, Sarah."

Mark appeared in the doorway. "Sheriff, you're needed inside."

Blake gave his friend a nod and a knowing smile.

"We'll have your quilt done as quickly as possible." The town's seamstress looked from Mark to him. "Not to worry, Sheriff. Come on, ladies. We have work to do." She led the group toward the church.

Blake entered the office and went to his desk. "Appreciate the rescue." He shuffled through the papers, looking for the map they'd drawn. It depicted where Mark's men would be located.

"Looked to me you needed one."

"Yep. Jake here?"

"At the livery. Something about a horse coming in on the afternoon train."

Blake's hand almost stilled. Life would've been different if that horse had come earlier. "That's Jessica's horse."

"The one she was waiting for so she could leave town? I don't expect her to be headin' out now. How's the wife this morning?"

But would she? Blake glanced at the boardinghouse. He hadn't thought she'd still leave, but Mark's words forced new fear to surge in his heart. No, he had to trust her, trust what they had shared as husband and wife. An image of Jess sprawled on their bed, her hair unbound, made him clear his throat.

Mark shot him a smile. "Say no more." He pointed to the papers Blake was shuffling. "Searchin' for the diagram we drew out? Top drawer. I tucked it there last night after a final look."

The back door opened, and Jake walked in. "Tom is heading to Fort Worth to pick up Jessica's horse, but you can tell he's not too happy about it. Never seen the big man shake like that in the summer heat."

"Tell me about this Tom fella." Mark eyed Jake, suspicion drawing his stance taller. "You think he has something to do with the Cliff Gang?"

"Relax, Mark," Blake said, lifting the diagram from the drawer. "Tom's wife was killed at the train station during a stampede." Blake could have sworn a cold shiver ran through him. It was only days ago his own life had flashed before his eyes. Blake's jaw tightened at the memory of the stampede and of his dead horse. "We should go over these plans one final time, but with an additional man."

Jake grabbed a chair from the wall and sat. "Who?"

"Tom. You heard him yesterday. He wanted to help, but he'd be tendin' to his children."

"Was that the burly Irish blacksmith?"

"That's him. Jessica and I made atlatls for his boys and plan to take them over this afternoon. We'll offer for the boys to stay with Jessica during the activities. With Pete, John, and Nick keeping an eye on her, they'd be the safest group on the ranch. Besides, Matthew, Tom, and the other cowhands can keep everyone safe. Not to mention, it will help Jessica keep her mind off Cliff, even if only for a little while."

"I like it," Mark said, now leaning over the diagram.

They continued discussing the time they planned to arrive in town to meet the marshal and deliberate the what-ifs. Everything on the map, activities on the ranch, and where Mark's men would be stationed on the ranch and in town were addressed.

They continued for another hour before Jake stood. "I need to stretch my legs. I'll take a stroll around town."

Blake rose from his desk. "I think we're covered. If anything changes by tomorrow, send word. I'll be walking Jessica to the general store and talking with Tom about what we discussed. Mark, you good?"

"I'm good." Mark's gaze swung after his deputy. "Jake, I'll go with you."

Jake paused at the doorway. "Sure. Hey, Blake, is Jessica carryin' her little breads to the general store?"

Pride soared at the question. Everyone loved Jessica's little breads. "That she is."

Mark looked between them. "Little breads?"

"Just you wait." Jake smiled. "You never tasted anything

like them."

Blake's gaze followed the men out the door and settled across the street at the boardinghouse, beating him there. He stepped off the boardwalk and pictured Jess finishing up her little breads and stuffing them in baskets. This wasn't permanent—she'd be back to baking her breads for Henry soon, but until Cliff and his gang were captured, they needed to be cautious. Cliff would never hurt Blake's wife again. No man would.

He found Jess in the kitchen doing just what he'd expected. The baskets were full and waiting. "You've been hard at work."

She beamed at him, and he went weak in the knees. "Perfect timing. Ready to take these to the general store?"

"I want a kiss first." He leaned down and took one, then two, before he lost count.

"I've missed you," she breathed, her cheeks turning a lovely pink as she glanced around the kitchen. "I've not told Mrs. Briggen yet."

"That we kiss? I think she'd suspect."

Her eyes widened. "Blake! You know that's not what I meant."

He chuckled, enjoying the full blush on her cheeks. "Once we explain why we'll be leaving for the ranch, she'll understand. She cares about your safety. We'll be back to stay while the house is being built."

"Who will help her with the meals?"

"It's only for two, three days, at most," he said. She had to see this was for the best. "Let's get these baskets to Mr. Vines before Jake and Mark start pacing the store."

"Jake? Mark?" Wrinkles creased her forehead. "I think I'm missing something." She hurried to the door and held it open for him.

Blake filled her in as they walked to the general store,

keeping her close. "Still plan to take the atlatls to the boys today?"

"If you have time. I can't wait to see their faces. Do you think they'll like them?"

"What boy wouldn't?" They were nearing the store, and he wanted to run his idea past her. "How would you feel about looking after the boys while the women are shooting? It would free Tom up and give us an extra set of eyes and ears at the ranch. He'd mentioned wanting to help but not being able to because of needing to watch the boys."

Her steps slowed. "Do you think they'll be safe with me? I mean …"

He leaned close, keeping them walking. "Jess, with three of the sharpest shooters watching over you, you'll be the most protected woman in the state. I think the boys will be safe."

"If you're sure." Her tightened mouth loosened into a grin. "Then they can practice with their atlatls."

It did his heart good to see the strain in her expression slip away. She loved children, and being with Tom's boys seemed to fill a void she'd lost after leaving the orphanage. Perhaps, the good Lord would allow them to have children, a need he felt in his own heart when he thought of Trent and Rosalind's children.

The bell over the general store door rang as they approached, catching them off guard. Mark stood with the door open. "Are you two ever going to get here, or am I going to sample these tiny-bites Jake and Mr. Vines keep talkin' about?"

"Tiny-bites. I like that." Jess nodded at Mark as she passed him.

Blake was on her heels, laughing at his friend.

Mr. Vines pivoted on the ladder he was standing on and smiled. "I hear congratulations are in order, Mr. and Mrs. McKenny." He descended the steps and headed for the counter.

"I knew Blake was a caught man when he came in here with the doc and ate half a dozen and still flipped a coin to buy the last breads."

Jake appeared from the back of the store with a box and set it on the floor by the ladder.

"Never going to let it go, are you, Henry?" Blake set the baskets on the counter, sensing Mark over his shoulder.

"What's the fun in that?" Mr. Vines winked. "Mrs. McKenny, thank you for bringing these. When you're ready to make more, please do."

Mark's brow rose, disbelief painting his features. "She snagged you with these. Must be some bread. You and I were the last ones standing."

"Was," Jessica said to them as Henry opened the register. "Mr. Vines, I'd be happy to make more. Thank you for agreeing in the first place."

Blake lowered his voice. "I was a goner before then, but this might have sealed the deal."

"Sealed the deal on what?" Jess slid her arm through his, the motion so fluid a grin lifted to his mouth.

Mark winked. "I believe it."

Blake stuffed his smile away and pegged his friend with a stern look. "I have to warn you, you'll want to carry enough back with you to Fort Worth. This is her last batch for a time, and they'll be gone by tomorrow."

The doorbell jingled, and several ladies entered, heading in the direction of the little breads, causing Jake to step to the counter to secure his spot in line.

"Mark," Jake called.

"Ma'am. It seems I have some samplin' to do." Mark tipped his hat. "Blake, we'll see you tomorrow."

Blake took Jess out of earshot of the men. "Do you need

anything before we leave?" He had thought of a few things, but at the shake of her head, they didn't linger. Soon he'd provide for the things she needed, and if some of those things were ribbons, beautiful dresses like Rosalind's, or boots to wear while they rode, he'd be happy to oblige.

Once at the boardinghouse, they headed upstairs to their room, and now that they were alone, Blake planned on kissing his wife. But Jess sat on the edge of the bed, her shoulders falling forward. She didn't want to leave, and he understood, but it was for the best. He'd have to wait on that kiss. Instead, he began packing. "There's not much since your trunk is at the ranch, along with most of my things."

"I should go talk with Mrs. Briggen." She rose and headed for the door.

"Jess, wait." He gently caught her hand. "We'll be back."

She avoided his gaze.

"Don't be upset with me." He lifted her chin with his finger and found moisture in her eyes. "Jess?"

She wiped a fallen tear. "I'm scared," she whispered so quietly he might have missed it if he hadn't been focused on her lips. "I feel safe here with you."

He pulled her close and kissed the top of her head, his own fears finding their way into his thoughts. He wouldn't give in to them, but he'd yet to tell her about the horse. "As soon as the marshal leaves with the prisoners, I'll find you. We can return a day or two afterward. You'll see."

She held him tighter, and his gut wrenched.

"Tom went to Fort Worth today to get your horse."

She pulled back slightly and gave him a partial smile. "It's finally come. It seems so long since I spoke to Tom about the horse. A lot has changed since that day."

"For the better?"

Wrinkles formed on her brow. "Yes, for the better." She tilted her head and searched his eyes. "What is it? Did you think I'd ride off now after everything we've been through? Now that were married?"

Seeing the heat rising in her face and the strength of her words, he didn't want to answer. "It did cross my mind."

Her hands fell to her hips. "Blake McKenny, what kind of woman do you think I am? That I'd marry a man and then leave town at the first sign of trouble?"

Blake held back his smile and enjoyed this feisty side of his wife. She let him have it and poked him in the chest with her finger. He resisted as long as he could before nabbing that finger and stepping in for a kiss. "Worry started hounding me once I heard about the horse. You're a part of me, Jess, and I … I shouldn't have let my fears get the better of me. I'm sorry. Forgive me?"

She wrapped her arms around his neck and stood on tiptoes. "I do. And will, for the rest of our lives."

Her kiss was sweet, tender, driving a prayer of protection from within his soul. For the rest of the afternoon, he would bask in his Father's goodness and in the love of his wife. Life and marriage were a gift. He wouldn't waste a single moment. Starting now.

Jessica's back rested against Blake's chest as they rode to the ranch. One of his arms cradled her midsection, while the other held the reins. They said little as they left the boardinghouse, their time spent in each other's arms still fresh in their minds. Both wished they were back there now. Blake had admitted as much before they left, and though they needed to leave, his loving touch and gentle words filled her heart full.

"I think Mrs. Briggen took the news fine," Blake observed.

Mrs. Briggen. How she loved the older woman. "Not until you promised we'd be back. A smile finally showed when you mentioned we'd be staying while the house is being built."

"I'm sorry Tom and the boys weren't there to give the atlatls to. They probably weren't back from Fort Worth."

She knew he was right, but it didn't stop the disappointment.

As they topped the hill that overlooked the Easton ranch, Blake slowed to a stop.

"Wow." She was amazed at the changes since they'd been gone. To the right of the barns and corrals, the field that had held longhorns now hosted massive bullseyes a couple hundred feet apart. Long rectangular tables with benches stood farther into the field and stretched beyond her sight.

"The men take pride in their work. It looks to me like everything is ready."

Movement by the barns caught her attention. She squinted. "Blake, there's a horse in the corral. A buckskin."

"I was waiting for you to notice. When we rode up, I saw Tom and the boys head into the barn with Pete. They must have parked their wagon on the far side of the barn." Blake moved them along, and as they neared, Jessica's stomach swarmed with delight. Her horse was here, and so were the boys.

When they reached the barn, Blake swung down and took her by the waist. She was becoming accustomed to his gentlemanly ways. Her father would have loved Blake as his own.

"Atlatls first or see to your horse?" Blake unstrapped the gifts from the saddle.

"The boys. I might not leave my horse once I see it." She neared the barn door, and sweet voices rose, an Irish brogue strong in them.

"Yes, Da," the boys said in unison.

"Sons, I've asked ye to behave. I will not have any folly come to this barn or ranch. Do I make meself clear?"

Pete was the first to notice them entering the barn, but they said nothing to interrupt Tom's discipline of the boys. It wasn't long before all eyes turned toward them, then slid to what they held in their hands.

However, Tom jumped right to business. "Blake. Ma'am. Yer horse has been delivered as promised. She's a wild lass, so I'd be right careful with her. Blake here knows about these fillies. He could tame her for ye."

At her side, Blake suggested, "Or we could do it together."

"I'd like that." She looked back to Legend, where Blake had stuffed her satchel in the saddle bags. "I need my satchel. Will you hold the other atlatl?"

Blake didn't budge. "Tom, we have something for the boys and a question to ask you before we settle the horse. Is that all right?"

"Sheriff, Miss Thompson ain't severin' our deal. This horse cost me more than expected after she plunged a hoof through a door and almost killed a man."

Jessica blinked several times. "A little wild?"

Blake whispered, "Legend was the same. Nothing tender love and a gentle touch can't tame."

Why did she get the distinct impression he was also referring to her? "Tom, I'm not trying to get out of the deal." She huffed under her breath. *Who's the stubborn one around here?* It certainly wasn't her. She shoved the atlatl she was holding into Blake's arms and went to Legend to retrieve her satchel. As she walked back toward Tom, she counted out the bills, then handed him the money. "The other half as agreed upon." She looked to Pete. "Isn't that correct?"

He gave a hard nod. "Looks to me it's a done deal. The sheriff here is also a witness."

Tom stuffed the wad of bills in his pocket. "Now, what's this about me boys?"

"Tommy and Chase," Blake called the boys over and set the gifts on the ground. "Jessica wanted you to have these. She'll explain while I take your pa over to the other side of the barn to talk a few minutes."

They nodded, excitement registered on their faces.

Jessica waited until Blake and Tom exited the barn before offering the boys a smile and kneeling in the dirt beside the gifts. "Blake and I made these for you. They're called atlatls. They have spears, so you have to be careful."

"Can we try them?" Tommy asked, quickly picking up one.

"Well, not today, but maybe tomorrow. Blake's asking your dad if it will be all right."

Chase lifted one of the hooks. "What do ye do with this?"

Jessica took the spear from Tommy and tapped the spear's end. "You place this part in the base of the wooden plank. There's a crevasse here. It's called a hook." She pointed to each piece, then began to demonstrate. "Then hold the spear at eye level and aim. Snap your arm forward to release."

"Me pa won't mind if I try it." Tommy looked to Chase. "Tell her."

"Tomorrow, lads." Tom reappeared at the barn door with Blake. She looked to her husband for confirmation that Tom agreed, but he gave nothing away. "I'll be helpin' the sheriff and Pete here on the ranch. You'll be with Mrs. McKenny and can practice yer throws then." Tom gave a nod in her direction. "Dinna know about the marriage. Congratulations to ye both."

Jessica stood and brushed the dirt from her knees. "Thank you, Tom. And I look forward to spending the day with the boys."

"Best be keepin' their presents, or they'd be broken by tomorrow."

Tommy's face fell, but the gleam in Chase's eyes spurred Jessica's hope that they were looking forward to tomorrow. Without a farewell, Tom limped his way through the barn, his boys following.

"See you, boys." She gave a small wave.

Chase turned and waved back before dashing after his father.

Pete chuckled. "You got a way with them, Jessica. Too bad they don't have a woman in their lives. Wonder when that mail-order bride is coming on the train."

Blake lifted the atlatls from the ground and held out her satchel, which she collected. "Not sure. Hadn't heard more about it," he said. He found an empty shelf in the barn and set the atlatls down. "They'll be here for you, Jess. Can you reach them?" He winked.

Tom's wagon clattered past the open barn, stealing her retort.

Blake swept an arm toward the exit. "Ready to say hi to our new family member?"

"Of course!" She lifted the hem of her dress and hurried past him through the doors at the side of the barn. Her mustang ran across the corral, then darted in the opposite direction. She'd never seen an animal so majestic in all her years. Perhaps it was because this was her horse. The buckskin saw her and stopped. The creature raised her head high, her dark mane her crown. Blake came to stand beside Jessica. "She's beautiful," she said.

"She is."

"We can keep her here?"

"Of course, and we'll train her together."

Jessica grinned at that. "Thank you."

"What do you think you'll name her?"

She already knew. "Majestic."

Blake slipped his arm around her waist. "It fits." They watched Majestic prance and dart for some time and were about to head in when the sound of a wagon neared. "Surely it's Trent, Rosalind, and the twins."

Jessica stepped out of the barn, and at seeing Rosalind and the twins, her heart jolted with delight. She hadn't realized how much she'd missed them until then. "Let's welcome them home."

CHAPTER THIRTY

"Everyone is in place," Matthew announced to Pete and to the men who would stay with Jessica during the day. "The town folk should be arriving shortly." He probably intended to be reassuring, but his statement had a different effect on her. In the barn, the men continued talking, unaware she was nearby, standing along the corral fence.

Since Matthew's arrival at the Easton ranch, his set jaw and no-nonsense demeanor had been a constant. Clearly he was concerned, and he gave orders like a sergeant, but it did little to ease Jessica's brittle nerves. Fear twisted her belly in a way she'd not allowed since her father's death. Her attempt to outrun Cliff and his gang had given her focus and direction. But now that she wasn't running, how could she not fear the worst? She loved her father and separation from him was unbearable, but to think of losing Blake sent tremors through her soul. Somewhere deep within her, she sensed Cliff was near, even now as she stood watching Majestic. Cliff wasn't going to leave without seeing her, or worse.

A touch at her arm made Jessica jump. Her gaze flashed to

Blake. "I didn't hear you come up." The concern she saw in his eyes, the slide of his hand to her cheek, made her feel worse, knowing she caused him worry.

"I can send Matthew in my place."

Jessica almost agreed but thought better of it. "The marshal is expecting you. Besides, Tom's boys will be here soon." She tried to sound upbeat, but Blake saw through her.

"If you want me to, I can stay."

"It's best if you go. We both know it's true. The town is counting on you."

He reached for her, and she went to his chest, relishing the feel of his arms, his protective embrace. "Pete, Nick, and John will be with you. You'll be safe." He placed kisses at her hairline. "I need to pray for us."

Last night, after saying goodnight to Rosalind and the twins, Jessica caught Blake in their room on both knees at the foot of the bed. He'd been asking the Lord above if He'd see fit to protect them today and always. She'd never witnessed a man pray at his knees, even her father, and it brought fresh emotions she'd been burying for as long as she could remember. She never wept when her mother died, choosing to be strong instead for her grieving father. Then watching him die before her own eyes ... She'd hardened her heart toward the truth her father had instilled in her as a child.

God will never leave you or forsake you.

She'd remembered her father's admonition as she hid in the shadows listening to her husband pray. Tears were rarely shed until she met Blake, but last night the gates of her heart broke. She hadn't meant to cry, but when Blake heard her, he carried her to bed and prayed until she'd fallen asleep. She loved the Lord, but never knew how far she'd drifted until that moment. Blake's prayer was a bridge she needed to cross to return home, a home where the Lord Himself was waiting for her with open arms.

"… and Lord, thank You for this day You've given us. We thank You for Your love and protection. Amen."

"Blake." Trent called out in the distance, summoning.

It was time for her husband to go. "Be safe." Her voice came out small.

He cupped her cheek. "This is hard for me too, but remember what we talked and prayed about. We must trust Him, Jess. The Lord is with us. He's our help in times of trouble. Our protection."

"There you are." Trent's smile wilted at seeing them. "I didn't mean to interrupt."

Jessica hid her face in Blake's chest to hide her tears.

"Give us another minute."

She peeked out from over her husband's arm as Trent left the barn.

"He's gone. Now kiss me."

Jessica gave him a teary smile, leaning in to press her lips against his. Jessica tasted the sweetness of his kiss and the finality in its parting. "I love you, Mr. McKenny."

"And I love you, Mrs. McKenny. I'll see you soon." Without a backward glance, Blake strolled from the barn and took a part of her heart with him.

Jessica's legs wobbled. She was drawn to crumble right there on the bare floor and have a good cry. The taste of the salt building on her tongue told her she was close to giving in, yet she forced herself to remain standing. Her husband was about to face one of the toughest days a lawman could have. He didn't need to get word his wife had fallen apart and lost her mind in his absence.

Blake was right. She knew God would never leave her, and

somewhere along the way she'd forgotten. It was time to live like she believed that. No, she didn't need to face her fears alone. God would be there to face them with her. All she had to do was trust Him.

She looked to Majestic, who seemed to be eyeing her from the other side of the corral. Perhaps the mare was able to see the transformation taking place within Jessica's heart. Granted, it was only a portion of her heart since Blake held the other.

She recalled her vow to never love another lawman, but now that she had, with God as their Protector, she was ready for the fight of her life.

Nick had arrived with John, and they were talking outside the barn. They had yet to see her, but she felt, rather than saw, Pete from behind.

At the sound of wagon wheels nearing the house, Pete came to stand alongside her. "Are you all right?" He looked into her eyes. "No matter what happens, I won't leave your side."

"Thank you for being my friend, Pete. I never would have made it here without you."

He gave her a cocky grin. "I know." He nodded toward the barn door. "Let's take a look-see at who's comin'."

She and Pete went to where Nick and John stood, watching the wagons crest the hill. There were a mix of families heading her way, but seeing Tom and his boys within the mix brought a much-needed smile to her face.

Strains of piano music waffled in the air as Blake looked out over Main Street and inhaled a calming breath. Except for the saloon, the streets were deserted, and the town was eerily quiet. He didn't like it, hated how outlaws could instill fear in his townspeople's hearts. Not only them, but in his life with Jessica.

Mark had sent three men ahead of him to let Blake know of the marshal's arrival in Fort Worth. Those men were now stationed at either the entrance to or exit from town, while Jake's post was at the livery. Blake took to leaning against the sheriff's office near the restaurant.

His gaze scanned the town, landing on the boardinghouse where Mrs. Briggen refused to leave—either because she'd sustained an injury from her fall or because Mr. Briggen didn't want to attend the Women's Day of Shooting. She claimed someone needed to cook for her boarders, but between Rosalind, Jessica, and the women folk providing the food at the ranch, there wouldn't be a hungry soul in the county.

Jake's short whistle caught his attention.

He turned to a man on horseback riding into town. Blake shouldered his long gun and eased his way to where the stranger stopped his stallion in front of the restaurant. He dismounted. "Hate to be the bearer of bad news, but they're closed."

The man withdrew a gold pocket watch from his single-breasted frock coat and looked at the time. "Closed?" He stuffed the watch back into his front pocket and glanced around. "Expecting trouble?"

"Company. So the stores and shops are closed."

He nodded and looked toward Jake. "You have a small town here, Sheriff. Do you get much *company*?"

Blake eyed him. "Sorry, but I didn't catch the name."

"That's because I didn't give one. Name's Braxton." He glanced over his shoulder and nodded to the saloon. "Heard it's for sale. Came to see if it was worth buying."

Blake stifled his surprise to the news. "Hadn't heard." He noticed Matthew coming from the general store.

"Good. Means I might be the only buyer. If I'm not under arrest, mind if I stay in town? I had heard your *company* is coming through, and I admit, I'm a bit curious. Besides, I'd like to see the saloon."

How had he heard about the Cliff Gang coming through? He wanted to tell the man to be on his way but stopped himself. Blake's intuition told him something was off, and Braxton might be hiding something, but that wasn't enough to force someone from town. "Depends. Which side of the law are you on?"

The side of the stranger's mouth lifted into a smirk. "Yours, of course."

"Blake," Matthew said as he neared, nodding to the stranger. "Who's this fella?" He asked the question as if the man wasn't standing there.

The man's mouth tightened. "Name's Braxton."

"He's here to see about buying the saloon." Blake added.

Give it to Matthew to raise a brow and meet the stranger's gaze dead on. "Today of all days?"

Unspoken tension stretched between the men, and now wasn't the time for foolishness. "Braxton, we're asking everyone to remain inside until the marshal rides through. You're free to head to the saloon."

He tipped his hat. "Thank you, Sheriff." He avoided Matthew's stare, took his horse's reins, and led the stallion away.

Matthew waited until Braxton tied his horse to the post before he said, "Do you believe him?"

"No choice at the moment." Blake turned to his friend. "Why are you here? I wanted you at the ranch. Is everything all right? Jessica?"

"She's fine." He gave a slight shake of his head. "Teaching Tom's kids how to shoot that caveman weapon."

He grinned. "I take it you tried it?"

"That woman of yours can shoot. A pistol. Rifle. An atl-whatever. When I left, she was teaching several women how to shoot."

"She's that good?"

"Better than Pete."

Blake raised a brow. "Then, Pete? He's…" The sound of horse hooves in the distance caught his attention.

"I know. Your wife continually surprises me."

Blake's shoulders tightened. "We have company."

Jake must have noticed, for he straightened and turned toward the posse entering town by the general store.

William, the owner of the saloon, came out onto the boardwalk with his Winchester to his shoulder. He knew better, but there was nothing Blake could do now. They had arrived.

Two armed men on horseback led the posse, followed by the marshal. A wagon rolled in next, carrying two guards. One was John Reed, the man Blake had met in Fort Worth, then there was the driver. Sitting in the bed of the wagon were Stevens and Tommy, bound. At the back of the posse were two more guards. Mark wasn't with them.

Blake hadn't expected them to stop, but as they slowed near the sheriff's office, he stepped from the boardwalk to meet the marshal. "Hello, Franklin."

"McKenny." He tipped his hat. "Mark wanted me to let you know he was detained."

"What happened?"

"Some sort of ruckus down at the saloon."

To his left, Blake caught sight of Matthew's slow movements heading toward the saloon. Matthew would handle William, but within the next breath, the newcomer's face came to mind. Blake spoke quickly. "Marshal, we have a newcomer that rode into town moments before you arrived. He's in the saloon. I suggest you get these men out of here."

His face hardened. "Men, arm yourselves. Let's move."

A gunshot cracked the air, and the earth seemed to jolt at the noise.

Matthew dove for cover.

Horses whined, and guards fought to move from harm's way.

Shielded by the posse's horse, Blake ran alongside the moving wagon. The shot came from the saloon, he was sure.

"It's William," Matthew shouted.

Another shot rang out.

In moments Blake would be in the open with nothing to shield him. He sought William's position behind a barrel next to the saloon. Seeing the opportunity, Blake lunged with his rifle, taking cover behind several water troughs next to Matthew, landing hard on the ground.

"William, put your gun down."

"Sorry, Sheriff. I have my own marching orders."

"Who gave them? I never pictured you as a killer."

"Gambling makes a man do strange things." William fired toward the general store, where Mark's deputies took cover. Glass shattered in the distance.

Blake caught sight of Jake sneaking past the boardinghouse, moving toward the saloon. "William, you won't walk away from this!"

"I'm already a dead man, Sheriff." He shot at them.

Matthew dropped his gun and slumped forward against the trough. "Hit," he moaned, hugging his arm. Blood soaked his sleeve.

"Hold on." Blake turned toward William when an exchange of fire with Mark's men pushed Williams back toward the saloon.

Blake saw an opportunity to take him as he neared the saloon door. He quickly aimed and fired, striking him, but another shot cracked. Williams fell to the ground.

Hurrying to Matthew, Blake knelt at his side and yelled out, "Somebody get the doc!"

"I'll go." One of the Lampkin boys ran for his horse.

Jake crouched beside them. "How bad is it?"

Pale and sweaty, Matthew blinked up at them. "I'm still alive."

Blake took off his coat and pressed it against the wound. "I'm not sure. We need to stop the bleeding."

Matthew moaned, "Blake. Go to the ranch. I have a bad feelin'."

So did Blake. William hadn't shot at the marshal or deputies with Guy and Tommy, but at him, Matthew, and Mark's men. Things weren't adding up. Mark wasn't here because of an incident at the saloon in Fort Worth, where Cliff and his brother had been, and now Graham's saloon owner was looking dead. Blake glanced across the street. Braxton was standing over William's body. "Jake, make sure you hold that man standing over William for questioning until I get back." He rose. "I'm heading out."

CHAPTER THIRTY-ONE

Seven women, Rosalind among them, now stood in front of their targets, and down the line, each held their guns with steady aim. With an impressive show, they all hit their mark within an inch of the bullseye.

Jessica joined the crowd in giving a roaring applause. The grin she wore spread to Trent, who stood at a safe distance with a group of other men. Jessica couldn't be prouder of what her group of women had learned. She hadn't meant to take over training from one of the cowhands, but while he was a decent shooter, as she'd witnessed before the festivities, but a trainer he was not.

At first, she thought Matthew was going to be one of the trainers, as he and Trent had opened the event, but halfway into the shooting, he disappeared. She hoped he hadn't left because of her. Their marksman challenge with the atlatl hadn't gone as he planned—she won every time.

Mrs. Lampkin, one of the ladies from church, rang the dinner bell. "Come and eat," she called.

Five wooden benches were laden with food while five others

were arranged as seating, while others preferred to have picnics on the ground. She scanned the yard and found Tommy and Chase tucked away in their father's wagon eating dessert. She'd already fixed them plates to keep them busy while she helped the women. As soon as they finished shoving cake into their faces, they'd want to go back to shooting their atlatls, she was sure.

Her stomach growled, and she looked to the long line of families. It was pointless for her to wait near the end of the line when she could be shooting with the boys. She could always return a little later.

She strolled over to the wagon where Chase wiped his mouth with his sleeve, chocolate staining his dingy blue shirt. "Dinna know pudding cake could taste so good."

Tommy was laid back with his arms sprawled out over the edge of the wagon. "I had my fill of those there walnut bars. Ye tried them yet?" he asked her.

"Can't say I have." She looked over her shoulder at the growing line wrapping around two of the targets. *And I probably won't have a chance.* She turned back to the boys, and in Tommy's hand was a square bar, one walnut perched on top.

"It's a free gift for ye," he said, smiling.

She chuckled, wanting to draw him into her arms, but she knew that wasn't her place. Instead, she took the offered bar and ate. "Mmm," she sighed. "I haven't tasted anything this deliciously sweet in ... I can't remember when. Thank you, Tommy." She finished the last bite, and as she did, the boys jumped down from the wagon.

Chase looked up at her with large green eyes. "Can wees go back to shootin'?"

"Of course. But maybe we should move closer to the house since everyone is eating. We don't want to hit anyone." She glanced around for Tom and Pete. "Boys, do you see your father anywhere? We should tell him and Pete where we're going first."

"I see 'em!" Chase ran off.

Jessica reached into the wagon and grabbed the arrows. Tommy gathered his and his brother's atlatl. "Mrs. McKenny, do you believe in Jesus? I mean, the man you were talkin' about when ye gave us those little breads?"

She stilled and met the young boy's face, his brow furrowed in thought. "I do."

"Me da has taken us to the church. We hear about this Jesus. But how do ye know he's real when you can't see 'em?"

"Well, Tommy, that's a good question. Have you ever tried to look at the air or the wind?"

"Nope." He shrugged, looking to where his brother had gone.

"Why is that?"

He met her gaze again. "Because there's nothin' to see."

"But the wind and air are still there. You can feel it on windy days, or breathe it in—"

"Or suck it in, like after I'm done racin' me brother."

"Right." She grinned. "Even though you can't see the wind and air. It's still there. Like Jesus."

Chase came running back, but Jessica knew the Lord had given her just the right amount of time to answer the boy's question. She looked toward Tom and waved. He nodded in return. "Did you tell Pete?"

"Aye, ma'am. Pete, Nick, and Johnny were next in line for their grub. Said they'd be comin' after."

"All right, then, let's be on our way." Jessica glanced at the boys, and her heart filled with love. She couldn't wait to start a family of her own. *Hopefully, we'll do that soon.*

The thought brought heat to her cheeks, and she looked toward the corral. Majestic grazed, taking two small steps, then stopped. "Isn't she beautiful?" Jessica sighed, still in awe she'd finally arrived, and soon she and Blake would train her.

"Me da said he wished he could have kept her for our new mathair."

Tommy stopped cold. "She's not our ma. Da hasn't even seen her."

Chase huffed. "But he will, and so will we. She said so in her writin's." He skipped ahead toward the barn.

Jessica wasn't sure what to say, so she waited to see if Tommy might respond. When he didn't, she wasn't about to press him. "Nick made a simple target for Blake and me to use to see the accuracy of the atlatls before bringing them to you. Want to help me drag it out? We can set it up past the house and face it toward the sunflower fields. What do you say?" She gave him a smile.

He shrugged and followed her to the barn by the corral.

"Chase," she called, entering, and walking through the row of stalls. "We're going to ..." Her words died on her tongue, and her skin grew cold.

Cliff stood behind Chase's stiff body, his arm against the boy's chest. He held a Smith & Wesson in his hand. His other hand was securely fastened to his holster.

"'Bout time you came. I was fixin' to worry I'd have to start another stampede with all them fine folks out there. Ne'er can tell what might have happened to those children." Cliff knew her weakness, and he'd do whatever he could to control her.

"Please, don't hurt him."

"You got a real soft heart for urchins." Cliff looked off in the distance, a sadness rolled over his features. "You tried to protect me back then, like this boy here. It's why I knew you were going to be mine." He met her gaze and smiled like he knew a secret. "Let me go on and guess. Brothers?" He looked to

Chase. "Boy, is that your brother hidin' behind Jessica?" When he didn't answer, Cliff began shifting his gun from one hand to the other.

"Aye, I'm his brother." Tommy stepped out from behind her.

She immediately pulled the boy back. "Cliff, please let them go."

"I can't do that. They'll run and tell the law. I came for ya and nothin' or no one is goin' to stop me this time."

Jessica had to think fast to protect these boys. "I'll go with you," she blurted, forcing strength into her joints and praying they'd hold. "We can tie them up, and then we'll head out. No one will be the wiser."

Cliff pointed his gun at her. Though she knew he wouldn't use it, she played along. "You give me your word? And that you'll come quietly?"

Until we're clear of Tom's children. "Yes."

Cliff smiled. "Grab that rope hangin' off that peg there beside ya. Tie them together. Put them in a stall." He pushed Chase toward her, and the poor child almost tumbled to the ground but then caught himself.

Tommy yanked him close and held him. Fear shook their little bodies as well as her own.

Jessica worked to nab the rope from the peg, then moved the children from gunpoint into the stall. "Sit on the ground," she said softly. "You'll be all right. Pete or your father will come and find you."

Tears ran down Chase's face. "I'm scared."

Tommy wasn't faring much better as he held his brother close.

"I'm so sorry."

"Hurry," Cliff hissed. "We planned a diversion in town to

buy us more time, but only a few minutes. We got no time for blabbin'."

Jessica tied their hands but left them side by side instead of back to back. She hugged them quickly, then rose to her feet. Cliff watched her closely as she pushed herself toward him.

He yanked her by the arm and drew her close. Her body curled into itself against his chest. He inhaled deeply into her hair. "We'll be perfect together. You'll see." He yanked her arm and with a grip of steel, pulled her away from the children and out of the barn.

Two horses stood ready at the side of the house. "Is Bryan with you?"

Cliff glanced around and darted for the house. "Inside."

Jessica had to make her move now, or she'd never get away. Cliff wouldn't shoot her, but Bryan wouldn't think twice. She went limp, becoming a dead weight. Cursing, Cliff stumbled. It was just enough time to reach into her pocket for her weapon.

The instant her fingers curled around the pistol's handle, the pressure from Cliff's hold increased, and she was yanked to her feet. The gun almost slipped from her grasp, but she clasped it for all her worth, keeping it hidden within the folds of her skirt.

Cliff almost dragged her, tugging her along. "Stop makin' this harder than it needs to be."

They were nearing the porch steps when she heard horse hooves galloping in the distance. She wasn't sure of their direction, but she had to let them know there was trouble. She jerked her arm free. In the same move, she rammed the pistol barrel toward Cliff's chest.

He grunted his displeasure, then smiled. "We both know ya won't shoot me, Jessica."

She took a step back to put some space between them.

"We've been through too much for ya to kill me this way."

He took an easy step toward her.

"Don't!" She took several steps back.

He started to close the distance.

She fired a warning shot above his head, stopping him cold.

He glared at her. "Now, you promised me you'd come easy."

Bryan bounded from the house and drew his gun on her. "See what trouble this woman has caused? I told you she wasn't worth it. Not a lick! What now? The whole dang town will be comin'."

"Shoot her in the arm, so she'll drop that toy gun."

"Bryan. Please. Don't do this." She began backing up even more. She was tempted to turn and run, but he'd still shoot her and probably dead center in the back.

A sneer curved Bryan's mouth as he cocked his pistol. "My pleasure."

She dropped to her knees. A crack sounded. Rolling onto her hip, she swung her gun up, aimed at his chest, and shot.

Bryan's weapon fell at his feet, and his body began to sway. Cliff ran for his brother, but it was too late. Bryan stumbled forward. She gasped as he fell down the porch steps.

Jessica gripped her gun still in her hand and ran for all her worth back into the barn for the children. She didn't know what Cliff would do to them now. But as she entered the stall where she tied them, all she found was the rope tossed along the ground.

"Jessica!" Cliff wailed. "You killed my brother! When I find you … you're gonna pay." He rounded the corner to the stalls, and his dark angry gaze held hers fast.

She was trapped. There was no other way out. "Are you going to kill me like you killed my father?"

"No. I'm going to beat you to the near end of your life."

"Miz Jessica. Are ye in there?" Tom called. Too close.

Tears pricked her eyes as she gripped her gun tightly in her palm, ready to protect the burly man if he entered this section of the barn. Outside, hoofprints told her more had joined him.

"We ain't over," Cliff said as he ducked from view. After a moment, she stood on the tips of her boots. A quick glance over the stall's ledge told her Cliff wasn't there.

She wanted to yell out, but was Cliff setting up a trap for Tom when he walked in? He'd be ambushed and those boys would lose their father at Cliff's hand, like she had. She remained silent.

"Tom, did you find her?" Blake's hurried speech set her pulse to racing and moved her from where she stood.

Gunshots rang out.

Jessica ran from the barn, her boots thudding against the ground to where Blake and Pete flanked the left side of the Eastons' home. Tom entered the house. Nick and Johnny ran to the right, then disappeared around the building.

Two shots sounded, then a lull.

Her breath caught as she neared the men, everyone seemed to be standing, but ... Cliff was sprawled out on the ground by the back door of the house, his leg bent in an odd way. Something drew her. She wasn't sure what, but she found herself there, at his side, looking down over him.

Cliff gave her a half smile. "I knew you'd come. You always came."

And in that moment, she saw the little boy she had protected, the boy who needed someone to love him. She knelt to the ground and felt Blake's watchful eyes, but she had to speak her peace. "You took my father away from me. I miss him every day, and I hated you for that for so long."

His frown deepened. "That wasn't meant to happen. I was plum mad at him for separatin' us. He wouldn't back down, and it raged me more. And then when I couldn't find you, I went crazy. I went from town to town searchin'." He groaned and inhaled deeply before blinking several times. "The things I did … I'm not proud of 'em, Jessica. Killed a lot of men. I'm paying the price for my ways of livin'. But I'm sorry for all I've done."

She lifted her eyebrows. "Are you?" Or was he merely afraid to meet his Maker?

He nodded. Tears running down his face. "I am. Will you forgive me?"

Jessica's mouth twitched open to tell him he didn't deserve her forgiveness. Killing her father. What he'd done to her, making her live in fear for so long. He was a murderer of who knew how many.

Yet, wasn't Moses? King David? Murderers? She began a quick list in her mind. Then her own past sins flickered in anew. It was Jesus who'd died on the cross for her sins, and those of everyone else who ever took a breath. She was no better than Cliff. It was only that she'd been taught at an early age about the love of Jesus. Like what she told Tommy and Chase, it's a free gift for anyone who'd accept it.

And what did the Lord ask of her? To love her enemies, to love others like Jesus loved her. Her heart pricked, and the anger and the hurt she'd held for so long seeped out. In its place, forgiveness came in, and for the first time, she saw Cliff not for who he was, but as a lost man in need of Jesus.

"I forgive you, Cliff," she rushed to say, seeing he was slipping and fast. "But it's not my forgiveness you need. That forgiveness comes from Jesus."

He coughed and blood filled his mouth. "Jesus would never forgive me. Not after what I've done."

She leaned closer and placed a hand on his shoulder. "But you're wrong, Cliff. He loves you. Just like others in the Bible who committed murder. There was Moses, King David, Paul, and more. They all sinned in His eyes, yet God forgave them when they asked because they meant it with their hearts. You have to mean it when you ask, but Jesus *will* forgive you." She shook his shoulder again. "Cliff. Did you hear me?"

His eyes flicked open, and he seemed to stare into nothingness. "Jesus ... please. I've sinned. Killed. Forgive me for what I've done." Tears rolled down his face, and he coughed, splattering blood on her sleeve.

"Rest. Until we meet again."

With that, Cliff closed his eyes.

She felt a hand on her arm, helping her to stand. Blake was leading her to a waiting wagon. She didn't know where they were going, but she didn't care. Numbness was settling into her bones. Blake lifted her into the wagon, placing her on the bench seat. He said something, but her mind was a fog. She tried to focus, and when she did, Blake was gesturing at the men.

"Mrs. McKenny."

Jessica felt a tug at her hand, noticing for the first time Tommy and Chase sat on both sides of her. "Oh, boys." She hugged them to her. "How are you? Are you all right?"

"Aye. Da said we should come and sit with ye while he helps the men." Chase wrapped his arms around her and squeezed.

"Are ye all right?" Tommy's wide eyes held her gaze. "I ran as fast as me feet would take me for our da. Pete was with him."

Jessica nodded. "Your father was the first to come. Thank you for being so brave."

Tommy leaned into her shoulder but said nothing.

She closed her eyes and inhaled a long breath, but Cliff's face, Bryan's body tumbling, flashed in her thoughts. Her lids flipped open, and she shuddered, wishing the images away. "So tell me. How did you get out of those knots I tied you up in?

They had to be good ones because the man would have known." They weren't as tight as they should have been, but they hadn't unraveled. The boys had loosed them.

"We practice tying each other up."

"Chase," Tommy chastened. "We're not supposed to tell anyone."

The youngest shrugged. "She asked," he said, looking around. "I'm ready to go. Can't ye take us home, Mrs. McKenny?"

She opened her mouth to speak just as Blake and Tom came to the wagon.

Blake shook Tom's hand. "Appreciate your help today. In many ways."

"Glad ye're safe, ma'am." He looked to his sons. "And me boys." He collected Chase in his arms and smacked a kiss to his cheek, then reached for Tommy.

Tommy moved from her shoulder and avoided his father's care. The boy hopped down on his own and started for the field where their wagon stood in the distance.

"Bye, boys. Don't forget your atlatls." She forced a smile, fully aware they were frightened today, and soon they'd all be home trying to deal with day's events. Hopefully, Tommy would allow his father to be there for him.

Horse hooves sounded quickly behind them, and her pulse sped up. She straightened in her seat and gripped Blake's arm.

"It's Pete and Nick." He covered her hand with his. "They'll be staying in town for a few days."

A moment later, Blake climbed into the wagon next to her. After he set the conveyance clattering toward town, he pulled her close. She tucked her head against his chest and thanked the Lord above for her husband.

Jessica had been in the sitting area in her and Blake's room, waiting for her husband to return. Mrs. Briggen had been with her for an hour, and in that time, she learned what had happened today in town. Matthew was injured, and the saloon owner was killed. She'd never been in the saloon, but she'd seen William a time or two walking to the livery or leaving town. "What do you think turned him?" she asked Mrs. Briggen.

"From what I heard, he owned money. Gambling. I wish they'd tear that place down, but no. We already have a new saloon owner."

"How is that possible? William just died."

"A man came into town, said before William died, he sold him the saloon."

Jessica glanced at the window, the light fading outside. A thought of what Cliff had said earlier came to mind. *A diversion.*

"Are you tired, dear?"

Her gaze swept to Mrs. Briggen. "Yes. I'm sorry."

"Nonsense. Blake should be back soon from checking in on Matthew. He asked me to warm you some bath water."

"I'd hate for you to bother."

"No bother, I—"

A knock sounded, and Jessica went rigid.

Mrs. Briggen hurried to the door and cracked it open.

Pete stood on the other side, his hat in his hands. "I'd like to speak with Jessica. If she'll see me."

She turned questioning eyes to Jessica, who nodded.

Pete entered, running his fingers around the brim of his hat. "Jessica."

Mrs. Briggen cleared her throat. "Mrs. McKenny. You need to remember that when I leave her alone with you. I'll check on dinner and see how your uncle is doing without me." Her mouth tilted into a smile before she went out the open door.

"Your aunt is one of a kind."

"That she is." Pete tapped his hat against his thigh. "Jessica." He lowered into the seat Mrs. Briggen had occupied. "I should have been there for you. I let you down. You could have been killed because of me."

"Pete…" She shook her head and looked to her hands. "I've not even processed all that happened. And right now, I don't think I'm able. But I had thought about Tom's boys. If you or anyone else would have been there with us, Cliff possibly would have killed you without a thought. As it was, it was just us, and he allowed them to live. He knew how important children are to me." She met the sadness in his eyes. "It's all right, Pete. We're okay."

As Blake entered, Pete glanced up and stood. "I wanted … I'm sorry, Blake. I let you both down." Tears filled his gaze.

Blake walked to him and held out his hand. "We're family."

Pete accepted and nodded. "Family." He turned to Jessica, nodded once more, then left.

Blake went to Jessica and held out his palm. "Bath is ready."

She'd prefer to stay right where she was and sleep. Instead, she placed her hand in his. "Will you carry me?" She chuckled, standing.

"If you need me to, I will."

And he would.

He directed her into the hallway and led her to the extra room Mrs. Briggen used for bathing.

On entering, she glanced at the tin filled with water and found herself hypnotized by the steam waffling in the air. In awe of her bath, she almost missed what looked like a blue dress folded on a stool. "What's this?" She fingered the fabric.

"I ordered a couple of wedding gifts for you. A new dress to match your blue ribbons, and some type of Turkish toweling that Sarah from the seamstress shop had recommended. It's not been sewn or hemmed, but we can still use it."

"Blake ... thank you. I wish ..."

"I know. And I also know how tired you are." He came to her and gently unbound her hair from the bun she wore. At his tenderness, her eyelids closed, and moisture threatened. "I'm here, Jess. You're not alone."

Tears slid down her face, and she leaned into his chest. "The boys, they almost lost their lives because of me." The day fell heavily over her, and she hiccupped. "Cliff ... I thought I'd never see you again. I ... I killed a man." She wept.

"Shhh," he whispered, holding her close.

Several minutes passed before she could gather herself. "The water is getting cold." She tried to smile, but it took too much effort. When she fumbled at the buttons on her blouse, Blake took over and helped her undress. Then he guided her to the tin tub, taking her hand, and assisted her in.

The warmth of the water was delightful as she slid farther under.

"Let me." He took to washing her hair. His fingers worked slowly through her scalp, and her shoulders relaxed at the motion. He rinsed her hair, then continued to her shoulders and arms, when she finally spoke.

"I can finish." She took over where her husband had left off, feeling the weight of her limbs like bags of flour.

"I'm proud of you, Jess."

She paused and looked to him, the last hours clouding her thoughts and how she could have done things different. She remained silent.

"You're the strongest woman I know. In fear, you forged

through, even speaking the name of Jesus over a man's soul." He ran a thumb along her chin. "You amaze me. I can't thank the Lord enough for saving you."

She wiped at her eyes and was about to speak, but Blake's mouth opened, then it closed. Whatever was on his mind, she'd wait for him to continue as she finished washing.

"I thought one of the reasons He gave you to me was to protect you, but I wasn't able to protect Abigail. I know now that was wrong thinking. He was showing me—us—that He was the One to protect our lives, and that our guilt from the past isn't ours to keep, but to be given to Him. To be set free from."

She thought on his statements as she finished washing. He was right, she decided. Hadn't the Lord been showing her all along her father's words were true? He was directing her path. Right into the arms of this man at her side. "We are set free."

Wearing a tender smile, Blake collected the Turkish material. A cold shiver ran across her flesh when she stood. "Here," he said, wrapping the cloth around her body. "This should keep you warm."

The material was the softest she'd ever felt, but it was the love of her husband, and his gentle care, that would keep her warm for years to come.

EPILOGUE

"Three. Two. One."

Rosalind leaned over and blew out her birthday candle on her chocolate cake. She chuckled. "What a surprise. Thank you, everyone."

A roar of congratulations rose from the Eastons' closest friends—Oliver and Catherine Hadley, Tom, Pete, and the rest of the cowhands. But it was the children's shouts and laughter that echoed in the air.

Jessica looked on as Trent and Rosalind's twins ran for the sunflower fields. Although Timothy and Steph weren't up to the task of playing chase, the Hadleys' ten-year-old daughter, Lilly, and Tom's boys ran through the sunflowers after them.

Blake reached over and squeezed Jessica's hand in acknowledgment of their hearts' desire, the one they spoke of the night before. She hadn't realized then that, while theirs was having children, Tom's heart's desire was being fulfilled—his mail-order bride was on her way from South Carolina by train. And that wasn't all that was happening in Tom's life. God had used the incident with Cliff to lead Tom to question his mortality.

A week after the near kidnapping, Tom accepted Jesus into his life. She still couldn't believe how God had used the bad things in this life for good.

Tom carried his plate of cake, and two others, to the bench across from Jessica and Blake. "Young'uns, ye cake." Tom set them down and sat. Lifting his fork, he cut a large piece, and stuffed it in his mouth." When his lips closed around the fork, he moaned.

"Good." Blake smiled. He looked to her. "I'll be back with our plates."

Jessica cupped his arm. "I should be getting them."

"Partners, remember. In everything." He kissed her cheek. "Besides, the way Tom is moaning, I want a big piece."

She chuckled, turning her attention to Rosalind and Catherine who sat on each side of her. Catherine leaned over the table to look at her and Rosalind. "You both must come to our home next month. I'm almost finished moving our things into the kitchen. We can make several pies. I have six apple trees in the yard. Besides, Oliver will be back to overseeing the railroad and I know Lilly and I would love the company." She took a bite of cake.

"Thank you for the invitation, Mrs. Hadley."

"Please, Jessica, we're friends now." She patted her hand. "Call me Catherine."

Rosalind wiped her mouth with a napkin, leaning in. "Believe me, just say yes. She can be quite convincing. Too convincing at times."

"Rosalind! You'll make her think I'm up to no good."

Rosalind winked, eating another bite.

Tom shook his head. "'Tis what it will be like when me bride meets you lasses?"

"I'm afraid so, Tom," Rosalind agreed. "At least you might

get some pies out of the bargain with Catherine offering her apple trees."

Blake returned with her slice of cake, setting it on the table for her. Trent and Oliver joined them. It wasn't long before the men started chatting about horses and she'd eaten half her cake, talking with the women.

Jessica noticed Pete was carrying a platter of cake to the house. Matthew had been staying with the Eastons and doing well after his gunshot wound in his arm. Doc said he planned on him making a full recovery, and Jessica couldn't wait, because once he did, Blake was ready to hand Matthew the reins as sheriff.

"Excuse me, ladies and men, but I'd like to take my wife for a stroll." Blake held out his hand for Jessica.

She grinned as she accepted. "What is this about? You seem a little mischievous." She gave a playful wink as they walked.

"Can't a man have some time alone with his wife?" He led her to the other side of the barn but glanced back from where they'd come.

"Do you plan to kiss me?"

A wide grin lifted his mouth. "You know I didn't wear this bowtie and vest for nothin'."

She reached up and was sliding her arms around his neck when hoofbeats and wagon wheels sounded coming down the hill.

Blake took a few steps with her still in his arms and glanced around the barn. "Well, I'll be."

"Who is it?" she asked, looking at the older couple as their wagon slowed to a stop. Right off, Jessica noticed the man's resemblance. "Is that Trent's father?"

Blake tucked them back behind the barn. "Yes, now where were we?"

"Blake." She smiled, shaking her head.

"They've been in Boston for some time. They won't miss us." He slid his hand into his pocket and withdrew a gold ring.

Jessica gasped at the diamond. "What did you do?"

He shrugged. "You need a ring for that finger." He gently took her hand and slid it on her fourth finger. "Do you like it?"

"It's lovely." She turned it to catch the sun's rays and smiled, tears pricking under her lids.

"I thought Mr. Vines was going to give it away when you took your little breads last week."

"He did look like he ate a canary." She gazed at the ring again. "Oh, Blake. I've never had anything so beautiful before. I'm at a loss for words."

"Good. No need for words." He brought her close and kissed her softly, lingering. He ran a finger down her jaw, his smile faded as his gaze fell to her mouth. "I love you, Jess. Our lives … this is just the beginning."

As Blake leaned in for a kiss, she knew God's ways weren't her ways, and she was all right with that. Look at where He'd sent her. Right into the arms of the sheriff.

Acknowledgements

Heartfelt appreciation to my encourager, April Gardner, for always being there. I would not be the author I am today without her endless love and support. Thank you for pushing me to never give up! To my dear friend, Mary Hamilton, my critique partner from the very first word, from the very first novel. This book was only a dream at one time. God is so good! I also want to give a special thanks to Elizabeth Kitchens, Christy Distler, and Lee Carver. Their support and friendship over the years has meant so much. I couldn't have published this book without any of the ladies mentioned. Lastly, I want to thank my readers for their enthusiasm and support of my novels. You are a special blessing to me. I'm so glad we're on this journey together!

ABOUT THE AUTHOR

TANYA EAVENSON is an award-winning Christian romance novelist. She enjoys spending time with her husband and their three children. Her favorite pastime is grabbing a cup of coffee, eating chocolate, and reading a good book. You can find her at her website www.tanyaeavenson.com.

Sometimes the path to freedom is found in an unexpected future.

Don't miss book 1 in the All Roads Lead to Texas series—
The Rescue

When Hope Michaels decides to face her past, she unknowingly purchases the house across the street from her former fiancé—the man her twin sister married, then widowed. Fire Captain Carl McGuire can put out any flame, except for the one Hope sparks within him— some things never change.

Don't miss book 1 in the Gaining Love series—
To Gain a Mommy

As Valentine's Day approaches, will Patrick and Amabelle miss out on the love they've always desired? Or will their love take flight under the stars on this very special night?

Don't miss book 2 in the Gaining Love series—
To Gain a Valentine

Undercover ICE agent Madi Reynolds has spent years infiltrating a human-trafficking ring, but when her life is threatened, she is forced to walk away and advised to leave the country. War Veteran and ICE agent Brice Johnson faces the biggest assignment of his life— protect the woman he loves.

Don't miss book 3 in the Gaining Love series—
To Gain a Bodyguard

When a cat walker visits a dog park, sparks fly. The road to love is paved with paw prints.

Don't miss book 4 in the Gaining Love series—
To Gain Forever

To one, hope is a gift. To the other, a lie. To both, it's what binds them.

Don't miss book 4 in the Georgia Peaches series—
The Heart of Mercy

BE THE FIRST TO HEAR ABOUT NEW BOOKS FROM TANYA EAVENSON!

Sign up for announcements about upcoming titles at www.tanyaeavenson.com/

www.ingramcontent.com/pod-product-compliance
Lightning Source LLC
Chambersburg PA
CBHW030924260626
47169CB00002B/372